# Hellbent
by Maggie Maren

Copyright © 2024 Maggie Maren

Published 2024 Rivermoon Publishing,
Bucksport, Maine, USA

ISBN: 979-8-9886727-2-2

Library of Congress Control Number: 2024917219

All rights reserved. No portion of this book may be reproduced in any form without permission from the publisher, except as permitted by U.S. copyright law. For permissions, please email at: Contact@MaggieMaren.com

This is a work of fiction. Unless otherwise indicated, all the names, characters, businesses, places, events and incidents in this book are a product of the author's imagination or used in a fictitious manner. Any resemblance to actual persons, living or dead, or actual events is purely coincidental.

Edited by Norma Gambini at Norma's Nook
Cover & book design by TW Designs

# Note to the Reader

Hellbent is a bit grittier than my other books **but isn't considered a dark romance**. As an author, I've tried to balance brevity with authenticity in my characters' experiences as adults grappling with everyday struggles. This novel is intended only for a mature audience and contains strong language as well as frequent and fully described sexual acts.

These characters have frank discussions regarding abusive relationships, a narcissistic mother, abortion, the death of a parent due to cancer, nonconsensual drug use (roofying), nonconsensual condom removal during intercourse (stealthing), and racism.

Other content warnings include alcohol and cannabis consumption, attempted sexual assault, violence, internalized body shaming, mentions of blood and menstruation, police brutality, and slut shaming.

**Your mental health matters to me.** If you have any questions about these content warnings before reading this book, feel free to email me at contact@maggiemaren.com

# Hellbent Playlist

## Contents

Chapter One ..................................................................... 1
Chapter Two ..................................................................... 5
Chapter Three ................................................................ 10
Chapter Four .................................................................. 16
Chapter Five ................................................................... 22
Chapter Six ..................................................................... 41
Chapter Seven ................................................................ 47
Chapter Eight ................................................................. 55
Chapter Nine .................................................................. 66
Chapter Ten .................................................................... 75
Chapter Eleven ............................................................... 91
Chapter Twelve ............................................................... 98
Chapter Thirteen .......................................................... 106
Chapter Fourteen ......................................................... 109
Chapter Fifteen ............................................................ 119
Chapter Sixteen ............................................................ 123
Chapter Seventeen ....................................................... 128
Chapter Eighteen ......................................................... 134
Chapter Nineteen ......................................................... 143
Chapter Twenty ............................................................ 152
Chapter Twenty-One .................................................... 158
Chapter Twenty-Two .................................................... 168
Chapter Twenty-Three ................................................. 185
Chapter Twenty-Four ................................................... 194
Chapter Twenty-Five .................................................... 208

Chapter Twenty-Six ............................................................. 220
Chapter Twenty-Seven ........................................................ 225
Chapter Twenty-Eight.......................................................... 228
Chapter Twenty-Nine........................................................... 232
Chapter Thirty ..................................................................... 239
Chapter Thirty-One.............................................................. 242
Chapter Thirty-Two ............................................................. 246
Chapter Thirty-Three........................................................... 250
Chapter Thirty-Four ............................................................ 257
Chapter Thirty-Five ............................................................. 263
Chapter Thirty-Six............................................................... 269
Chapter Thirty-Seven.......................................................... 276
Chapter Thirty-Eight ........................................................... 279
Chapter Thirty-Nine ............................................................ 290
Epilogue............................................................................... 298

# Chapter One

### September

I had three goals. One, to get through my best friend's wedding without blubbering. Two, to make sure as the maid of honor I was, you know, honorable and shit. And three, to not punch a certain groomsman in the face—or sit on it.

If I was being completely honest with myself, I could manage maybe one out of three.

By society's standards, I should hate weddings. I was unconventional, freshly thirty, and newly divorced. All three of those should put me firmly in the wedding-hating column, but that wasn't the case. Nothing was more revealing than a big event. They were ripe petri dishes for me to examine humanity. I might not be a blushing bride, but I was a nosy Nancy, that was for damn sure. Consider my popcorn already popped.

"Do you want another Diet Coke?" the bartender asked, ripping me from my worry.

"Yes, that'd be great." I smiled at him as he slid a plate of French fries in front of me as I shifted my bony ass on the maroon cushion, hearing it deflate slightly.

I was told to visit Tilly's Tavern before leaving Pine Bluff, and now I knew why: the service was quick and the inside looked like something out of Middle-earth. I glanced over my shoulder, spotting a roaring fireplace that should have Aragorn sitting beside it, but instead had a bunch of blue-collar guys inhaling French dip sandwiches.

Yep, I was in Maine alright.

As the bartender returned with my second Diet Coke, I heard the front door scrape open behind me. I flashed another look over my shoulder and there he was. Dane *motherfucking* MacCloyd. The dreaded groomsman in question. We'd met last night at the engagement party, and things had ended with me literally kicking him square in the chest. His best friend, Harley, was marrying my best friend, Kaylee, next spring, so unfortunately, we'd be spending lots of time together.

I couldn't romanticize the idea that we could be something more. I couldn't wait around for a man like my mom had with my dad. I'd seen the absence of him eat her alive and ruin my childhood. I knew I had to get out before the pattern repeated.

Waiting on a man to change was like going to Vegas sober—useless and maddening.

When he spotted me, Dane's mouth pulled to the side in a cocky grin. I rolled my eyes and turned back to the bartender. "Hey, if a girl tips you fifty bucks, can you refuse service to a certain local?"

"Sorry, can't," he said, drying a glass with a rag as he left.

Dane purposefully dragged his wide chest against my arm as he settled onto the stool next to mine. I leaned away, refusing to acknowledge his shamelessness.

"Hey, Maisie." His low voice covered me like warm honey. He was one of the few guys who hadn't butchered my name by calling me Macy the first time we'd met. As much as I didn't want to admit it, the slow rasp of May-zee escaping his mouth made my blood jolt.

I shot him a glance, trying my best to look unbothered. His light skin with golden undertones was still clinging to the tan he must've earned from being outdoors all summer. The backlight from the windows darkened his sandy brown hair, which was buzzed short along with the scruff framing his jaw. He was in jeans and a gray shirt with a camel-colored Carhartt jacket over it. I knew underneath it all, he was jacked from wrenching as a mechanic, with tattoos filling his arms clear up to his thick neck.

"Hey, dude." I loved calling grown-ass men *dude*. It was my petty way to humble and friendzone them.

It didn't work on Dane though. His smoky green eyes scanned my tousled, neon-pink pixie cut. "I dig the pink hair. Did I mention that?"

I picked up a French fry and offered it to him. "No, you somehow left that out yesterday between laughing at me and grunting."

"I didn't laugh at you. You know that's not how things went." He plucked the fry from my hand with calloused fingers. The sight of them brought back the memories of how sinful they were dragging down my body.

I hid a shudder as my nipples pebbled in my bra. "Did you come here just to harass me?"

"No, I came here to talk. I don't like how things ended last night."

"That won't be necessary. You showed me exactly what kind of man you are."

A wry smile brightened his face. "So you're just going to act like nothing happened? Like there isn't something here?" He looked away, nodding. "Okay, darlin', we can play it that way." I snorted into my Diet Coke as he rounded his gaze back to me, his expression more intense than before. "But we both know it's just a matter of time."

"A matter of time until what?"

"Until you're crawling into my bed at night, pulling off some little sundress you're wearing and begging for it." His nose wrinkled slightly when he hurled the word *begging* at me.

I fought an uncomfortable laugh. "You've really thought this out. I mean, the whole sundress detail and everything."

He shrugged. "I just have a feeling, that's all."

"That's cocky."

He stole another fry. "Last time I checked, you were perfectly okay with my cock."

I shoved at his beefy arm. "Fuck all the way off!" I slid off my stool, making eye contact with the bartender while gesturing at Dane. "Sir, he'll pick up my tab, thank you!" Looking back at Dane, I grabbed his stubbled jaw, leaning in close. "If you breathe a single word of what happened in that forest, I will make your life a fucking nightmare. Do you understand?"

His stupid face crumpled in a grin around my fingers. "I love it when you're pissy." With his proclamation, he planted a kiss on my forehead.

I scoffed, releasing his face as I slung my purse over my body to leave.

Before I could fully retreat, he slapped my ass. "See ya next May!"

# Chapter Two

## DANE

She was a squabbling little tornado of a woman. She strutted out of Tilly's with a huff. The air right in front of me still smelled like her, all sugary sweet, like a waffle cone on the boardwalk in the summer. I'd seen a couple of flashes of her sweet disposition last night, but it had melted away as quickly as it'd come. Now I was in a sticky situation.

Watching her cute, little pixie ass bolt from the tavern was painful. Trust me, I wanted to chase her, but after last night, I didn't know how much pride I had left to lose. I was so used to people leaving, I'd gotten used to it. But I kinda, maybe, wanted Maisie to stay.

It was a foreign concept to me. I'd just have to wait for this whole thing to sort itself out next spring at the wedding. I wasn't one to play the long game—life was too short. I'd lost too much already. I didn't let a single moment pass wondering if I should take a risk or not. I just did it. Sure, it'd gotten me to some interesting places, but those always had the best types of friends and even better lovers. Maisie was neither to me right now. We were in some murky gray area I'd never been with a woman. A half-hearted hatred and a full-blown obsession.

    I lay in bed last night thinking of her mahogany-brown eyes lit by the autumn sun when we'd first met. They were so large and curious as they scanned my face with slow blinks. I loved how the warm, tawny skin of her cheeks blushed to almost match her hair when I made her laugh. She reminded me of a faerie with her little swoop nose with a golden ring fit snug against the left nostril. She was short and slender, with a delicate frame. On the contrast, her voice wasn't high and airy, but instead packed a punch with a confident tone accompanied by a slight Southern drawl.

    She was smart as a whip, with instant comebacks and jokes. I could've talked to her for days. I got the feeling she was just as taken aback at me as I was her. Kaylee had really downplayed her best friend all these months. I was starting to think it was on purpose.

    But everything had gone sideways last night, so when Maisie had strutted in front of my shop before entering Tilly's moments ago, it was like a Hail Mary to go talk to her. I'd only known her for less than 24 hours, but we'd been through it. I'd seen her stunned, playfully horny, and completely crestfallen. I'd also had her little foot square in the middle of my chest as she kicked me away with a string of curse words even my buddies couldn't replicate.

    Things weren't great right now, but that was fine. That was the lie I told myself while I snarfed down the rest of her French fries before leaving some money on the counter and returning to my shop.

    A stench immediately slapped me in the face. "Lennie, what the fuck did you cook this time? It smells like a god damn biohazard in here!" I sucked in another puff of air, willingly torturing myself. "Dear lord, it's like something died in something's ass that was already dead!"

    Gangly legs stuck out from underneath an old Toyota Camry, the same shade as flat Champagne. Digging his heels into the shop floor, he rolled his creeper out from the car, crunching up to talk to me, a wrench in one hand, a sandwich in the other.

"Hey, man, it's pastrami, gouda, and some sprouts. Want some?" He shook the sandwich, letting the meat flap a little.

Lennie looked like John Lennon if he got caught in a bog for too long. I'd told him that the first week he'd worked for me and it had cracked him up. So the nickname Lennon had slid into effect, then over the years had shortened to Lennie. With the little, circular glasses, hawkish nose, and feathered hair, I wasn't wrong. His hair was now white with age and his skin had leathered to a nice maroon shade since the man had never heard of sunscreen. He was a sight that caused sore eyes.

"You're hella old. Why do you eat like a frat bro?" I asked.

"Because I never went to college. So why not?" He chuckled before chomping into a side of the sandwich, causing sprouts to sprinkle out like Listeria-ridden confetti.

He hadn't gone to college because he'd bought a VW van to drive to California to be a hippie, then he'd followed the band Phish around America. The last place his van had broken down was Maine, so now we claimed him as some artifact. He still couldn't keep a VW running, but in his defense, who could?

"Open a bay or window if you cook. Now it smells like sketchy cheese and motor oil. And while I'm bitching you out, which you know I hate doing, I want to remind you to lock up when you leave. Just because Maine has the lowest crime rate in the nation doesn't mean you can just leave without shutting the door, okay? This isn't some Burning Man shit where we *trust our tribe* or whatever."

The man didn't believe in doors. It was horrifying.

"Fair enough, brother." He tucked the sandwich in the breast pocket of his coveralls and slid back down under the car. "So did you get to talk to the little lady?"

I pulled coveralls out of the washer, wringing out the damp fabric before hanging them up. "Yeah, she wasn't much for talking."

"You couldn't convince her to stay a couple extra days? That's usually your specialty."

I glowered at his legs sticking out of the car. "Guess I'm losing my touch," I said dryly.

"What's her name?"

"Maisie Quinn. She's Kaylee's best friend from Texas and a real pain in my ass."

"I like her already," Lennie said. "So is she your date to the wedding?"

"No." I shut the washer with a loud thud. "She's unfinished business."

"Yeesh."

"I meant what I said, lock up and don't stay past six o'clock. You deserve a life."

"Okay, boss."

I went upstairs to my loft above my shop. Harley had helped me fix it up a couple of years ago, but sometimes I disliked living so close to where I worked. I hated living in Pine Bluff in general. It wasn't a secret I was friendly to the tourists. People around here thought I was a manwhore, but I didn't think I was doing anything a normal 31-year-old guy wouldn't be doing anyway. I just so happened to be one of the few people in town single and not old enough to be on Medicare. So what if I dated some of the women who rolled in through town. Big deal.

My biggest secret? I kind of wanted to leave.

My family? Dead.

My career as a mechanic? Dead end.

My social life? Slowly dying.

So when I'd met Maisie last night, I'd gotten a little carried away. She was different. Instead of batting her eyelashes and playing the coy card like most visitors, she was bold, busting my balls and challenging me immediately, all while remaining playfully alluring. She was this intoxicating mix of *come hither* and *you better back the fuck off*. For a simple man, it was a complex brew I couldn't help but partake in.

I thought maybe she could be my last bang, my send-off. Then maybe I could put my dick into retirement and stop putting it in every willing participant.

But Maisie wasn't out of my system yet.

I still needed to unpack that.

# Chapter Three

### January

"Sir, this can't go up your ass." I wrangled the gummy dildo like an eel as I stood behind the counter of my adult boutique.

His white, broom-handle mustache twisted as he cleared his throat. I swore under his cowboy hat, his cheeks deepened to match the bright red toy in my hand.

I held it out horizontally in a demonstration. "No flared base, no trace. The muscles in your bum will suck it up. Only flared base things can be used anally."

"It's for my wife." His eyes darted around the store.

"Zero judgment here, sir. I just want to make sure you or your wife don't end up in the ER. They have my number on speed dial. I can't be on their shit list."

*I guessed the term shit list was a bit too specific for this situation.*

I popped on a bright smile. "It's my job to educate my customers for safe usage. Can I recommend some lube and a plug?"

"Do you have something that vibrates?" he whispered.

I whispered back, "You bet. Ten different speeds. Oh, and I have a sale going for nipple clamps. Buy one nip, get the second one free!"

My joke didn't even earn a chuckle, but that was okay. His cowboy boots clunked on the hardwood floor as I guided him over to the wall of options, launching into the rundown of what would work best. A little, triumphant warmth rushed over me when I witnessed his shoulders drop as he relaxed a little.

You see, my store wasn't the typical sex shop. It was first and foremost a safe place for everyone to explore their sexuality, especially women. Instead of rows of bleached bimbo porn from the 90s and blow-up dolls with comically huge tits and gaping mouths, I had more tasteful options available that didn't objectify women.

Whenever I'd gone into a sex shop in college with my friends, I'd left feeling like most of the place was geared toward the straight male gaze and experience, so when I'd opened my boutique, I'd gone out of my way to change that. I'd tried to keep it mysterious with dark plum walls, sexy music, and moody lighting. No buzzing fluorescent lights and blaring glam rock under my watch.

I also had lingerie with inclusive sizing and did my best to order toys in shades other than just pale white. As someone who didn't exactly know their genetic makeup and heritage, I could attest to feeling weird when I didn't see my own light tan shade represented.

Along with local art, I also sold Kaylee's pottery. The boob mugs and butt vases were a huge hit. My newest addition was a rental studio space in the back portion of the store where people could hold events, like mixers for swingers, bachelorette parties, and tantra classes. No orgies though. I even had that listed in the rules and on a sign in the bathroom. The state of Texas would throw a hissy fit, and I was already pushing the boundaries operating this debauchery.

After I rang up the rancher, the landline chirped in the cradle.

"I can get that," my employee Dominique offered, pushing some dark curls over his shoulder as he finished hanging up some new satin robes on a rack. He wore cobalt-blue, sequined booty shorts, pink cowgirl boots with fringe, and a white cropped shirt that stated *Your Dad is my Cardio*. He finished the look with disco ball earrings that reflected light on the deep bronze skin of his neck.

"No worries, I got it." I picked up the call and forced my peppy customer service voice. "Pretty Kitty, this is Maisie. What can I help you with tonight?"

"Huh?" A man's voice filled the other line. "Pretty Kitty?"

"Yes. Do you have the right number, sir?"

"Are you a veterinarian?"

I rolled my eyes. This happened a lot. I launched into my regular script. "No, this is a boutique in Austin. I carry local art, lingerie, and adult toys that encourage a more sensual lifestyle."

"Explain the name to me, darlin'."

The use of the word *darlin'* rang in my memory. "Dane, you motherfucking menace! Why are you calling me at work?"

He let out a gravelly chuckle. "That was too easy. I had to pull out the big guns. I never got your number, and Kaylee won't give it to me. You've blocked me everywhere else."

"I didn't block you. I've been banned from most apps."

There was a pause for what could only be amusement. "For what?"

I sucked in a deep breath, turning to the wall to mutter, "For cyberbullying Ted Cruz."

A bark of laughter shot out of Dane. "That's my girl. Oh god, I forgot how funny you are. Is this a good time?"

"Time for what?" I asked, baffled.

"We have to talk, Maze."

"Listen, don't call me Maze or darlin'. Don't call me your girl. And especially don't call me at work. Don't even perceive me, okay? For all intents and purposes, I am just a sack of warm, gooey flesh to you."

"Oh, baby, I love it when you talk dirty like this."

I rolled my lips into my mouth to fight a laugh while holding the phone away from my face. Gaining composure, I shot back, "Get the fucking hint, dude!"

"Get off your high horse and I will!"

"I'm not on a high horse."

"You are. And you're rewriting what happened to make yourself feel better. That's pretty shitty. The wedding is coming up and we have to be a united front."

"No, we don't. We only have to get through a rehearsal dinner and the actual wedding day. As long as you fake a smile in the photos and leave out any low blows aimed at me in the toast, I'll call it good."

"Maisie . . ." he said in a chiding tone. "You've known Kaylee since you were teenagers, right?"

I moved the phone to my other ear, pinning it between my cheek and shoulder so I could organize the tins of edible body dust near the register. "Yeah, we bonded in high school after getting kicked out of ceramics class for trying to recreate the pottery wheel scene from the movie *Ghost*."

He chuckled. "Of course, it was something like that. Well, don't you want her to have a nice tension-free wedding day? I mean, Harley and I go back even further. He's been a good friend through some gnarly stuff. I don't want to ruin his day either."

"You're so full of it! You have a guilty conscience and you're trying to smooth it over by weaponizing a wedding. That's some next-level bullshit."

"You made fun of my dead dad," he snapped back, all forced detachment evaporating.

"You laughed at my body," I countered.

"No—"

"Bye, *darlin'*," I said in mockery before I smashed the button of the phone with a deep exhale.

Dominique approached the counter. "Who was that?"

"Some fucking idiot I met in Maine. We had a thing; it didn't work."

Dom pointed at me conspiratorially. "Listen, it was hard to eavesdrop on that call, but best believe I managed. Did I hear he laughed at your body?"

"Yeah, cute, huh?"

"What a bastard. And you have to fly back for the wedding? That's going to be awkward as fuck."

"Yeah, tell me about it."

"If you need a hot date, I can find a tux." He stuck out his tongue playfully.

I opened some of the pixie dust, tapping the poof only to dab some on his arm. "Oh, you'd like that, wouldn't you? Fresh man meat?"

He ran from my attack, grabbing a flogger with black leather tassels. "You can't blame me! I'm sick of the guys here!"

"You think they're better in New England? Fuck no!" I chased him as he ran to the other corner of the store, the sequins sparkling on his tiny ass.

"At least let me decide for myself!" Dom hit me on the hip with a playful swat of the flogger.

I struggled to get close enough to dab him with the glittery poof again. "What do they even have in Maine?"

"Lobster?" he replied, dodging my attempt by running around a clothing rack.

"You want to fuck a lobster fisherman?" I screamed in outrage.

"Oh yeah, gurl! See what's under those rubber waders?" He chuckled at his idea, shimmying his ass. "Have the crew bend me over the edge of the boat to see who has the best sea legs. Tell 'em to crack me open and dip me in butter to eat instead."

"Oh my god, you're so deranged!" Leave it to Dom to make me laugh. If it wasn't for him and Kaylee, I'd be depressed as hell. "Besides, I can't take you. Who will run this place? Hmm? All these housewives need their toys. We can't deny them."

"Like their limp-dick husbands do, golfing every fucking opportunity and yanking it to creepy babysitter porn."

"Damn straight." I gestured to the wall of vibrators and dildos with the glittery poof. "Besides, who needs a man if you have these?"

Dom gave me an incredulous look, running the tassels through his hand. "I don't know, those won't keep your bed warm at night. And who will you fight with when you're all saggy and I've moved on to be rich and famous and shit?"

"Sad and saggy. Sounds 'bout right. You know me though. My picker is broken."

"That sounds like a personal problem."

I chucked the poof at him, hitting him square in the chest. "Hush!"

The truth was, I had terrible taste in men. I'd missed the boat when it came to love and marriage with probably the worst pick possible—my ex-husband Conner. He was a cowboy who'd promised to whisk me away but had only given me regret.

Considering Dane was also charming as hell, he was without a doubt a terrible choice.

I moseyed back to the counter. "For starters, I don't want this fucker." I glared at my phone, wondering if I should scrawl down his number from the caller ID. Blinking back the memory of his face cracking in a laugh as he hovered over me in that forest last autumn, I jammed the clear button on the call history.

# Chapter Four

# DANE

I stared at my phone after she all but hung up on me. "Fuck this," I said to myself, shoving it in my pocket and grabbing my keys from the bowl on my coffee table.

One of the only perks about living on Main Street above my shop was that I could walk just about anywhere I needed. As a mechanic with a truck, a car, and a motorcycle, it felt excessive to own all three some days, but oh well.

It was a bitterly cold night, three days after a massive snowstorm. Grayish snow piled up to knee height lined the streets and salt crusted the sidewalk. Making my way to Tilly's Tavern, I contrived my plan. I would find someone to be with tonight. By filling a woman's void, I literally filled my own. Call me a red-blooded male, but sliding into a warm pussy made everything feel all right in the world. We all came out of a woman hoping to get back into another one our whole lives. It was a known fact, kind of like how food while camping always tasted better and nothing good ever happened after 2 AM. These were the untamed truths you didn't get from Buddha.

Besides, I liked most women. There was a certain mystique only women could conjure—a distinct smell, a lightness in laughter. It was addictive. They were insightful and funny. They actually talked about things that mattered, unlike some of my guy friends. Sometimes I just needed to literally feel not so alone, like there was someone beside me, witnessing the same reality as me, breathing in the same air. Plus, the sex wasn't a hardship. Were mornings a little lonely? Yeah. Did I wonder what it would be like to have the consistent aroma of a woman I loved on the sheets? Sure. But I just couldn't say no to the quick yeses I got from tourists.

I tilted my neck to the side, letting the crack calm my nerves. The din of the tavern welcomed me along with a couple of townies. The bartender, Bronn, picked up a glass for my usual whiskey with raised brows. I nodded, silently confirming that was what I was drinking tonight.

Waiting for my drink, I looked over my shoulder. There was a gaggle of women chatting over wine. Ever since a lodge nearby had started offering weekend spa packages, more and more women tourists flocked here in deep winter. I scanned their shoulders for ribboned sashes, like what they'd wear at beauty pageants. Usually, sashes meant divorce or bachelorette parties. I'd learned they couldn't stand to celebrate without accessories. The divorce parties had black sashes and were down for hate sex. The bachelorette parties had hot pink or white and were usually more competitive, so you got the potential of a threesome. They unknowingly color-coded themselves for me.

Without a sash in sight, I continued inspecting my options. All eight or so women blended in a mass of pastel-blue crew neck sweaters with something cheesy scrawled across the chests. Ah, so they'd elevated from sashes to sweaters, fucking fantastic. I was sure they were keeping some Etsy shop in Iowa in business with this embroidered bullshit.

One woman in particular caught my attention. She seated herself in the center of the semicircle booth, ensuring all eyes were on her. She had dark hair at the roots that morphed to brownish blonde at the ends that I'd seen on other women. I'd been told it was called ombré. As a guy, I didn't really get it, but I could tell she'd curled it in a way that must take skill, so I'd give her props for that.

She forced her laugh, making it extra loud along with how she threw her head back. A few other women, more even-keeled, sat toward the edges of the booth, watching her with either annoyance or envy. I didn't care. My sight was set. A couple more seconds confirmed her ring finger was empty and it was time for liftoff. As I got closer to their table, their conversation quieted.

"Excuse me, miss. I couldn't help but notice you're having the time of your life."

Her hand flew to her chest as she looked around at her friends in amusement before answering, "I *am* having the time of my life."

"Care to make it better? I'd love to buy you a drink at the bar."

"Um, sure."

Enjoying their eyes on me, I remembered my manners. "That is, of course, if you ladies are okay with me stealing your friend for a bit?"

The other women bobbed their heads with airy agreements. The one next to her shooed her by tapping her hip. Three of her friends had to get out of the booth to free her, but I stood there, waiting to take her hand to help her stand, knowing damn well I'd just started some silent reverb of gossip that would fuel her ego for the foreseeable future.

"I'm Dane, by the way."

"Cami," she said breathlessly.

As we walked away, the murmurs of her friends made her smile. Once at the bar, she ordered a Moscow Mule as I took off my jacket and pushed up the sleeves of my thermal.

"Wow! Oh my gosh, I love your tattoos." She ran a nail up the black-and-gray scissors and roses just below my elbow, not bothering to ask me what they symbolized. "Do you have a lot?"

I held up my other arm and then tugged at my neckline. "Yeah, covered. Well, not entirely. Maybe you'll see what I mean." I winked at her, bringing my whiskey to my lips.

A half hour later, she was leaning into whisper, "I leave tomorrow. I've always wanted to hook up on vacation. Wanna fuck?"

"Yeah, I live just down the street." I rubbed her back. "I've been tested recently. You're clean and single, right? No surprises?"

She nodded, twirling her hair. "No surprises."

"Well, then let's go have some fun."

She leaned in again and whispered in a baby voice, "I want you to gag me with your big cock, Daddy."

*What the actual fuck?*

I couldn't be limper if I tried. I never wanted to shame anyone, but baby talk grossed me out. Pairing that with the whole daddy thing gave me the biggest ick. To spring that on a stranger seemed extreme, even for me.

Completely at a loss, but not wanting to embarrass her, all I could say was, "Oh yeah?"

Her flat eyes drifted to my lips as she traced them with a fingertip. "Yeah, and I want you to call me filthy names."

I leaned in closer, moving some hair off her shoulder. "Only if you live up to them." I gently pulled her face to mine for a kiss, immediately comparing her lips to the last person's I'd felt. This wasn't as electric or consuming as kissing Maisie. My mind didn't melt away the second we touched. The world didn't go silent with only the low thud of my own pulse. Instead, it was a hollow, transactional moment I'd easily forget. Sure, Cami was sexy and fun, but she wasn't my Maisie.

She let out a little coo of pleasure when I stopped kissing her, a smugness pinching her features. "I'm going to go say goodbye to my friends."

"Meet me at the front door."

I watched her walk away, only mildly intrigued. Pulling my gaze back to the bar to hunt down Bronn to close my tab, I was met with my own reflection in the stained-glass window behind the taps. I could've sworn shadows hung under my eyes as I held my mouth in a miserable line. I wasn't used to looking rough. Something about seeing myself hunched over a bar, nursing a whiskey while a 20-something-year-old stranger filled in her friends about her fling made me feel like my face was a roadside attraction. Sit on it and take a selfie, prove to your friends you saw it.

A sour taste filled my mouth while an indistinct dread frayed my nerves, like when you realized you'd overstayed your welcome at a party or slept in too long. I didn't belong here. I could just feel it.

"She deserves better," I mumbled to my reflection, realizing I wasn't talking about Cami.

"Huh?" asked Bronn.

I pushed the tumbler across the counter. "Close me out when you get a chance."

Catching Cami at the door, I put on my friendliest tone. "Hey, I'm sorry, but I can't do this tonight. I swear it's nothing personal."

She balked. "What do you mean it's not personal?"

"There's this girl I'm realizing I still have feelings for, and this just doesn't feel right."

She rolled her eyes. "What kind of pathetic excuse of a man are you?"

"Guess I'm trying to figure that out myself," I said, shoving my hands in the pockets of my jacket.

"Listen, Dean—"

"Dane," I corrected, trying my best not to let that sting.

"I don't need some asshole embarrassing me in front of my friends. How dare you lead me on!" She stomped her foot.

Feeling petty, I leaned in. "Hopefully you can find some *daddy* to gag you and burn that snazzy sweater while the night is young."

She gasped in outrage as I brushed past her to open the door. "Fuck you!"

"You wish you could, sweetheart!" I shot back, not even looking at her.

# Chapter Five

## May

    I rolled into Maine feeling in control and focused. Since I hadn't flown this time, I wasn't dependent on Kaylee picking me up and didn't have to survive her chaotic driving. That was the only thing I didn't miss about her. Surviving as her copilot left you with unseen scars and fun coping mechanisms. Plus, she was a busy bride who didn't need to worry about me. It was the least I could do.

    Last autumn, for the engagement party, I had stayed at Kaylee's cabin with her and her fiancé, Harley, who I'd affectionately nicknamed lumber daddy since he was a forest ranger. But with the stressful nature of a wedding, I'd snagged a rental of my own to not be in the way, much to Kaylee's displeasure.

    The drive from Texas to Maine was a whopping thirtyish hours that I had broken up over the past couple of days, but I didn't mind. I was doing some soul-searching, and I had some interesting baggage.

Arriving in town, I decided to check in and drop off my luggage before visiting Kaylee at her shop. I was wearing my favorite purple-velvet bell bottoms, a vintage *Goosebumps* shirt I'd found at a thrift store, and my trusty denim jacket covered in kooky patches. Bringing a bit of Texas with me, I made sure to wear my favorite cowgirl boots.

Pine Bluff was a beloved destination because of its dense forests, rock climbing, flowing rivers, and pristine lakes. According to Harley, after the lumber boom, the town had found a way to bounce back by creating an artsy Main Street along with some lodges and a winery.

It was early afternoon, and the late spring day was glorious, even by Maine standards. Golden light filtered through the lush trees, urging me to roll down my window for a whiff of crisp air that had the distinct pinch of pine. It was dangerously relaxing, to be honest. Maybe that was why people here were in no rush—they were literally pine-drunk.

I followed my GPS, pulling up to the small cottage nestled in a sleepy, historic neighborhood. It was bright white with dark green shutters with hearts cut out in the middles of the planks. Ivy grew up the side of the house while big, shady trees and tall pines surrounded the property, along with a tidy yard and two rocking chairs to the left of the front door.

When I got out of my car, a crow flew close to me, so close it created a slight gust as it landed on my hood.

"Hello, crow," I said, feeling amused at how it tilted its head at my words.

I'd been dreaming of crows, come to think of it.

Feeling rude, I reached into my center console and grabbed a bag of Corn Nuts I'd been snacking on. The ranch-flavored kind was my go-to road trip treat. I placed four on the hood of the car for my new friend, who gobbled each one up and flew off.

My crossbody purse cut into my shoulder as I bent over, typing in the code for the lockbox. It beeped in denial with a red flash. I sighed and tried again. Denied. I pulled up the PadHopper app on my phone and sent a request for the host to help me. In the meantime, I sat down on one of the rocking chairs and replied to some work emails.

A rumbling made me look up from my phone just in time to see Dane park a classic muscle car by the front garden gate. Its shiny black hood mirrored his profile as he rounded it to make his way to me, his black T-shirt tight across his chest, his inked-up arms on full display.

"Oh my god, you've got to be kidding me." I whimpered under my breath. Gesturing to him, I raised my voice so he could hear. "What in the *Supernatural* wannabe Dean Winchester shit is this?"

He glanced back, putting his hands in his pockets with a shrug. "It's not a '67 Impala. It's a '68 GTO. Plus, my dad had this before that show was even a thing." His eyes flicked to my car in the driveway. "That's pretty rich coming from a girl who just drove into town in a fucking hearse. Where's the funeral, Maisie?"

"Don't diss the hearse." I shot up from the chair, pointing at my shiny ride that had a black cherry custom paint job. I used it as a cargo hauler. It was much cooler than a truck or some utility van. "Why are you here?"

He met me at the steps. "You tell me. You booked my cottage."

"I did not!" I swiped on my phone to find the reservation, ignoring how good he smelled standing this close to me. A hint of leather mixed with oakmoss, if I had to guess.

"Yep, and based on your reputation, I know you've already run an FBI search on me. What's my middle name?"

I was known for digging up dirt on people. I had receipts, files, and screenshots galore. Information was power. In a world where I had little, I'd take whatever I could get. But after my recent antics of cyberbullying senators, I'd laid off snooping because I was worried my nosy ass had landed on some watch list.

Plus, if I was being honest, I'd purposefully refrained from lurking on Dane because ignorance was bliss and I was already flirting with fascination. I didn't need any more material to hyperfixate on this man. Now I wished I had. Surely, I would've found property records of him owning the cottage. I was kicking myself in the ass for not finding a way around it.

"Fuck, fuck, fuck!" I hissed, staring at the email reservation. At the bottom was Francis Mac, the host's name. "Is Francis your middle name?" I asked, finally looking up at him.

He typed in 0404 for the code. "Yep."

"Why did— Did you use my birthday as the code?" I sputtered, pointing at the lock. That wasn't the code he'd given me in the reservation, the rat bastard.

"You're not the only one who knows how to dig up dirt on people, Maisie Quinn Collier. Or did you revert to Adams after the divorce?"

I flashed him a fake smile. "Charming. Kaylee said you lived above your shop."

"I do."

"Why don't you live here? It's adorable."

"Bad memories." His eyes narrowed, the friendly demeanor clouded for a moment. "Both of my parents died here. Doesn't feel charming to me."

"Oh great, so not only does it have a shitty host, but it's also haunted?" I blurted then winced, realizing how rude I was.

Dane just cocked an eyebrow, unfazed. Opening the door, he ushered me into the cottage.

"Sorry, I wasn't thinking. Listen, I don't want to make things weirder between us. I'll go—"

"Lodging is an issue right now," he interrupted, stepping toward me so I was forced to walk backwards and even farther inside. "People are flying in from all over for the wedding. I think Kaylee's dad claimed the last spot at Stonebriar Inn."

"Oh, he loves me. Maybe he'll switch." I attempted to dodge back toward the door, but his arm was outstretched, bracing on the wall next to me. With it, his bicep twitched in a way that caused a flutter deep inside me.

"Stay. Please. I promise it won't be awkward." He was feigning being casual, but I could tell by how hard he swallowed after that sentence it was all an act. And goddamn did he look good. In the nine months apart, he had filled out more, in a good way. He'd put even more meat and muscle on his glorious body or something. The man dwarfed me in height and sheer size. I wanted to pull him down for a kiss and let him fling me on the couch and have his way with me.

His scruff still covered the little dimple in his chin I loved so much. Not to mention his lips. Oh god, there was also a little dent in the middle of his bottom lip. It made them all pillowy and kissable. I knew right behind them were straight, white teeth. Not your average white, but the kind you'd see on fucking Colgate commercials. I still remembered how they'd nipped my bottom lip before he'd whispered the sexiest things all those months ago.

Pushing myself out of ogling, I flipped back into outrage. "You wanted this all along, didn't you? You wanted me trapped where you'd have access to me. It's kinda creepy actually."

He stepped in closer to me as he lifted his other arm to cage me, all but pinning me to the wall. "I don't mind that I know where to find you." His lashes flicked as his green eyes darted to my lips and back up to meet my gaze. "I think you want to be found."

And just like that, he set all the blood in my body on fire. I fought for a steady breath as I stared at him, not knowing if I wanted to drop the act or run.

With a smirk, he stepped back. "Now let me in the back door."

"Pardon?" I shrieked.

He sauntered to my car. "Unlock your deathmobile so I can help you with your bags."

"No need!" I chased after him.

"It's the least I can do as a host."

"I've got it. Really. I didn't pack much. I'm only here for four days."

"Maisie, let me help."

I let out a horrified squeak as he lifted the hatch, freeing a waterfall of sex toys to spill out. We stood there staring as box after box bounced off the hitch and onto the pavement.

When the loot finally stopped pouring, he looked at me in bewilderment. "Let me get this straight. You rolled into town driving a hearse filled with vibrators to attend a wedding? What kind of bachelorette party are you planning exactly?"

A loud cackle ripped through me.

"Jesus Christ woman!"

"I warned you!" I said, trying to sober.

He eyed the carnage. "The real question is which one is your favorite?"

I lunged to grab a box and slapped his arm with it. "Stop! They're for Harley's mom! I'm hosting a workshop with her while I'm in town."

Maxine was a sex therapist. If anyone needed discount dildos, it was her. I'd done the math, and by the time I'd bought plane tickets, a rental car, and shipped her the lot, it would've been double than just driving them to Maine myself. Two birds, one stone. Or rather, a bunch of dildos and one road trip to clear my mind.

"What kind of workshop? The care and feeding of your battery-operated boyfriend?"

"Pretty much. How to operate, clean, and store it. I have several models that are open so guests can decide which one is best for their anatomy and arthritic hands. It's for senior citizens at the community center tomorrow. Maxine is buying the rest for her clients."

"Grannies have needs too," he said with a shrug.

Dane made a few more cracks at me while he carried my bags into the house while I restacked all the inventory. I could feel that my cheeks were flushed, and I wished he weren't so funny. It would be much easier to hate him if he were dull. But I didn't think Dane had ever been considered dull. Was he maybe a little surface level? Sure, but that was just because he didn't want to pry. I got the feeling he was hiding his own shit.

He gave me a quick tour of the small cottage that had a certain shabby chic charm you couldn't replicate even if you tried. It was from years of collecting, and if anything, it gave me more questions about Dane's late mother because her style was flawless. Everything was soft pinks, bright whites, and white oak. No trace of a man, children, or anything practical in sight.

After showing me the bedrooms and bathroom, he stopped in the middle of the short hallway leading to the living room. "Why did you change your hair?" he asked, picking up a piece that swung just above my shoulders. I had to curl it every day into these beachy waves, and it was a real bitch. Along with it being longer, it was now back to my natural onyx black color. A stark contrast from when we'd met and it had been short and pink.

"I didn't want to look like a neon highlighter in Kaylee's wedding photos. You know, stick out like a sore thumb."

"But you don't look like you," he whispered, tucking it behind my ear. I fought the buzz of his fingers trailing the rim of my ear.

"Kaylee said the same thing. She said she wanted me to look like *me* on her big day. Oh well, I don't want her to regret anything."

His brows pinched together.

"Chill, dude." I sighed. "It's just hair."

He opened a linen closet. "Since you're tiny, I'm going to go out on a limb and assume you run cold. All these blankets are clean. The warmest ones are on this bottom shelf."

I rolled my eyes at the mention of my size as he turned to lead me back into the living room. I was barely five foot one, big fucking deal. Everyone liked the idea of being quite spritely until you were scaling your kitchen counters daily to get

Cheerios. He already made me feel small in more ways than one. Hearing the observation just felt like another nail in the coffin that would be my ability to trust him.

He scratched his head. "Come to think of it, you might get cold at night. Do you know how to work a wood burning stove?" He gestured to the metal contraption in the corner surrounded by worn stones.

I dropped my shoulders. "Does it look like I know how to use a wood burning stove?"

We fought a laugh, staring at each other.

"No, you sure don't," he said. "It seems the guest before you used the last of the wood. Let me get you some and I'll show you how to light it."

"Wait." I grabbed his arm to stop him. His muscles against my palm were so warm and dense. The slight contact felt like a current of electricity between us. Alive, strong, and undisputable. I knew he felt it too by the way he cast a quick look at the skin-on-skin contact. I gulped, jerking my hand back to shove it in my jacket pocket where I wouldn't be tempted. "I don't want to trouble you. I'm sure you have to get back to work. Don't worry about me," I offered.

Unperturbed by my objection, he made his way into the kitchen. "I want to know you'll be warm. Hang tight. There's Diet Coke in the fridge for you, help yourself," he said over his shoulder before shutting the back door.

I opened the fridge wearily. He knew I loved Diet Coke. It was my vice. I didn't drink alcohol that often because I'd had a bad experience in college, plus my mom was an alcoholic, so it was probably for the best. When we'd first met at the engagement party last autumn, he'd asked if he could make me a drink, and I'd said just a Diet Coke. Instead of making a huge deal about it, he'd put down his beer and drank soda with me. I found his social grace and adaptability sexy.

Snapping a can open, I brought it to my lips, reveling in the familiar tingle as it hit my throat. The fact that he'd thought of providing Diet Coke for my stay in his cottage made my head spin with possibilities I had no business considering.

Combating my urge to swoon, I pulled out my phone to text Dominque some details about Dane so he could dig up dirt for me. I'd taught him all my tips and tricks over the years. I knew I could do it myself, but quite frankly, I needed Dom to filter through any information that might be lurking out there. You know, like leaked dick pics, bad reviews about his auto shop, maybe an ancient Facebook profile with awkward photos of him sitting next to some dead deer like a trophy. I couldn't go down that rabbit hole. I needed to keep my head in the game and stay in maid of honor mode.

Taking another sip as I turned around, I had to fight from spitting it out. Dane was heaving a huge round of wood out of a shed. In the process, his muscles shifted, bunched, and released as he plopped it on a stump. With his back to me, the sun lit up his broad shoulders as he reached inside the shed to produce an axe and chain. Turning back to the log, now almost facing the house, he wrapped the chain around it. I took another sip and pretended to look at my phone just in case he caught me ogling, but out of the corner of my eye, I continued to watch as he planted his feet and lifted the axe, swinging it down in an ear-splitting crack.

"Sweet baby Jesus," I whispered under my breath, literally wiping the Diet Coke and drool off my mouth. "Now I get why women agree to live in this godforsaken place."

He continued to hack into it with long, practiced swings, the wood splitting but remaining neatly together due to the chain around it. Each time he'd lift his axe, the long-sinewed muscles of his tatted-up forearms corded and veins bulged, creating a mesmerizing display of strength that I simply couldn't look away from.

When he put the axe back, I scampered with my phone and Diet Coke to the family room, where I leaned against the wall, trying my best to play it cool.

"Ah, the log has a belt," I said wryly as he walked past holding the load of heavy wood by the chain like it was nothing.

"It helps," he said, unhooking it and dumping it into a wrought-iron holder next to the stove. "Okay, rule one of fire making is always start with dry and small."

I crouched down with him in front of the stove. "Dry and small," I repeated with a determined nod.

"This is kindling." He held up strips of wood, and from there I zoned out because he smelled amazing, and our knees kept touching, and watching his calloused, working hands maneuver the wood was super distracting. I guessed I'd have to bury myself under the blankets if I got cold.

Could I ride a horse bareback? Sure. Had I passed advanced business calculus in college? You bet. But could I risk my chaotic Aries ass burning down this cute cottage because I didn't listen to simple fire safety instructions? No way.

I pretended to understand, nodding along to appease him. When his spiel was over, he stood, brushing off some stray flecks of wood from his shirt. "And if you can't figure out the stove, just let me know, and I'll come over and keep you warm." He flashed me a sexy wink.

I swatted his chest. "Very funny." I took a step back, needing my space so his charm didn't soften me. "Hey, but on a serious note, thank you for letting me stay here. This place is so lovely, and I appreciate you trying to make it comfortable for me."

"It's the least I can do," he said with a shrug, making his way to the front door, stalling as he stepped onto the porch. "I want you to settle in, but I'd love to talk things over now that you're in town. I'll pick you up at 7 for dinner." I opened my mouth to refuse, but he swooped in with another line. "And don't say you have plans with Kaylee because I already know she has a meeting with Harley and their high priestess.

Something about jumping over a broom during the handfasting."

Knowing my bestie, that tracked. But I was super annoyed by his certainty that I'd cave and go with him.

"What makes you think I want to have dinner with you?" I asked.

His face pulled in a bright smile. "I'm delightful."

"More like delusional."

"You really don't like me?"

"You literally can't imagine someone not liking you?"

"No, people love me. I'm friendly."

"You're a bit too friendly."

He leaned against the doorframe with an amused look. "One dinner, Maze. Everyone needs to eat."

"I've been on the road all week. I should really take it easy tonight. Plus, I have some things to help Kaylee with for the wedding. Then the bachelorette party is tomorrow night."

"Great, so we're still acting like nothing happened. Fooling everyone with fake smiles and lies?"

I grabbed the door handle, officially over his shit. It would take more than a dinner date to repair what he'd done to me. "Yeah, you're good at that." And with my proclamation, I shut the door in his handsome face.

After settling in the cottage and freshening up, I visited Silver Springs Coffee & Crystals, the shop owned by Kaylee and her new friend, Rosie. It was located on the picturesque Main Street that was lined with mature trees wrapped in twinkle lights and speckled with wrought-iron bistro tables, colorful awnings, and quirky shops. The entire street was on a slight incline leading up to one of the bluffs encircling the town, giving it its namesake. It was the epitome of cutesy yet historic New England charm, and I wanted to soak up every second I could.

Eyeing the purple sign with moons, I couldn't help but smile while opening the door. I heard Kaylee's girlish squeals as she ran toward me with open arms. We clashed in a fierce hug, and just like that, a chunk of my heart was back with me. I breathed her in, tears filling my eyes as her familiar scent and energy permeated my being.

Kaylee and I were platonic soulmates. The second I'd met her, I'd thought to myself, *There you are*. We'd had countless lifetimes together, were thick as thieves. It was something you could feel. A familiar glint in someone's eye, the easiness of their presence. I was pretty sure we'd been handmaids and harlots together. You know, birthing and bathing together over and over again until we were stardust. Our bond would survive beyond arguments, men, and far-off distances. I was her sun, and she was my moon. And one thing was for damn sure—I would always love Kaylee Waters.

"I missed you so damn much," I said, fighting tears.

She hugged me tighter. "I missed you, too."

"I can't believe your wild ass is getting married." I sniffled, breaking the hug.

Her gray eyes watered as she blinked back unshed tears. "Yeah, pretty weird, right?" She flipped her long blonde hair off her shoulder and fanned her eyes to prevent mascara rivers running down her porcelain skin. Today she was wearing a flowy tie-dye dress with cap sleeves and a long, beaded necklace that, if I had to guess, was sandalwood.

This was the longest we had been apart. The time before was when she'd gone to India for yoga teacher training. We'd gone to high school together in Texas, and then college together in Florida. When her dad had gotten in a motorcycle accident, she'd had to move to Maryland to help him recover, and by that time I'd been consumed by marriage and trying to keep Pretty Kitty afloat.

"Hey, Poe!" I said, greeting a barista I recognized.

She had locs that were dyed a lovely teal that complimented her deep umber-colored skin. A delicate choker with a pale blue sea glass charm floated over her clavicle. It jiggled when she spoke. "Hey, good to see you." She finished watering a plant by the front window to give me a quick hug.

"How's school? I bet having Maxine as a psych professor is entertaining."

"Very. I actually just survived finals, so I'm in between terms. I decided to take summer semester," Poe explained.

"I remember summer semesters were always a bitch, but worth it just to knock out credits. Major props for signing up."

Her slender fingers wrapped around the brass gooseneck watering can as she sighed with a pensive look. "Yeah, I'm already regretting my decision."

I couldn't help but smile, remembering those exhaustingly hard college days.

Finishing an order, Azalea rounded the coffee bar. "I'm so glad the maid of honor has arrived! Now the real party can start!" She pulled me in for a hug. She was a tall, leggy brunette with sun-kissed cheeks. When I'd met her last autumn, I'd immediately liked her. She was so wholesome and warm.

"Hi, Azalea!" I said as her boobs smashed my cheek for a split second in the hug. "I don't know how much of a partier I am now. You're giving me too much credit."

"No, she's not!" Kaylee demanded.

I beamed at her adoration, feeling all my walls fall this close to Kaylee.

"How's Stonebriar Inn?" I asked Azalea. "You're still helping run it until you inherit it, right?"

"Yeah, I'm just waiting for my aunt to commit to retiring. I keep telling her to stay in Florida, but she comes back every summer." She flashed a quick wide-eyed expression relaying her annoyance. "So I bounce between here and the inn in the meantime."

"Well, that's nice of you to help her."

She batted away my compliment. "It is what it is. Can I make you a drink, hon?"

Kaylee interjected, "Oh, make her that new one." She snapped her fingers, trying to recall the name of it.

"The Horny Hag?" Poe offered with an amused smile.

"That's the one! Rosie came up with it last week. It's so good iced!"

"Well, that's an appropriate name because I sure feel like a horny hag lately. I haven't gotten any dick for ages," I quipped.

A middle-aged woman at the table behind me gasped. I peered her way over my shoulder. "Tell me about it," I said, milking the joke as she buried her face deeper into her book, which made the other women giggle even more.

A mob of tourists in outdoorsy clothes streamed into the shop. Kaylee gave me an apologetic look as she followed some of them through the archway that led to the crystal shop side of Silver Springs.

"I've got all day. Don't worry!" I said, waving her off.

Azalea set to work making my drink as Poe tapped her phone to change the music to something more upbeat to match the suddenly crowded energy of the shop before diving into taking orders.

Azalea slid the drink across the counter for me, committed to watching me try it.

"Oh, that's dangerously good!" I said after the first sip.

"Right?" Poe agreed, pumping syrup into a cup. "It was an instant hit."

I took another sip. "It's like kettle corn at first then it morphs into that coffee taste."

"I'm telling ya, Rosie is a total mastermind," Azalea said. "She can make these drinks no one else can. It's a gift."

Hmm. I had my reservations about Rosie, but I couldn't help but admit this gave her some brownie points. "Sounds like she's in the right business," I offered. My eyes darted up to the chalkboard above Azaela's head. "Is the Wi-Fi password seriously FlickYourCoffeeBean?"

"Yep!" both baristas said in unison with a snicker.

"God, I love it here."

I took a corner seat at a small table next to an intricate mural of a mystical forest. I checked in on some work stuff and got lost in my own little world. When I got up to pee, I tried to twist the handle on the bathroom door, but it was locked.

"Sorry!" I yelled.

Clomping and a bang sounded off behind the door before it cracked open. "Hey, I need help!" Azalea whispered, looking around suspiciously.

"Are you out of toilet paper?"

"It's stuck!" she hissed in horror.

"Uh, I'm gonna need more context clues, babe."

"My menstrual cup is stuck! Inside me!" She winced through the crack in the door. "Oh god! It's my first time wearing it, and I feel so stupid."

I wasn't a stranger to menstrual cups. Or people frantically coming to me with things stuck inside them. My customers were fucking wild, and I always sent them to the ER for legal reasons, but Azalea was just a woman at work in a very real predicament.

"I . . . Can't you just leave it inside you, and when it fills up with blood, it will weigh it down so you can reach it easier?"

She whimpered. "I have really impressive Kegels and a high cervix."

"Okay, humble brag, love that."

"I think it flipped inside me or something. It's making my cramps worse somehow. I am in so much pain." She sighed, bumping her forehead on the doorframe.

Her confession tugged at my heart. I eyed the small line at the coffee bar, knowing time was of the essence. "Listen, can I maybe help in some way? I can try to break the seal."

"You'd do that for me?" she muttered.

"Yeah, you know, girl code."

She made a little noise that sounded like a gasp or cry while I racked my brain. *What would a doctor do?* I dodged into Kaylee's office for the first-aid kit to get some gloves and fetched my emergency pouch from my purse.

The next thing I knew, a pantsless Azalea was letting me into the bathroom that had a single toilet and a sink. The poor thing was almost in tears.

I reached up to hold her shoulders. "I've totally got you, and you're in luck because I always have lube. I get tons of testers for my store. I'll put it on my gloved finger so it won't be as uncomfortable. Oh, and I have a pad for you to wear when we're done."

She gave me a small smile before bobbing her head with a determined nod. "Right, so, I guess I'll crouch on the toilet?"

"And I'll go fishing," I said, putting some paper towels down to kneel on.

I distracted her by talking about the wedding, but the second I got up to a knuckle inside her, she murmured, "Dane was right about you."

"Beg your pardon?" I asked shrilly. The last thing I expected from this trip was to be digit-deep inside a townie while talking about Dane.

She stared down at me, still squatting like some shark week version of Spider-Man as she braced herself on the handrail and the sink. "He said you're a cool chick. I mean, I knew that. You're friends with Kaylee, so that's a good sign. But this is like next-level kindness."

"Wow, you weren't kidding. This little fucker isn't going anywhere. It's not upside down though, so that's good news." I couldn't look at my hand or her face, so I stared at the ceiling as I blindly tried to push the side of the cup to collapse the wall and break the seal. "Bear down for me."

With a loaded pause, she finally gasped. "You got it. I felt it. It worked."

Not knowing social etiquette on what to do when pulling out a menstrual cup from an acquaintance, I slowly slid it down her vaginal canal, presenting it to her like a wedding ring during a proposal.

Azalea sighed in relief, grabbing it with a wad of toilet paper as she sank onto the toilet with a manic laugh. I joined her in the absurd moment before I stood to clean up, rolling off the glove and turning on the sink.

"Oh god! We're definitely friends now! I owe you!"

"No offense, but I don't know what would even be in the realm of period cup removal when it comes to favors," I said, snatching another towel to dry my hands.

"We'll consider it a running tab."

"Sounds good."

"Oh, and Maisie . . ."

I stood in front of the door to strategically open it. "Yeah?"

She ripped open the pad. "I'm really glad you're here."

I fought a clash of emotions and put on my friendliest smile. "Thank you, me too. And I hope you feel better."

A few minutes later, Kaylee and I exited the coffee shop to get our official wedding nails. As we walked into the nail salon, the familiar scent of acrylic made me even more giddy. It was weird that certain smells were tied to certain memories.

Kaylee opted to abandon her usual dark polish for a pale pink set that would look timeless as a bride. I went with a pale cream color that looked better with my tan skin. We gabbed about every final detail for the wedding, and afterward, we ran some errands before she was supposed to meet her high priestess, formally deemed Lady Geneva Gravedust.

"Are you sure you don't want to come with? Lady Geneva Gravedust lives in a yurt. It's really cool. She has a therapy llama. We're using some of its wool in our handfasting cord."

I'd learned to filter out about thirty percent of the unhinged details Kaylee gave me. If not, we'd get distracted with side tangents. This was one of those cases.

I stopped mid-stride on the sidewalk to look at her. "No, I'm okay. I'm going to call it an early night. By the way, did you know I was staying at Dane's cottage?"

A mischievous smile lifted her face. "Maybe. But after everything I went through with Rosie, I've sworn off meddling when it comes to other people's love lives."

I playfully swatted her hip with my purse. "Okay, blondie! Abandon me when I need you most!"

She started to giggle, which meant I was on to something.

"Oh god, you didn't have one of your visions, did you?"

Along with astrology, energy, and past lives, I believed in her visions. She was eerily intuitive. She'd known when things had gone sideways for me in the past without me even needing to send her a text. She'd just showed up on my doorstep with a plan and a cold Diet Coke. I'd never be able to fully thank her.

She scrunched her nose. "I haven't had any visions lately. I can promise you that. I've been so stressed about the wedding and the shop that I'm barely dreaming, let alone getting intuitive hits." She wiggled her eyebrows. "Luckily, Harley's been providing me with some stress relief, or I'd be a tangled ball of nerves."

I started to buck my pelvis toward her in a mock attempt of air humping. "Oh yeah, lumber daddy is giving you some *good wood*."

She joined me, gyrating right there on the street. "Yeah, girl! Morning wood, lunch break wood, good night wood." She stopped mid-hump to hold up her pointer finger. "Oh, that reminds me! You can't call him lumber daddy in front of his hella Greek grandparents. It will give his yaya a heart attack."

I scoffed. "They have Maxine as a daughter-in-law. Hasn't she broken them in by now?"

"Maisie! It's a formal event. Please!"

"Okay, fine. But he better be thankful for me. Oh, that reminds me, I brought his favorite flavor of edible panties for you to wear on the honeymoon. They're TSA approved, I checked."

"Peach?" she exclaimed gleefully.

"Yep!"

Kaylee looped her arm back in mine, clearly pensive as we walked. "He can never know that you know that."

# Chapter Six

After saying goodbye to Kaylee, I walked to my hearse that I'd parked in front All Booked Up, which was a bookstore right next to the coffee shop. While fishing out my car keys, a distinct buzz hit my temples, the telltale sign of someone watching me. I looked up, catching an old granny smiling at me from where she dusted a window display. Something about the way her smile reached her eyes drew me in.

"Hello there!" her little voice quaked as I entered. She was barefoot, in a dress with a faded apricot cardigan dwarfing her frail frame. Even with her white hair formed into a little poof on her head, she was about the same height as I was, which was nice.

"Hello, ma'am. How are you?"

"Oh, I love that Southern drawl. I'm good, honey. I just saw you walking with Kaylee. Are you one of her friends from back home in Texas?"

"Yes, I am. Here for the wedding. My name is Maisie." I extended my hand for her to shake.

"Viviane." She smiled, her pink, thin lips curving as she placed a small, cold hand in mine to shake. "Oh, I love your *Goosebumps* shirt!"

I chuckled, opening my jacket to further reveal it. "I didn't even plan on wearing a bookish shirt in here. I'm just a 90s kid that grew up."

"For the record, all my *Goosebumps* books are down in the basement along with the mass-market paperbacks. They're on sale for a buck right now before summer really ramps up and the tourists take over. I'm open for another hour, so feel free to wander."

"Sounds great, thank you."

I meandered deeper into the rows of books, feeling her gaze on me the whole way. I wasn't exactly sure what I was searching for. Admittedly, I wasn't much of a reader. Ever since college, I'd felt like my attention span was shorter. Academic stress had rotted my brain, so I stuck mostly to trashy reality TV shows and true crime documentaries.

The spine of a lilac book caught my attention, and tilting my head, I read the title: *The Seat of the Soul* by Gary Zukav. That sounded a bit airy fairy, but something about it made me pull it out for further inspection.

It was a book on secular spirituality and tapping into reverence for life. I could get behind that. Opening it, I found a strip of paper from a fortune cookie serving as a bookmark. I thought I was the only one who did that. In faded blue, it stated: *Be bold and totally worth the chaos.*

I snorted, feeling like that had been written for me. Turning the book over, I saw the used price was $4.44.

Okay, now this was just getting weird.

Being born on the fourth day of the fourth month of the year, my lucky number had always been 4. I had it on my softball jersey, and Kaylee said since I was always seeing 4:44 on the clock, it was my angel number.

The book was in fairly good condition, with a tight binding, its pages only slightly yellowed. There was a receipt clinging to the backside of the cover. The book was traded for credit with several cheap paperback Westerns. And there it was, at the very bottom right of the receipt, all the damning evidence I needed.

**Account holder: MacCloyd, Dane**

Why would he have read a book about this? He didn't strike me as a spiritual person, but the further I read, I could see why he liked it. It wasn't overly flowery or steeped in doctrine. It seemed unpretentious and like a good starting point.

I reasoned with myself that it wasn't illegal to buy a book before shutting it to walk up front. Viviane was perched in an armchair, waiting for me while light classical music trilled from her laptop.

"Ah, good choice! Even Maya Angelou loves this one!" she said.

"Always a good start." I flashed her a friendly grin, pulling out my wallet. "Hey, are you familiar with the class tomorrow over at the community center?"

A ding sounded. My eyes sliced to the intruder, my blood jolting as I saw Dane strut in with a paper bag stuffed with books, the seams threatening to rip. He'd changed into his coveralls, clearly returning to work since our little interlude this afternoon. The navy fabric was littered with oil stains and dirt as it stretched across his wide chest with his name stitched over one of the breast pockets. To make matters worse, he wore a backward baseball cap, and a touch of grease was smeared on his neck next to his Adam's apple. I had to look away, feeling fucking feral.

"Hi, Dane honey!" Viviane said.

"Sorry, I know you're about to close. I'm hoping to grab something to read tonight since I don't have any plans." He shot me a loaded look before returning to her. "Did you get the loot?"

"Yeah, some old geezer in Skowhegan croaked. Found these at his estate sale." Her little, arthritic hand slapped a box on her counter. "You're gonna shit yourself when you see some of these titles."

"Perfect!" he said, flopping the sack next to it.

This close, he smelled like grime mixed with the faint hint of manly musk layered with the existing oakmoss and leather from earlier. My instinct was to flare my nostrils for an indulgent whiff.

*Girl, get your shit together! You are not swooning over motor oil and sweat.*

Viviane's bluebonnet eyes darted between the two of us. "This pretty, little gal was about to tell me all about her class tomorrow."

Dane leaned on the counter to join the conversation. "My apologies. So sorry to interrupt. Please, go on." He pulled his mouth in a cocky grin, undoubtedly loving my torment.

I focused my attention on Viviane. "It's a class I'm hosting with Maxine about senior sexuality."

She wrapped her cardigan around her body. "I love that woman. She does great things for our aging community."

"She's great. I own an adult boutique down in Austin— "

"It's called Pretty Kitty," Dane interrupted, causing her face to wrinkle even further with an amused smile.

"I've brought several different models of adult toys for people to look at and a personal lubricant that has squalene in it. It's very moisturizing and great for aging skin."

"Ya gotta keep it wet and ready," Viviane said with a wink.

I let out an appreciative chuckle. "Yes, exactly, you get a toy and a bottle of the lube when you sign up. It's included in the cost of the class."

Viviane's jaw slacked in awe. "What a lovely idea!"

"Yeah!" I beamed.

"Want to carpool?" Dane asked her jokingly.

I smacked his arm. "Stop!"

Straightening up from the desk, he towered over me. "She doesn't like to drive. I was offering her a ride. You know, being a gentleman."

I stepped closer to him, not letting him intimidate me. "It's for seniors. You can't come."

"Are you being an ageist?" He tilted his head with his question.

I stepped even closer, damn near chest to chest. The hint of his body heat drew me in as I fought a steady tone. "It's more for women—"

"So only women can use sex toys?" he countered.

Viviane's little laugh tittered between us.

Even in the unflattering light of the bookstore, he was irritatingly handsome. His smirk traveled up from his kissable lips to his knowing eyes. He lifted his hand, causing me to hold my breath under the assumption that he was about to tuck hair behind my ear again. Instead, he grabbed the book I'd just bought, flipping through it in consideration. "Great choice by the way. Loved this one."

I snatched it out of his hand, slapping him on the chest with it. "You're not welcome in my class! Do you hear me?"

"Why not?"

"Because . . . I have my reasons."

"And they are?"

I looked to Viviane for a lifeline, but she just handed me my receipt.

"I don't have to tell you."

"Okay, well, Maxine loves me, and Viviane here needs a ride."

She gave us an innocent shrug of her frail shoulders.

*Oh how quickly the granny turned on me!*

"I guess I'm outnumbered here. Thank you for the book, ma'am." I nodded to make my exit, but before I could, he held open the door, forcing me to press past his chest at the threshold.

"Oh, and Maisie . . ."

"Yeah?" I said, turning around in a huff.

His eyes flicked to the book in my hand. "If you wanted a piece of me as a souvenir, you could've just asked."

# Chapter Seven

DANE

Viviane's knees cracked as she settled down on the bench next to the back door of her bookstore. The sun was setting behind the pine trees, casting an electric orange swirl in the sky. The brisk late-spring weather allowed the scent of pine to hang in the air mixed with the heavenly aroma of coffee wafting from next door. The low hum of cars driving on Main Street on the other side of the building created just enough white noise to feel private.

"Well hell, Dane, she's adorable!" she said, plucking a joint from somewhere in her poof of hair and handing it to me before she dug into a pocket of her cardigan, presenting a lighter. This was our ritual: I'd start it and leave her the rest.

"I know. I'm so screwed," I said through gritted teeth as I held the joint between my lips, cupping around the flame while I inhaled the distinctive earthy smoke.

"That sweet little accent. That petite figure of hers. Oh god, she's cute! Those big brown eyes would make any man sign their fortune away with a bat of an eyelash."

"You're not wrong," I said, taking another drag, grateful both of our shops were closed for the night so I didn't have to worry about getting too high to literally operate heavy machinery.

Her bluish, drawn-on eyebrows scrunched as she wrapped the cardigan around herself. "What happened between you two?"

I blew out the smoke, watching it mix with the clouds streaking across the sunset. "You know I don't kiss and tell."

"I haven't seen you with anyone else in a while. Have you been holding out for her?"

"I'm not sure. She's just kind of taken up my mental space."

Flickers of the engagement party dashed into my mind. Seeing her for the first time, laughing with Kaylee as they walked in with pure carefree confidence. Her little drawl as she said *I'm Maisie* right before she went in for a hug instead of a handshake. Her legs resting over my lap as we sat on a garden bench and talked for hours. The little noise breaking in the back of her throat while we kissed as I picked up her and laid us down on the forest floor as bright yellow autumn leaves lazily fell around us.

"Tortured. I get it. That's how I was with William." She pursed her thin lips, deep in thought. "But I can see why she's hesitant. There would be a life here, ready to swallow her up."

"Yeesh, well, when you put it like that." I handed her the smoke.

"Oh, don't take it personally, honey. You know what I mean."

"I do."

"Your mom would've loved her."

A burning beyond the weed filled my throat. "Yeah, I've already thought of that too."

Viviane had watched my mom grow up. My mom had been the hairdresser in town for decades. When she'd passed away, her nail tech, Ginger, had taken over. The salon was only three doors down from my shop and a constant reminder of what I'd lost.

"Is she close with her mom?" Viviane asked.

"Not really. From what I remember, her mom sounded kind of self-absorbed."

"Poor thing," she said reflectively before taking a drag.

Thinking of Maisie made my stomach churn. She had changed so much. Who knew nine months could do that to a person? Of course, she was still gorgeous. Her dark hair was beautiful against her warm skin, and her big doe eyes looking up at me made me want to cradle her face in my hands and promise her the world. She was still wearing funky clothes, just like the time before, even down to her denim jacket covered in patches from different places she must've visited. But looks weren't everything. I worried more about what was haunting her. She was impatient, defensive, and detached, three things I hadn't witnessed at all that first night.

I liked women who lived in their instincts, who went with the flow and bent so they didn't break. Spontaneity was one of the sexiest things in a woman. With Maisie in front of me today, it was nothing but protocols, plans, and her guard up. I wanted to shake her, to help snap her out of whatever game she was playing. Even if I hurt her, which I didn't mean to, I wanted to urge her to stop living small.

Even worse, she was in my cottage. In the house that once had my finger-painted pictures on the fridge and dings from baseball bats along the wall. When my dad had died after my mom and sister, I'd scrubbed the place of our life there together as a family. I'd needed to. It had been part of the healing process for me.

I'd needed everything gone.

Now, everything was a bit too far gone.

The only thing I couldn't scrub away was my dad's auto shop, which was mine now. I still used his tools and his old radio in the window above my tool chest. I even kept the cobwebs that had been there since before I was born. In some sick way, they felt like his. I even kept his crusty coffee mug from a fishing trip to Vermont we had gone on together. It had stains rimming the lip and remained by the sink in the breakroom still to this day. If it wasn't for the shop and some good friends, like Harley and Noah, I wouldn't stay here in Maine. God knew the winters were rough, the summers were short, and the town was quiet.

"Maybe you two should go for a drive," Viviane said with a shrug, flicking some ash. "I remember when I was dating, it was always so fun to drive up and down Cumberland Avenue. That was when gas was twenty cents a gallon but still."

The innocence of her suggestion tugged at my heart. I wished it were that simple. Not wanting to shut down her suggestion, I flashed her a grateful smile. "That's a great idea, thank you. Oh, by the way, are you going to that class tomorrow? I really could give you a ride."

"Nah, seeing her squirm was enough entertainment to last me a month." She let out a dainty smoker's cough. "Plus, I don't need another vibrator. William refilled his Viagra for little willy."

I blinked hard, wishing I were stoned enough to forget I'd just heard that.

The next day, I was at work, cursing at a beat-up Suburban. I was good at my job. It was either simple or complex, not too much in the middle. I'd realized that was how I like life, either straightforward or something that makes me work for it. Today, it was making me work for it.

Lennie was back on his bullshit, talking about how the earth was flat and no one had ever seen baby eels so that must mean we live in a simulation. I asked if he'd ever finished the movie *The Matrix* and he couldn't remember. You see, Lennie had lost most of his long-term memory on his fourth acid trip. If I wasn't an honest man, I could probably get by without giving him raises.

A diesel rumbling outside my bay along with a deep bark made me roll out from under the Suburban to see Harley hop out of his truck. His olive complexion was already darkening with the oncoming summer. His tan work shirt was untucked and unbuttoned at the top, his black hair longer than usual and a little disheveled.

I got up and wiped my hands, snatching a dog treat.

"Hey, man, what's up?" I gave him a quick hug and walked to his back seat window to pet his work dog: a German Shepard named Storm. "Such a good boy! Yes, he is!" I said in my dopey dog voice, earning a low woof.

"I'm running around like crazy with all this wedding stuff. I want to give you Kaylee's key before I forget."

I grabbed the key from Harley, pocketing it. "So we're cool to put the normal shit on her Jeep? Tin cans tied to the hitch, *just married* scrawled on the window, all that jazz?"

"Yep, have at it." He scanned me up and down with a hazel, hawkish squint. He was the kind of man who already knew everything, so you rarely had to fill Harley in. "Why didn't you tell me she booked your cottage?" he asked, silently referring to Maisie.

I shrugged, still petting Storm from where his head hung outside the window.

Harley raised a dark eyebrow. "Was it on purpose?"

I shrugged again. "I just saw her reservation and let it unfold. It doesn't have to be a big deal. We had a thing. It's over." I tilted my head to the side, hearing my neck crack. For a split second, the sensation eased the knot of anxiety in my stomach. It had been there since the second I'd seen how fucking pretty she looked in the rocking chair on my porch, her little cowgirl boot dangling with how she crossed her legs. I'd immediately pictured myself sitting on the rocking chair next to her, all old and grizzled, just like all the hypothetical futures country singers crooned about. I tilted my head to the other side, letting the second crack snap me back to reality. "I promise we won't ruin your wedding or anything. I already saw her, and we seem cool."

"Cool?"

This was the part about Harley I didn't like. Sometimes, I felt naked around him. He was a good friend, always loyal, didn't judge me, and most importantly, the man was a vault. Any info I gave him would die with him. That was hard to come by, but I paid the cost by having almost zero privacy.

"We're two grown-ass adults that will be civil with each other. You have my word."

"I'm not worried about that. I'm worried that ever since you met her, you've been different. You clam up when Kaylee mentions her. You won't tell me what happened between you two. I've just been assuming you guys had a one-night stand and it went wrong but—"

"We had a disagreement. Shit happens."

Hell, even I could hear how evasive I was being. I felt like a worm dangling on a hook.

He crossed his arms to lean against his truck. "Does she know about your past? About Boston?"

"No, that didn't really come up." I stopped petting Storm to lock eyes with Harley, silently sparring. "I don't think she needs to know. It doesn't affect my life much nowadays."

"Bullshit," Harley said with an amused laugh.

"That's what you've cooked up in your head? You think that's why she's mad at me?"

He extended his arms wide. "You're not giving me anything else to work with. Plus, people always love you. I can't think of why she would be avoiding you so much other than she found out—"

"We had a disagreement about something else," I interjected.

"You should try to smooth it over with her."

I puffed air out of my nose. "For Kaylee's sake?"

"No, because she clearly struck a chord with you. If she can do that and keep up with a friend like Kaylee, she must be one hell of a woman. You'd be a fucking fool to let her prance out of town without some closure. Trust me, I know how painful it is to watch a woman leave."

"That's just it, Har. She's going to prance out of Pine Bluff, just like the rest of them."

"It might be different with her. She has Kaylee here, too."

There was no way that was going to happen. When she'd stood in front of me at the cottage, I could see so much disdain in her eyes, it had gutted me. Each time I'd tried to help or compliment her, she'd walled up.

"We're past the hook-up stage and she hates my fucking guts. If I make it out of your wedding with my nuts still intact, I'll call it a success."

"We'll see."

His doubt caused my blood to hum with a slow burn. I had to change the subject to ensure we weren't fighting during his bachelor party tonight.

"Enough about my bullshit. Where are you off to now?"

He pointed to his head. "Haircut, then I have to get a bigger suitcase for our trip, and I'm supposed to track down mead for the ceremony. Did you know the term honeymoon comes from the honeyed wine they used in handfasting ceremonies in Europe? It's like some ancient Viking shit where the bride's family would provide mead to the couple during the first moon phase of their marriage."

"The things we learn from your girl."

"Right? I had no clue."

"If it's so important, why doesn't the high priestess have any on tap in her yurt?" I teased.

Harley flashed me a smile. "That's a good question!" He clapped a hand on my shoulder, squeezing it. "See ya in a couple hours?"

I scrubbed Storm's head affectionately as a goodbye. "Sure thing."

# Chapter Eight

Kaylee hovered over me from where I sat next to her register. She was doing my makeup while we waited for the rest of the girls to meet us at Silver Springs for the bachelorette party.

"I'm not gonna lie, it's a trip seeing you without your implants. I mean, it's not like you had huge honkers before, but you know what I mean. It's different. I forget you had them sometimes," she said.

"You saw me without them before, at the engagement party, remember?"

"Oh, you're right." She bobbed her head, recollecting. "You look great. Are you still feeling better now that they're out?" she asked, swishing a brush in the dreamiest lavender eyeshadow.

"Yeah, it's like a night and day difference." I grabbed my breasts, which barely filled up my palms. I was a modest B cup now. "It's weird if you think about it. I've spent most of my adulthood with fake boobs."

"Oh, I remember. I was so mad at Conner for gaslighting you into thinking they weren't making you sick. I could kill him." She blew on the brush and then tilted my chin.

I'd spent years exhausted and in pain because of my breast implant illness. I'd presented with issues like fatigue, migraines, and arthritis. I'd even had to get on thyroid medicine at one point because they'd thought I had an autoimmune disease. No one had taken me seriously. I'd done what I always do and fell down a rabbit hole and found a whole community of women experiencing the same thing. Your body could react to the implants like a threat and turn on you with bizarre symptoms. After years of suffering and a bitter divorce, I'd invested in myself and gotten my implants removed. It had been quite an adjustment.

My mom, being the shallow hag she was, had made me feel super insecure about my petite body growing up. She'd gifted me breast implants as a high school graduation gift. She'd acted like it was a favor, sending me off to college with boobs so boys would actually like me. I remembered when I'd told her I'd started dating Conner after college, and she'd made sure to ask if he was a boob or butt man just to prove the theory correct. And when my marriage had been strained, she'd laid on the guilt for not keeping him interested.

She'd say, *Maybe if you looked more feminine, he'd want to lie down in the bed you've made for yourself.*

She'd always hated that I didn't look like I could belong to a country club. The pink hair, the occasional body hair, the nose ring, the expressive clothing I wore, she berated them all. I was too brash in her eyes. It just made me want to express myself even more. I'd spent so many years hiding from the very woman who should've honored and loved me at all costs. Now I was committed to living a life my younger self would've been proud of.

I had my own business. I owned my own townhome, filled with all the weird shit my little heart desired. My social calendar stayed full. I was part of a softball league, and I was always trying new exercise classes like Zumba and acro-yoga. And some nights, I'd order takeout and curl up on my comfy sectional couch and binge true crime documentaries with zero shame. Something I know my mother would've hated.

I squeezed my eyes shut as I pushed all thoughts of my mom and illness out of my mind. It was supposed to be a happy night.

Kaylee smacked her lips, which I knew meant she'd remembered something. I chanced a peek at what she was doing, only to find her searching behind her register with the makeup brush still in hand. "Before I forget, I have something for you."

"Oh?"

"Yeah!" She plucked a saffron-colored, beaded bracelet from a little wooden box behind her counter. "This is called golden healer quartz." She stretched it over my wrist with a little, pleased hum. The stone beads were cool against my skin. "I've been charging it up with reiki. The second I unpacked it for the shop, it was singing for you."

"Thank you," I said, giving her a quick hug. "Wait, I thought yellow quartz was just citrine?"

She pointed to the bracelet with the brush. "You're right, but golden healer is a hematoid quartz, which means it has a specific chemical makeup that includes iron, which citrine does not. So it's rare. Cool, huh?"

I twisted it on my arm, admiring how beautiful it was. Each bead was different, some clearer than others. Some even had inclusions with tiny rainbows reflecting in the lights. Whenever Kaylee gave me anything, I could feel the love she'd poured into it.

"What are the metaphysical properties of this stone?" I asked.

She dabbed the brush in the eyeshadow palette once more and knocked it on the edge to shake off the extra. "Oh, you know, healing energy."

I knew that tone. That was her forced-detached-evasive tone.

I tilted my head sassily, calling her bluff.

"And it, you know, increases confidence and helps clear blocks on your path." She shrugged, pulling her lips taut to look casual.

"And?"

She went on sheepishly, "It's been known to help foster forgiveness, feelings of love, and releasing old patterns."

"Kaylee!" I snapped. "Are you trying to crystalize me into liking Dane?"

She held up her hands, feigning innocence. "I'm just saying it might help let your guard down."

I continued to stare at her, half embarrassed, half amused, either way totally clocked.

She balked. "Oh, like you need a fucking crystal to be obsessed with that man! You don't need a rock to crave his cock!" Clearly done with my shit, she went back to doing my makeup, clucking at me like a mother hen. "It wouldn't kill you to try things again. Even if it's just to have fun. I mean, isn't it tradition for the maid of honor and a groomsman to fuck?"

"You're unbelievable," I said, my chest bouncing as I held in a chuckle.

"What does it say about you that you didn't take the bracelet off, hmm?" she jested.

I reached around to swat her ass. "Speaking of mystical shit, can I ask you to interpret a dream for me?"

"Of course, tell me everything," she said, dabbing the final shimmer on the inner corners of my eyes.

"So in the dream, I'm flat on my back, staring up at a dusky sky that's filled with all these crows flying above me in circles. They caw occasionally, but they don't seem hostile."

"Just kind of foreboding?" she asked, putting glue on a strip of false eyelashes.

"Yes. What freaks me out is I'm frozen there, stuck watching them. It's like I'm pinned to the earth. When I wake up, my heart is racing. It's happened twice since I've been on this road trip. What do you think that means?"

She delicately blew on the lashes. "The logical side of me thinks you're just tired. You've been on the road all week and not in your own bed. Who knows, maybe you heard crows outside your hotel room window while you were sleeping?"

"That makes sense. Like when you hear your alarm go off in your dream."

"Exactly. But the witchy side of me knows that crows are powerful messengers. Whenever I see one, I know magic is afoot. Some cultures view them as negative omens, foretelling bad luck or deception." She shrugged in consideration. "But others see them as intelligent and fearless. They're extremely adaptable. Either way, you know my advice—"

"Trust my gut?"

"Bingo!"

Kaylee stuck the tip of her tongue out between her lips slightly as she focused on applying the fake eyelashes on me. For such a wild card, she was quite gentle and calm most of the time. We always joked that she mothered me because she was a Cancer and my mom was a cold-hearted bitch, but all jokes aside, that wasn't wrong. Kaylee always came in clutch, and she never held judgment. I was pretty sure I could tell her I'd fallen in love with some elderly oil tycoon down in Texas and she'd just ask to bedazzle his Jazzy wheelchair.

"So the class with Maxine was a hit?" she asked.

"Yep. We went half an hour over the planned time because they had so many questions."

Little did she know, I'd spent the whole morning dreading Dane might show up. When both Viviane and him had no-showed, I'd been relieved.

"I'm sure you made their day."

"You have a really cool mother-in-law."

"You should hear what she says to embarrass Harley. She can make him blush so fast." She gently pressed my lid with the tiny eyelash clamp to ensure the lashes were on. "There you go!"

"Thank you!" I held up a mirror to inspect the final look. "When I do it, I always end up looking like one of those creepy dolls that has one eye stuck shut."

"Like that one we found at that estate sale in Sarasota when we were still drunk from brunch?"

In our best creepy voices, we leaned in closer and whispered, "Mildred!" together before cackling. It was one of our old inside jokes.

"What's so funny?" Rosie's silky voice came in from behind us. She was gorgeous, covered in tattoos and curves, her auburn hair in waves down to the crook of her waist. I instantly felt a little insecure.

"Hey, Rosie!" I gave her a little wave.

"Hey!" She leaned in for a quick hug that earned her brownie points. I'd only talked to Rosie for a quick moment at the engagement party last autumn, but I had mixed feelings about her. She'd lied to Kaylee most of last year. They said they'd settled their differences, but Rosie still had to earn my trust.

"Congrats on getting married!" I said, grabbing her hand to see the sparkly rock.

"Thank you!"

"And you're sure you're okay to be the designated driver tonight?" Kaylee asked, slathering on some lip gloss while looking in a compact mirror.

"Yep," Rosie said, her hand going to her stomach.

"She might be preggers!" Azalea gleefully yelled as she walked to us from the café.

Rosie rolled her eyes. "Zay, what did I say about using that word?"

"Sorry, I keep forgetting you hate that term."

From where I sat right at eye level, I glanced at Rosie's midsection, not wanting to be rude but craving more info.

She looked down at me, still protectively holding her abdomen. "We started trying for a baby on the honeymoon. It's only been a couple of weeks, but I just don't want to chance anything," she explained.

"I think that's really special. Good for you."

Kaylee snapped her compact mirror shut. "And even better for us!"

We shared a giggle and left for Tilly's Tavern. The men were going to some lodge tonight so we could steer clear of them. More girls from town met us there, most of their names turning into mush in my mind the second they said them. I found myself alone next to Rosie in a semicircle booth as Kaylee went full-on cheerleader mode for Poe, who was singing a Karaoke version of "Sk8er Boi" across the bar.

"So, you and Dane, huh?" Rosie asked. "Are you going to hook up again?"

"Wh-what do you mean?" I sputtered.

"I saw him stumble out of the forest at the engagement party after talking to you. I figured you guys, you know . . ."

It was like a brick dropped in my stomach. She'd seen? What did she know? Hell, not even Kaylee knew the full story. When she'd asked what happened, I'd told her the gist of it but downplayed it a ton. A townie having information I didn't know about wasn't something I'd factored into my situation.

"He stumbled out of the forest?" I asked.

"Yeah, he was doing up his pants and everything. I figured it was after you guys got all up close and personal." Rosie fiddled with the straw in her Coke, moving around the ice. "I'm sorry. I'm probably reading way too much into it." She sipped her soda uncomfortably.

"Who else did you tell?"

Her eyes scanned my face in genuine confusion. "No one. It didn't seem that important." Her eyes narrowed. "Is there something I'm missing? Are you okay? He didn't hurt you or—"

"God no! No, he's just pathetic." I slid out of the booth. "I'm so glad I don't have to rely on the dating pool here. No offense! Sounds like you and Kaylee got the last good ones." I hitched my thumb over my shoulder. "I'm gonna get another drink. Wanna come?"

She picked up her empty glass with a nod.

One Slippery Nipple later, I was swatting the phone out of Kaylee's hand. "Don't call him! He's at his stag!"

"Bitch, I miss Harley! I want to squeeze his ass!" she drunkenly yelled with her eyes closed. She'd always been a codependent drunk. And quite handsy.

"His ass?" I asked in amusement.

"Yes! He has the cutest ass cheeks. They're like coconuts." She squeezed the air with one hand in demonstration, letting out a little snarl.

Azalea swayed into me, wine drunk. "Girl, you're so pretty," she slurred. I wrapped an arm around her waist as she stared down at me, running her finger down the swoop of my nose. "Your skin is so glowy. I get why Dane likes you. Oop!" Azalea covered her mouth with a snort. "I don't think I was supposed to say that. Boy talk!" She smiled blissfully. "He talks to my friend Noah all the time about you. And Noah can't keep secrets, so I know everything."

Kaylee stopped molesting the air to point at me. "I caught him and Harley talking about you one time, Maze! They were fixing my Jeep. I was driving home and saw Hagrid, that bitch-ass moose, again. I tried to take a photo of him and kinda hit a curb and broke an axel or something important."

Rosie's mouth twitched in amusement. "Can I hold your phone for you so you can twerk properly?"

Kaylee joggled it with a devious, little laugh. "Only if I can make a dirty deposit."

Being a good sport, Rosie pushed her tits together and leaned forward, letting out a whorish porno moan the second Kaylee shoved the phone in her cleavage, causing all of us to break out into cackles of delight.

Another Slippery Nipple later, the girls swayed like a group of drunken lemmings as we watched Azalea serenade us with that song Aerosmith did for the movie *Armageddon*. She was taking it super seriously with choreography and everything.

"I got you this drink." A man's voice came from my right, so I looked away from the stage, spotting a blond guy standing next to my stool at the bar.

"Oh, thanks, but I've cut myself off for the night." I forced a polite smile, eyeing the drink that looked suspiciously cloudy.

His beady eyes flashed over to Kaylee, who had her back to us. "Take it you're here for the wedding?"

"Maid of honor." I gave him another brittle smile, hoping he'd get the hint that I wasn't trolling for a guy.

"Boyd," he said, extending a hand to shake. "Officer Boyd."

I refrained from rolling my eyes. He wasn't in uniform, so it was unnecessary to tell me he was a cop. Plus, I didn't shake men's hands, especially in a bar. They never washed them after pissing. I pointedly looked at his outstretched, dirty-dicked hand, sliding mine underneath my thighs from where I sat on the stool. "I'm here with my girls, have a good night."

He snorted, planting his hand on the bar in a blatant attempt to crowd me. "I guess you weren't raised with manners. When someone buys you a drink or tries to shake your hand, it's polite to be nice to them."

I fixed my eyes on him the best I could with my buzz. "It's also polite to leave women the fuck alone when they're clearly not interested."

My tone must've caught Rosie's attention because she turned around. "Everything okay, Maisie?"

Boyd let out a dark laugh. "Yeah, maybe reconsider the company you keep." He slapped the counter and swiped the drink to walk away.

"What the fuck was all that about?" Kaylee asked, catching the final moments of the exchange.

"He tried to force a sketchy drink on me," I said, flashing her a wide-eyed look that relayed *and it was spiked.*

Rosie guarded our drinks and kept watch on the other women as Kaylee grabbed my elbow to lead me to the bathroom. Her smooth hair tickled my arm as she leaned in, whispering conspiratorially, "Stay the fuck away from that guy, okay? I remember when I first crashed here, he gave me the creeps. Later on, Harley told me all about how he basically had to cockblock Boyd from taking me with him to the station. He knew he wasn't a good guy and didn't want me at his mercy."

"Stop!" I hissed in horror.

"Yeah! He has a dark aura. I've given his poor wife two tarot readings recently. It breaks my fucking heart because even the cards show betrayal. Everyone knows he's a cheater, but I worry he abuses her. And I can't call the cops because he is one!" she grumbled in frustration. "So I'm trying to find a way to help her out safely."

By the time we left the bathroom, Boyd was all but waiting for us in the hallway.

"You need to teach your friend some manners, Kaylee."

"The fuck I do!" she barked back, her voice echoing in the tiled corridor. Leave it to Kaylee to come back swinging.

He scanned me up and down, circling us. "Don't act like you weren't interested in getting free drinks, coming in here with a short skirt like that. It's like you're asking for it."

"I could be sitting on the bar, full pussy out, and I still wouldn't be asking for it. Especially from your creepy ass. Do you hear me? Leave me the fuck alone!"

Kaylee slid between us, facing me. "Let's go."

"You're a mouthy little thing, aren't you?" he said behind Kaylee.

"The only thing more pathetic than your pickup lines is that receding hair line, you fucking beady-eyed bastard!" I yelled as she pushed at my shoulders to hold me back from pouncing on him like a drunken, enraged, little Chihuahua.

Kaylee all but herded me down the hallway, other patrons breaking up our spat as they walked past to the bathroom. Right before he was out of my line of vision, I flipped him off with my best ugly face.

"I meant what I said. You better pull your bitch!" he hollered at Kaylee.

# Chapter Nine

# DANE

Kaylee had openly encouraged strippers because she was cool like that, but finding one around here was like a hot, sunny day in Maine—suspiciously uncommon. So we stuck to the classics: burgers, booze, card games, and darts.

As the night went on, all I could think about was Maisie. She was in my town and here I was, wasting my time with guys I could see any day of the week. I knew the fastest way to get to Maisie was through Kaylee, so I suggested we crash the bachelorette party.

"You have to go over there! That's half the fun!" I goaded Harley, punching him in the shoulder from where I sat with him at a rounded card table.

"I want to see Kaylee." He smiled over the rim of his glass of bourbon with glassy eyes. "I love her so much, dude. She smells so good." He dramatically lifted his chin to sniff the air. "I want to smell her. She's so soft and warm. And funny! God, she's so funny. Life is so good when she's around." He snorted as Noah, our designated driver, started to laugh at him.

I hadn't seen Harley this drunk since we'd stolen moonshine in high school. Seeing such a big, serious guy this hammered was unnatural. Like seeing a dog walk on its front legs or the inside of a bowling ball. Some things just felt wrong to witness.

The main difference was his older brother, Carson, was drinking with us and he was a surprisingly bad influence. From where he sat across the table, he said something to Harley in Greek that sounded mildly teasing as he poured water and a clear liquor called Ouzo into long, slender shot glasses.

"*Yasas!*" they'd cheered together in Greek before gagging it down.

Carson pounded his chest with a cough. "Dear god, that's it for me."

"I want cheese fries," Noah said. "Dane is right. We should go find the girls."

A few more of Harley's friends from college murmured in agreement around the table.

In a delayed reaction, Harley slurred, "Cheese fries? Fuck yes! Let's go!"

Tilly's was busy for a Thursday night. As we walked in, Azalea was singing into a karaoke mic, causing Noah to crack into a wide grin as he watched her.

"Go find your *friend*," I joked.

"Shut up," he said, straightening his posture and running his hand through his light ash-brown hair.

Carson took a seat, pulling Rosie onto his lap with a drunken grin.

Kaylee and Maisie let out high-pitched squeals then hollered, "Lumber daddyyyyy!" the second they saw Harley.

He ducked his head, blushing as he made his way to Kaylee. They melted into a quiet pool of drunken, mushy hugs and murmurs.

"Baby!" She giggled as he nuzzled her neck. "I've never seen you drunk!"

Harley looked at her with a dopey smile then whispered something in her ear.

He really adored that woman. I'd admit, their love story was unconventional. They'd been snowed in his cabin together after he'd rescued her from a car wreck. She'd almost killed Hagrid, the town moose. When she'd moved here without dating him in the real world, I'd had my reservations about how long they'd last, but it had quickly become apparent that Kaylee was good for Harley. And he was good for her. He kept her wild ass mostly safe.

As our best friends canoodled, Maisie and I looked each other up and down. I was in jeans and a nice shirt. Tonight, she was wearing combat boots, a little black skirt that barely covered her perfect ass, and a cropped Chicago Bulls vintage T-shirt. A piece of metal coiled around her neck in an intricate necklace, and her dark hair was half up in tiny buns on either side of her head. Shimmery lilac eyeshadow filled her lids along with wispy eyelashes that fluttered each time she blinked. It was like a faerie going to a rave in the 90s, kind of funky and unexpected. And the way her flat stomach and hip bones peeked out between her skirt and the rough edge of her shirt was driving me fucking crazy. I wanted to nip those hips.

"You guys aren't supposed to be here," she snapped.

"Thanks for the warm welcome," I said wryly.

Miffed at my snub, she put her hand on her hip as she popped it. "Wow, Dane! I'm so glad you pulled yourself up from licking some tourist's twat to join us. Your presence is such a gift!" she said loud enough for people to notice. Both the bachelor and bachelorette crowd paused what they were doing to eavesdrop.

"I dunno, most tourists seem to be just fine with my presence and unique *gifts*."

"Oh, I'm sure they flock here just to fuck you. Nothing says sexy like Maine. Get real. New England isn't hot. You probably sound like a Kennedy when you come."

The crowd chuckled around us.

"Well, based on how sexually frustrated your ex-husband left you, it's safe to say not everything is bigger in Texas," I shot back.

Some of the girls gasped along with her at that one. I swore her eye twitched. "You know what we *do* have in common though?"

I steeled myself. "What's that, darlin'?"

"We're both in the business of making sure dried-up premenopausal cougars don't burn their clits off with ancient vibrators."

The guys behind me exploded in howls of laughter, swatting my back.

She went on with a lethal squint, "Except, I actually get paid in the process. You just get chlamydia"

Kaylee pulled on her shoulder. "Hey, take it down a notch. This is Harley's best friend you're talking about."

"Keep going!" Carson drunkenly bellowed from his seat. Rosie's hand covered his mouth as she buried her face in his neck to hide her laugh.

"Is it really that bad if I take women out and show them a good time? If I give them a few orgasms and stolen moments of peace where the world isn't asking anything of them for once?"

Maisie rolled her eyes. "Oh sure, you're saving divorced women one pump at a time."

Noah held up his finger. "He usually dates women around his age or younger. Usually brunette and—"

"Noah!" Harley and I shouted in unison, cutting him off.

I continued to glare at my friend. "Not helpful," I added, frustrated at his overly literal ass.

Harley went on, "Maisie, that was a low blow. I think you owe him an apology."

Instead, she stepped closer to me, damn near chest to chest as she glared up at me with nothing but pure audacity. I stared down at her, wishing I didn't find it attractive. I couldn't look away. The entire bar blurred and all I cared about was her. She could make me feel so free yet fucked at the same time. Only I got her wrath. But I couldn't forget the fleeting moments I'd had in the forest with her. When I'd had nothing but her surrender.

"Look at them, it's like two alley cats in heat about to pounce on each other," Azalea muttered to Noah.

"My money is on the smaller one," Noah mumbled back, causing Azalea to snort.

"Hey! Take this shit outside!" Bronn yelled at us, whipping his bar rag around. "Your little lover's quarrel is causing a scene."

We barely ripped our eyes away from one another long enough to charge outside in heated silence. I led her to behind Tilly's, where an old wooden fence was half covered in ivy and a streetlight cast an amber-hued spotlight on one side of her face.

"I'm sorry for slut shaming you in front of everyone, but god damn, do you have to be everywhere in this fucking town? You're always ambushing me, wanting to talk," she said through gritted teeth before taking a tense sip of her drink.

"I know I hurt your feelings last autumn, and your friend is getting married, and it's really not an ideal time to work this shit out."

"You're right about that," she said, staring at her drink as she swirled it around in her glass.

A pause spread between us, only filled with far-off murmurs from inside the tavern and the occasional car. I'd spent months wanting to talk to her, and now that I could, I didn't know where to start. It was this tangled mess of misunderstandings and unsaid desires.

Her gaze lifted back to mine. "But you're impatient enough to push it."

"Right. I get it, Maze. I'm a bad man. I'm selfish and pushy, but god dammit, I don't want to wonder what could've been. And I know it doesn't make sense, but everything in me wants to protect you and care for you. To just be around you. It's that simple."

"Dane," she whispered.

"I only got a sliver of time with you, and it wasn't enough. Just a couple hours at that party and you changed me. You rocked me to the core, and I don't know why. All I know is you don't remember it as fondly as I do, but—"

"Don't." She stepped closer to me, her lips tight as she fought to hold back whatever words threatened to spill out.

"Don't what?"

Her chin quivered before she swallowed her emotions. "Don't speak for me. For the past nine months, I've thought of you often. I remember that night fondly. Right up until . . ."

I swallowed hard. "Yeah."

Her mouth sagged. "I don't know how to move on either. And all I have are questions. Why was it so easy to let my guards down that night? Why did kissing you feel so fucking good? Why can't I stop thinking about you even though you absolutely humiliated me? Do you think I enjoyed our time apart?" She sucked in a ragged breath. "Because I didn't. At all."

Hearing she was just as miserable as I was gave me a shred of hope.

With her legs and midriff exposed to the night air, she was trembling slightly with a chill. I opened my arms as an invite for warmth and was half shocked when she clutched her glass to her chest and stepped into my embrace. I ran my hands up and down her back and sides as she fought a shiver.

"I've got you," I murmured as she curled into me, resting her head against my chest, still shaking.

I breathed her in, loving her sweet scent and how she felt in my arms.

When she pulled back, her eyes searched for something in mine, but I didn't know what. I couldn't promise her love or to say the right thing. I could only offer up myself and my time. But I knew that wasn't enough.

A crow flew over us with a loud squawk at the same time as Bronn threw open the back door to toss a crate. Both made Maisie jump, dropping her drink, shattering glass everywhere.

"Shit!" she hissed, assessing the carnage.

"Unfuckingbelievable," Bronn muttered under his breath.

"If you bring me a fucking broom, I'll handle it, dude!" I barked at him. Turning my attention back to Maisie, I saw a shard of glass balancing on the edge of her combat boot, about to slice open her shin.

"Wait, hold still," I urged.

"It's fine. I'll kick it off," she said, shooing my hand away. "I don't want you to get hurt."

Both of our frantic actions caused the glass to cut my left middle finger. I fought a wince and tried to play it cool, but she saw the blood pooling out.

"Dane!" she said, cupping my hand in hers.

"It's nothing. You should see what happens to me at work."

"Nonsense!" she said with an adorable huff as she led me back into Tilly's, where she parked us at a pub table so she could clean up my hand. I didn't hate watching her fuss over me. She was so gentle as she dabbed at the blood with a cloth napkin dipped in cool water. And her lips were unintentionally enticing as she blew on the cut after using liquid bandage she'd gotten from a server. She continued to cradle my hand on the pub table when her ministrations were over, a concerned look softening her features.

"Thank you."

One side of her mouth lifted. "Don't mention it. Can I buy you a drink?"

I chuckled. "Let me, yours was destroyed."

I knew she didn't usually drink alcohol. If I remembered correctly, her mom was an alcoholic, but I figured it was a special occasion, so that was reason enough.

"If you insist." Her beautiful face radiated in a dreamy smile as she gave my hand a final squeeze.

"Oh, look who made up!" Kaylee teased as we joined her and Harley at the bar. Maisie bashfully shook her head and stayed by me, not giving Kaylee any more material to work with.

While Poe drunkenly told the group a story, Maisie's eyes flicked to someone across the bar, then her gaze traced behind me. Gnawing at her bottom lip, she positioned herself in front of me, using me as a shield.

"Everything okay?" I discreetly mumbled in her ear, rubbing my hand up and down her arm.

"Um, yeah." She fought to pull her eyes from whatever she was seeing.

I looked over my shoulder, but with the tavern packed, I couldn't narrow it down.

Kaylee slid past us, grabbing Maisie's shoulder to break her from her spell. "Are you ready to dance?" She wiggled her blonde eyebrows.

"You bet your sweet ass I am!" She took Kaylee's hand and shimmied onto the dance floor. I hung back for a second, purely enjoying the show as Harley pulled up next to me.

"I'm going to marry that girl," he said with a proud tone.

I slapped him on the back. "I'm happy for you."

Without a word, we both watched as they pranced around before committing to some mash-up of line-dancing and twerking.

Another drink in and I could've sworn I was hallucinating when Azalea came out of nowhere, jiggling a hot dog.

"It's time for swing the weenie!" she exclaimed with glee.

"Isn't that what got Harley in this situation?" I said, causing a few laughs.

"Look at Zay grip that sausage. Get it, girl!" Kaylee said to Maisie, causing more laughter as Azalea playfully stroked it with a wink.

Noah cleared his throat, unable to look away from Azalea's grip.

"Okay," Azalea continued, "so for this game, you tie a string around a hot dog and then you tie the other side of the string around your waist like a belt." Demonstrating, she attached her string, letting the hot dog dangle down the front of her, freely hanging between her knees. "Then you have to swing the weenie to hit this golf ball into the goal."

To the side of our group were two long strips of AstroTurf with putt-putt golfing goals at the end of each. Azalea plopped a golf ball down and bent her knees, bucking her hips, causing the hot dog to sail forward to skim the ball.

Kaylee and Maisie lost it, snorting and almost falling over in a giggle fit, knocking over a couple stools in the process as Azalea continued relaying the rules. "You have to keep your hands on your hips"—she paused for a determined thrust—"to move your weenie closer to the goal."

"Then what?" I asked, unable to tamper down my competitive streak as I tied the sausage around my body.

"Whoever gets their ball in the hole first with their weenie wins."

Maisie wiped away a tear from her red face. "That sentence has never been muttered in English, I can assure you!"

Azalea shimmied her hips. "Right? It's so fun though! Harley, are you going against Dane?"

"I think I need another drink," he replied.

Noah stepped up to plate.

"The hole is your goal!" Maisie heckled.

I stared downward. "Hold on! I'm just trying to synch up my meats," I said, swaying my hips.

"Oh my god!" Kaylee bellowed in horror, realizing what I meant.

# Chapter Ten

I woke up hungover as fuck, but luckily Rosie had left out water and crackers for me next to the bed. Once I pulled myself together, I checked my phone to see if Dom had texted me any updates on how things were going at Pretty Kitty or, even better, dirt on Dane. I figured no news was good news. An alert I'd set for myself flashed on my phone, reminding me to report Officer Boyd. Memories flooded me of how I'd suspected that asshole had roofied that drink he'd offered me, and his conduct had been wildly inappropriate.

I wasn't shy when it came to justice. I'd reported Tyler, the dirtbag who cheated on Kaylee and Rosie, last year because his misconduct as a lawyer had been concerning. I was pretty sure I'd gotten him fired. I'd also reported a creepy professor in college who kept coming up with stupid reasons for me to visit him during office hours. He'd eventually left me alone, but gave me a lower grade than I'd deserved, the petty asshole.

I knew better than to simply report Boyd to his department. Since Pine Bluff was a small town, I was sure the circles were tight and the corruption ran deep. So I reported his ass to Maine State Police through their Office of Professional

Standards. I stared at my email that outlined my concerns and request for a call back to discuss it further and felt like a Karen for a nanosecond. I reasoned with myself that if it wasn't me last night, it might be a different woman tomorrow and hit send.

The rest of the day was spent running around and getting everything ready for the wedding. Everyone must've nursed their hangovers for most of the morning because by the time we gathered for the rehearsal dinner, everyone was in good spirits. The event was squaring up to be unpretentious and intimate. I was proud of Kaylee and Harley for not losing sight of what weddings should be about—a couple and their love. Not showing off or, worse, going broke.

The wedding party gathered before the rehearsal dinner to go over the logistics of the handfasting, which was taking place lakeside in front of their cabin. The ceremony itself was on a wide T-shaped dock, while the guests were to be seated on the shore. They'd even arranged Persian rugs to line the wooden dock, a little, colorful touch only someone like Kaylee would've thought of.

I was wearing a flowy pale-pink dress about as long as my bridesmaid gown so I could ensure nothing snagged it tomorrow. Dane was wearing black dress pants and a black button-up shirt, that was unbuttoned just enough to tempt me, and no tie. He caught me staring at him from where he stood with the other groomsmen and gave me a wink. I flashed him a smile, grateful Lady Geneva Gravedust, a middle-aged goth woman sporting purple hair, interrupted the gathering to burn a bundle of herbs around the perimeter of the crowd to bless us.

From there, I got in line. Lady Gevena Gravedust kicked off the procession by strutting to the altar at the end of the dock. The respective grandparents and parents made their ways to where they'd sit tomorrow, followed by Harley, who joined the high priestess at the altar. Carson, Harley's best man, followed, then the rest of the groomsmen, including Dane.

After the bridesmaids, it was my turn. And since they'd opted out of having a flower girl or ringbearer, Kaylee and her dad were right behind me. When it was time to walk back, Dane offered me a hand off the dock, which was infuriatingly polite but admittedly appreciated.

"Thank you," I said, squeezing his hand before letting it go. "How's your finger?"

He examined it with a lopsided grin. "Totally good. I forgot it even happened. Thankfully someone really smart bandaged me up."

I swatted away his praise. "It was nothing." Out of my periphery, I could see Kaylee getting swarmed by Harley's yaya, who was insistently handing her a mysteriously thick envelope and pinching her cheeks. I pointed to the exchange. "I, um, better go save Kaylee from whatever that is."

Dane just chuckled, hanging back while I made my way over to the bride-to-be.

After shielding Kaylee from any other exchanges, I drove to the rehearsal dinner. It was at Stonebriar Inn since most of the guests were staying there to begin with. The inn itself was a three-story Queen Anne-style Victorian estate with crisp white paint and sprawling gardens nestled near the top of one of the mountains in town. I parked and entered through the wrong door, coming in through the kitchen by accident. Azalea was there, beaming with a smile while she wiped her hands on her apron that had mushrooms printed on it.

"Hey, girl! Let me show you where to go!"

"I'm sorry. I had a feeling I parked in the wrong spot." I eyed my hearse over my shoulder.

"Oh, nonsense! You're totally fine." She ushered me in through a narrow hallway, turning through corridors of rooms.

The inn had that quintessential Victorian charm with an edge of rugged details. The mix of historic Maine and cozy care was so evident. The floors were wooden with the occasional creaky board, and the walls were sprinkled with detailed molding, antique light fixtures, and oil paintings. Thankfully, instead of the old funk most historic homes had, it smelled like baked goods. It made my mouth water.

Azalea escorted me into the banquet hall, which was more masculine than I expected, with darker woods and hunter-green wallpaper. The chandelier above the table was dimmed, making the lighting intimate along with a fireplace at the end of the room with a moose bust above it.

"This place is lovely, Azalea."

"Thanks! I love hosting small events like this. Especially for friends." She clasped her hands together under her chin. "It's a pretty small crowd, so we're not doing assigned seating except for the bride and groom at the end closest to the fireplace. Feel free to pick a spot and help yourself to some water, wine, and a roll," Azalea explained cheerily before turning to leave.

I eyed the large oval table, picking a spot two seats from the end in hopes that Kaylee's parents would sit next to her and I could buddy up to them. A few people came in that I finally started to recognize after the festivities. We made a few jokes about the bachelorette party, trailing off our polite conversation when Rosie came in holding Carson's hand as he walked behind her protectively. He was somehow a broodier version of Harley, which I found amusing but a little intimidating. I had no clue how Rosie had tamed that beast. She must be braver than I was.

"Hey, Rosie!" I said as perkily as I could. The rehearsal was so quick, I hadn't even had time to say anything to her.

She looked up from where her feet dodged chair legs to squeeze between the table and wall. "Oh, hey, girl! Glad you recovered from last night!" she said, flashing Carson a pretty smile as he pulled out a chair for her.

Taking his own seat, he glowered at me. We had never been formally introduced so I held eye contact with him, finally earning a nod with a simple, "Hey."

A solid, warm chest skimmed my back. The scent of oakmoss and leather teased my nose.

"Hey, Maze," Dane's deep voice rumbled as he pulled out the chair on my left.

"I'm sorry, that seat is reserved for Kaylee's parents," I explained in my friendly customer service voice I was so accustomed to using at work.

"My bad," he said, dragging across my back again. I looked up at the ceiling, rolling my eyes as Rosie giggled, watching us. Now on the other side of me, he sat down with a smirk. I shot him daggers, fiddling with the cloth napkin on my lap. This was not the place to openly flirt with me. Not only did I not want to pull attention from Kaylee and Harley, I also didn't want to get all flustered. I was already experiencing enough emotions with my best friend getting married.

Sensing he should give me a moment, he turned to Carson and Rosie across from us. "Car-bro, didn't get a chance to ask you last night. How was the honeymoon?"

"Warm," Carson said flatly.

Wow, stunning response.

Dane went on, unperturbed. "You look tanner than normal. Did you get some good beach time?"

"Yeah."

Rosie elbowed her husband, breaking into another amused smile. "It was lovely, thank you for asking. Did you hear Kaylee and Harley are going to Greece for theirs? How cool is that?"

Dane unfurled his cloth napkin, putting it on his lap. "It's probably just an excuse for moose killer to dance around naked on some beach without being arrested."

We all snickered at that accurate observation as more people streamed in. Dane pulled out a Diet Coke from his pants pocket, snapping the tab with a playful glance at me.

"Why do you have that?" I asked as he poured it slowly into my wine glass.

"What do you mean? I love this stuff," he said, pouring the last half into his own. "To keeping a clear head," he said before clinking his glass to mine.

I took a sip, keeping my eyes on him. He was handsome as hell in the dim light, the fire casting a soft glow on his strong cheekbones and defined jaw.

Before I could ask him anything else, Kaylee inched by me, Harley right after her, their presence pulling my attention to the end of the table. They were both beaming, the happiness tangible. It filled up the room. Both of their moms and dads gave short speeches, and then Dane. He didn't deliver any jabs at me, only heartfelt memories of growing up with Harley and a couple of rowdy jokes to poke fun at him. He was charming as hell and had the entire room chuckling. At one point, I had to stare at my plate because the way he stood with one hand in his pocket and the other clutching his wine glass, the veins on the back of his hand on full display right by my face, made me tailspin into a bunch of naughty thoughts I shouldn't have in public.

When it was my turn, I recollected some memories I had with Kaylee and how I'd always known as a true bohemian who believed in love that she'd find it someday. I also mentioned I'd been her confidante while snowed in with Harley, and without even meeting him, I'd known he was a safe place for her. That made his mom cry, then Kaylee. I could've sworn I even saw a little shine in Harley's eyes, so I tied up my thoughts.

When the dinner was over, Dane stood and knocked on the table with a single nod to Harley.

"See ya tomorrow," Harley said.

"You take care, man." He bumped knuckles with Kaylee. "Get some sleep, moose killer."

"Thanks, Dane."

His green eyes flitted to mine, but he was unable to hold my gaze. "See ya, Maze."

"Bye." My farewell was barely a whisper as I watched his broad frame stroll out of the room, his large hand silently crushing the Diet Coke can.

I hung back to buffer Kaylee from any draining conversations someone might want to spring on her. Harley's family was kidnapping him for some Greek superstition, so Kaylee was going home to an empty cabin tonight. I walked her to her Jeep and gave her a goody basket of bath salts, sleep promoting tea, and her favorite chocolate so she could unwind properly.

She made a cooing noise while inspecting the basket. "You're a damn good friend, Maisie Quinn."

I hugged her. "So are you." Breaking the hug, I opened the door to her Jeep. "Alright, it's your last night as a single woman. Let me know if you need me to come over. I'll keep my ringer on."

"I'll be fine!" she said. Her brow scrunched together as she let out a breath. "It's actually you I'm worried about."

"What do you mean?"

She smoothed a piece of my hair. "If I forget to tell you tomorrow, please be extra careful driving back to Texas, okay? And wear that bracelet I gave you."

"I will, I promise."

She hopped up into the driver's seat.

"And hey, guess what?"

She flashed me a coy smile. "I get to marry my other best friend tomorrow?"

"Exactly! So don't worry about me. I'll be fine. It's your big day and it's going to be so lovely. Everyone is excited and ready to celebrate you guys. Now all you have to do is go home and rest."

With a tired nod, she shut the door. I sighed, watching Kaylee's Jeep take off down the hill at a breakneck speed.

And you know what? I believed what I said. Kaylee marrying Harley was a low risk. From what I could tell, no one was whispering *will they make it?* behind their backs like they probably had with Conner and me. Together, they were just easy. Meant to be. I secretly wanted a love like that someday. But I knew I'd missed the boat by settling for the first guy that had asked and blowing my chances. With everything Conner had put me through, I couldn't risk it again. With all the big changes happening in my life, I didn't have the courage to try.

I moseyed back into the inn's kitchen to help Azalea with dishes. When I opened the door, a cute guy was at the barn sink with bubbles almost spilling over. He had kind eyes and an athletic build. He was in earthy-colored clothing, his simple T-shirt exposing sinewed forearms that only an avid rock climber could sport.

I recognized him from the bachelorette party. His name was Noah, and he was one of Harley's buddies and a fellow ranger. He and Azalea were "just friends," but Kaylee was convinced there was something more.

"Hey, Noah."

"Hey there, Miss Maisie. What can I help you with?" he asked good-naturedly.

"I was just popping in to see if I could help Azalea with the dishes." My eyes bounced around the empty kitchen, Azalea nowhere in sight. "Um, can I help you dry or something?"

"Sure!" He nodded to a white towel hung on the oven.

"So, you and Dane, huh?" he asked, handing me a large platter. "You guys were really at each other's throats last night."

"He's just so easy to argue with." I smiled. "You're pretty close with him?"

"Yeah, I've been working as a ranger here for a couple years. I met Dane through Harley. He's a good friend, always down to help me." Noah carefully handed me a gravy boat. "But don't believe everything you hear in this town. People get bored, they come up with crazy things."

"I've also heard you and Azalea may or may not have a little romance brewing."

"Where did you hear that?"

"Everyone. Plus, I don't think most guy friends would do my dishes like this." I waggled the now dry gravy boat in front of me.

Noah shook his head bashfully, scrubbing a pot. "It's not like that. I live in the old groundskeeper's cottage out back and I come inside to use the kitchen, so I feel obligated to help out."

"Still, you haven't thought about dating her? She's so caring. And beautiful."

His lips pulled to the side for a split second as he gathered his thoughts. "Dane dated her in the past. I mean, granted, it was high school, but I'd still feel like I'm betraying my good friend by dating the first girl he fell in love with." He blinked quickly. "And I just don't feel like I have my life together enough. She deserves better."

I playfully nudged him with my shoulder to lighten the mood. "Hey now, don't sell yourself short."

Noah shut the water off in the sink, drying his hands. "I don't want to play matchmaker or anything, but I thought you should know. Maybe hearing it from one of his friends—the man is obsessed with you."

"But how much of a compliment is that really if I'm not the first tourist he's fallen for?" I asked. Continuing, I put on a more playfully mocking tone. "I don't want you to lie to me and convince me he's changed his ways and that he's cleaned up his act for me."

"I don't think there is an act *to* clean up. He's just a young guy living in a small town. Trust me, that's hard."

I could tell Noah was a nonconfrontational type, like a golden retriever. He was visibly uncomfortable challenging me this way and it showed. It was adorable.

He went on, "With all due respect, I think you haven't given him a chance and you might be surprised. Or maybe it will give you some closure. That's all I'm saying, Miss Maisie."

I whipped him playfully on the chest with the drying towel. "Fine! But will you do me a favor?"

"Sure," he said, catching the towel while I walked to the back door.

"If you want me to look past Dane's previous . . ." I picked the word carefully. ". . . transgressions, then I want you to do the same. Really consider things with Azalea. I think you'd be cute together."

He gave me a half-hearted nod, wadding up the towel. "Will do."

Accepting that I had helped Kaylee and Azalea as best I could, I decided to head back to the cottage for the night. Getting in my hearse, I wondered if I should just cut the shit and go talk to Dane at his shop. Or maybe invite him over to the cottage. The can of Diet Coke he'd brought tonight was a peace offering. That part was undeniable.

Flashbacks crept in my mind of him hovering over me in the forest, his hungry eyes roaming my body before his laugh echoed around the trees.

A laugh that had been aimed at me. He'd laughed *at* me.

I straightened my back, shifting the car in gear, reminding myself of that detail. *Fuck him.* In my humility, I floored my car, racing toward the cottage. Only a few blocks away from the inn, I ran a yellowish-red traffic light since I wasn't thinking straight. I only noticed my snafu flying through the intersection, blue-and-red flashing lights bursting in my vision seconds after.

"Oh, fuck me in the ass," I whined to myself as I pulled my car over, unrolling the window an inch before fetching my license and registration. When I opened my wallet, the blood froze in my body. The slots for my I.D. and credit card were empty. I remembered the bartender at Tilly's had asked to keep both my license and credit card to open the tab. Since my driver's license was from out of state, that was their policy.

I must've never closed it out. I racked my brain, trying to remember the details, but I couldn't recall much past swing the weenie except Rosie getting me inside the cottage and helping me unlace my boots. I hadn't partied that hard in years. With just Rosie watching out for multiple drunk girls, it was no wonder a little slip like this had happened.

I jumped as a knuckle tapped my window, glancing up. There he was in the annoying lights, the same asshat from last night. Officer Boyd. His light hair was receding on his unmoisturized forehead, his eyes a flat shade of blue, like the color of a Febreze bottle. He was in the habit of either smiling or mouth-breathing so you constantly saw his bad veneers.

*Wow, this fucker is so slappable.*

I knew the type. He looked like the kind of guy who'd peaked in high school yet still couldn't get into the Army. I was sure he'd married his high school sweetheart and knocked her up with several of his spawn who were probably sticky iPad kids.

"License and registration."

"I only have my registration. My I.D. is still at the tavern. I didn't close out my tab."

Maybe I shouldn't have told him that. Now he for sure knew it was me last night. The real question was, did he know about the email I'd sent his superiors earlier?

"Okay, so we'll start with driving without a license." He held out his hand. "Registration."

"I'm not familiar with the roads here and this wedding is very stressful. I promise I'll be more careful."

"Is there a reason you're withholding your information from me?"

I wasn't going to explain the obvious—that I didn't want him to know my whole government name and home address. I flipped into logic. He couldn't know I was heading back to the cottage. And even if he'd already scanned my plate, I didn't want him in front of me a second longer than needed.

Contriving a quick lie, I put on a pleasant smile, letting my Texas drawl seep in. "I'm sorry, officer. I was actually heading to Tilly's to pick up my I.D. I assure you I will be very cautious if you let me go with a warning." I gestured to the road behind me. "No one is even out right now. Surely, I didn't put anyone in danger."

"I don't care what your circumstances are. You ran a red light going over the speed limit."

I scanned the front of him, trying to find a body cam. He wasn't wearing one. With a small town, I guessed that tracked. "Given our history, I'd like a different officer to conduct this traffic stop." I gulped, hoping my nerves weren't showing.

"This is the last time I'm asking for your registration."

I shoved it through the slot of my window with a grumble.

Boyd read the paper. "And where are you staying in town?"

"With a friend," I lied.

He rolled his eyes. "Figures."

"Can you at least turn off your lights? It's going to give me migraine waiting for you."

"No," he bit back before turning to leave.

Twenty minutes later, I popped my head out from my window, flagging him to unroll his. "Hey, how much longer? I really gotta pee," I shouted back at him.

"Piss on the side of the road."

"That would be the only way you ever got my pants off!" I grunted, rolling my window back up.

I snapped a wide-eyed selfie with the police lights behind me and sent it to Kaylee.

**Kaylee: What the fuck? I leave you alone for ten minutes.**

**Me: I ran a red light. Officer Numb Nuts from last night is giving me a ticket and it's taking forever. He's for sure Googling me.**

**Kaylee: Drunk with power. Let me know when you get back to the cottage safely.**

Another thirty *fucking* minutes later, and yes, I counted, he strolled back to my hearse. Something deep down in my bones told me to record our interaction, so I did, propping up my phone on the speedometer, praying it was slanted enough to not catch his eye as he slid my ticket and registration through the crack in my window.

"Really?" I asked in indignation. "It took you that long to write a simple ticket? People give birth faster than this!"

He leaned against my car, both hands on the lip of the roof, palms digging into the tiny slant of space where the window was unrolled. "Listen, I don't like your kind in this town."

"My kind?"

"I just looked you up. Some magazine interviewed you when you opened your sex shop in Austin. Sounds like you're a pervert, sexualizing a perfectly good neighborhood."

I scoffed. "You've got to be kidding me, right? It's the twenty-first century. Everyone uses toys. And it's a boutique first and foremost. There's nothing wrong with lingerie, dude."

"I think you're a nasty woman, selling all those dildos. That sort of thing encourages women to neglect their husbands' needs."

Wow. Okay, he was one of those zealots who believed a woman owed her husband sex. Like a signed wedding certificate equaled continual consent. I was in too deep. This wasn't my town, and the odds were stacked against me. As much as I didn't want to, I had to play it vague. I had to make it to the wedding tomorrow, not jail. Lord knew I'd look much cuter in my bridesmaid dress than prison orange.

I shoved the ticket and my wallet in my purse with a tense, fake smile. "Well, bless your heart. Thanks for expressing your concerns to me. I will pay this ticket before I head out, sir."

"Did you hear me? You come into town acting like a fucking slut, you'll have to eventually deal with the consequences."

An icy sensation zinged up my spine. "What are you insinuating?"

"Your wild behavior shouldn't be rewarded in society. It would be a shame if you turned up missing." He stood upright, resting his hands on his belt that definitely had a gun and cuffs. Even more evidence of things stacked against me. "You came to town and got so drunk you don't even have your I.D. What respectable woman does that? Only a stupid slut."

"Am I free to go?"

He continued to glare.

"Am I free to go?" I repeated.

He slapped the hood of my car, right above my head, making me jump before returning to his cruiser. My hands trembled as I faked my route. I knew I could show up at Kaylee's and stay with her for extra safety, but I didn't want to stress her out before her wedding, so instead I drove around and avoided Main Street at all costs, snaking through side streets until I made it to my rental. I reversed into the driveway in a pathetic attempt to conceal my hearse. The last thing I needed was Boyd driving by and seeing it.

I texted Kaylee that I was safe, and it got me thinking maybe Dane could come stay with me. There were three bedrooms, so we wouldn't even have to share a bed. While brushing my teeth, I pulled up my PadHopper app, fully tempted to send in a help request to get him over here.

His big, brawny body could slide right against mine. He could hold me through the night. That idea alone got me flustered.

A part of me was kicking myself in the ass for not ever giving Dane my number.

Another part of me was kicking myself in the ass for wanting to see him in general. I didn't want to be some damsel. It was bad enough I was in his cottage.

Spitting out my toothpaste, I pointed at myself in the mirror with my toothbrush. "You're a fully capable, grown ass woman who doesn't need a man. Hell, you willingly lived in Florida for five years. You can handle anything! You didn't do anything wrong except run a red light in a sleepy town. Tomorrow will be fun, and Kaylee is going to look so beautiful. You'll do the wedding, sleep here one more night, and then it's all over. You've got this!"

I inspected the mirror. I didn't even look like myself. I hated my dark hair and the worry lines scrunched on my forehead. Even the way I held my shoulders was too high. I took a couple of deep breaths, willing myself to relax, promising myself a hot stone massage or something when this was done.

As I crawled into bed, I wondered if the room I was staying in was originally Dane's. I never wanted children of my own, and I didn't particularly like kids, but I bet Dane was cute growing up. I could imagine that his sandy brown hair was originally blond and he had little, chubby cheeks. And that his dad taught him fly fishing and how to fix up cars.

The idea of young Dane made me smile, and with it I shot out of bed. I found myself flinging every door open in the house until I found the one—it was the door to the pantry in the kitchen. Trailing up the doorframe, etched in pencil and marker, were stacks of different heights with dates, along with the names Dane and Jamie. My fingers trailed up the vertebrae of time. He'd been so little, then the last one hovered up at the top, well over six feet.

Something about it tucked away made me want to cry. Two children's whole lives shut away, forgotten. I'd never gotten the full story, but at the engagement party he'd mentioned his parents and sister had died within a couple years of each other. It had left Dane completely alone, the rest of his family down in Boston.

I could see why he felt obligated to stay in Pine Bluff. His auto shop was his dad's. I was sure a part of him felt proud it remained open, but if he didn't want to live in this house, it definitely felt like a piece of the puzzle was missing.

Why stay in a small town like Pine Bluff?

I still had so many questions about him. I was beginning to realize at this pace, I was never going to get any answers.

Maybe I should change that.

# Chapter Eleven

With Kaylee in charge, the wedding was just about as weird as you'd think. All jokes aside, she was a beautiful bride. She looked like Galadriel from *Lord of the Rings* on her way to Woodstock with her long bell sleeves and flowy dress, her golden hair down in curls with a flower crown to top off the look. On the very bottom of her dress, where it fanned out behind her, she even had embroidered moon phases, which was just so *her*.

There wasn't a dry eye in the crowd as she floated down the aisle. Even her tough biker dad wiped at his face as he gave her and Harley one last departing hug. I could tell Harley was trying to hold it together too. Like Harley and the rest of the groomsmen, I was in a fitted dress shirt along with a vest and brown pants. Kaylee wanted us to look *earthy* to fit the *whimsy-hippie-boho* theme. Whatever the fuck that meant. I was happy to not be in a full tux outside.

Maisie looked like a goddamn dream. Her drapey lilac dress hung on her body beautifully, with tiny straps barely visible on her shoulders. The front was tasteful, barely revealing her cleavage, but the back plunged, showing off two dimples low on her toned back. I wanted to fall to my knees to kiss them, only to turn her around and nuzzle between her legs. Her dark hair was loosely curled, one side pinned behind her ear with some flowers. With her natural grace, she appeared like a faerie, and I wanted her to lure me into the woods once more.

At the end of the dock, we each took our respective spots on either side of our best friends. I had to fight not to notice how the sunset lit up Maisie's cinnamon-bark eyes just like when I'd met her all those months ago.

The high priestess, Lady Geneva Gravedust, led an interesting handfasting ritual, and Kaylee's dress didn't snag on the broom when her and Harley jumped over it with their hands still bound by the ceremonial cord. That was what we were all told to look out for. The only real hiccup the entire night was when they cut the cake, Moose, their Golden Retriever, ran up to them wagging his tail, wanting a piece. It made everyone laugh, and he got to run around getting pets.

Maisie kept with the other bridesmaids, who were all in shades of mauves, pinks, and purples, but when it came time to dance, she picked up her flowy dress and moseyed in the direction of the cabin.

"Maisie," I semi-shouted to get her to stop mid-stride.

"What's up?" she asked with raised eyebrows.

"Are you in the middle of something?" I gestured to the impromptu dance floor set up beneath twinkly lights between their cabin and the lake. "Care to dance? I promise it's just to make them not worry."

A flash of emotion trailed her face that I couldn't place. Almost like something knocked the breath out of her. "If that's the case, sure. Let's put on an amicable show."

"Truce?" I asked.

"Truce," she echoed, walking closer.

"You make one hell of a maid of honor. You look gorgeous tonight."

"Thank you, you clean up quite nicely yourself."

I gestured at her reverently. "And this dress . . ."

"I look like some backup dancer for Florence and the Machine hate fucked a lace doily you'd find on a grandma's dresser."

"No, you don't." I chuckled, extending my hand until hers was in mine. Her nails were painted white, which was my weakness. She had dainty little gold rings and a necklace with a sun pendant floating high up on her décolletage. "That's a pretty necklace."

"Kaylee just gave it to me today." She forced a close-lipped smile. "As a thank you for being her maid of honor. She has a silver moon one to match."

We assumed the dancing position, my one hand on her waist, the other bent and holding out her other arm. It was nice having her back in my arms again in any capacity. I had to fight the buzz of attraction. The warmth of her felt a little too good. Mixed with the sugary sweetness of her perfume, I was back in the sticky trap of Maisie.

I knew I couldn't have her, but god did I want her.

"It must be a hard day, seeing your friend married off. I mean, for Harley and me, it's different. He has a brother. But you and Kaylee are both only children, right?"

"Yep, exactly. She's like a sister to me." She looked around at the wedding. "All of this just feels very final. She's never coming back to Texas. I'm happy for her, but it's still hard. She's my safe space."

"She probably felt the same way at your wedding," I offered.

She shook her head. "Nah, Conner didn't even want a formal wedding. That should've been the first red flag."

"So what did you do?"

"We were on the road for a rodeo, so we stopped in Vegas for a quick wedding. It was very impulsive. I didn't even get a proper gown. He gambled and lost five thousand bucks right after. Then he ate a huge breakfast burrito with too much Cholula sauce and bitched about the heartburn before passing out on the bathroom floor. I didn't even get fucked on my wedding night. He had whiskey dick."

"What the hell did you see in this Conner guy?"

"Money," she said bluntly. "He comes from a family of wealthy ranchers. Pretty Kitty was in those super-lean early years of business, and I honestly wanted some cushion." She pursed her lips, shooting a glance at the sky. "I was too young and dumb. I had no business getting married at twenty-two. I confused financial security with love."

"I'll be honest, I'm a little shocked at how unashamed you are about your gold-digging ways."

She fought a smirk, digging a knuckle in my rib. "Capitalism really fucks us all." When she put her hand back on my shoulder, it was in a closer embrace, her fingers lazily tracing the seam of my vest and collar. "Looking back on it, I think that's why I've been so determined to make Pretty Kitty successful. Conner hated it. He always thought it was a dirty business. Like I sold tobacco or something."

"I'm sorry he made you feel that way."

"What about you? Ever married?"

"No, not even close."

"Why do you think that is?"

"No one has haunted me like you have." I put my hand this time on her bare lower back. Her lashes fluttered on contact. "I meant what I said, you look beautiful tonight," I whispered in her ear.

"So do you." She squeezed my shoulder. "I really am sorry about the jabs I made at you at the bar. It wasn't cool of me, especially in front of everyone else."

"Thank you. That reminds me." I dropped her hand to tug my phone out of my pocket, pulling up the three PDFs I'd saved to throw in her face for a moment like this. When I swiveled the phone around, her brows pinched together as we wandered closer to the edge of the dance floor.

"Are those test results?"

"Yep, proof I'm clean and snipped. So you can stop making fun of me."

"Wait, snipped?" Her little white nail flicked on the screen, displaying a letter from the American Urology Association confirming a successful vasectomy. She looked up from my phone with her upper lip slightly curled, the screen's low light casting a glow on her face. "This past winter, Kaylee said something about you and Harley icing your nuts while camping out on her couch. I thought it was a metaphor for how cold it gets here in Maine."

"Oh no, we got buddy vasectomies and made the mistake of letting her chaotic ass drive us home." I grinned, knowing Maisie's head was spinning with this random info. "We had a *Breaking Bad* marathon afterward, spent the day with frozen peas on our nuts."

"Wait, what?"

I shrugged, taking my phone back. "We don't want to be dads, so we took the proverbial bullets out of the chamber. It's the least we could do, especially with how this country is going full *Handmaid's Tale* on its women."

Her eyes flitted around my face. "That doesn't earn you brownie points."

"I'm not saying it should. It's the bare fucking minimum, but please don't insinuate I put women's health at risk when I've obviously done more than most men out there. I get that a lot of things are stacked against you, and I know as a guy I don't always deserve a seat at your table, but don't for one second think I wouldn't fight to be there."

"No, you're right. And I've been tested too." She cringed at her admission, clapping a hand to her forehead before gesturing. "I'm just telling you that to be transparent. You know, 'know your status' and all that jazz. I wouldn't be much of a sex store owner if I didn't walk my talk, ya know?"

I smiled at her, loving the way it was making her squirm. The blush was coming back to her cheeks. God, I'd missed it.

"What I'm saying is after my divorce, I went and got checked. My ex did some creepy shit. I'm in the clear. Not that you need to know that." She went to bite her nails but ripped her hand from her mouth on second thought.

"Right," I mocked.

"Wow. Sorry, this is getting weird."

"Can I have another dance?"

"Smooth," she said, taking my hand. "But don't dip me. One quick move and this dress will be around my ankles."

"Is that a promise?" I asked, earning a giggle.

Azalea came by us and snapped a candid photo. Feeling caught, we both popped on cheesy grins for the next one. After that interruption, we just swayed to the music, letting it lull us even deeper into a reverie. Each step brought us closer until her breasts skimmed my chest, the flowers tucked behind her ear wafting their delicate scent toward me.

"So no dip, but how 'bout a twirl?" I asked, fighting the energy between us.

"One slow, deliberate twirl is in order."

"Okay, tornado, here we go." From there, I extended my arm, methodically turning her only to weave her back in, her back now to my chest. I planted a delicate kiss on her bare shoulder.

She made a gentle, little noise of pleasure. "Did you just call me tornado?"

"Yes."

"I'm not that destructive, am I?" She glanced up at me, fighting the hurt in her voice.

Gathering my thoughts, I extended my arm once more, straightening her out so we could resume our dancing. "Destructive is a harsh word. I'd say untamed, powerful, undeniable. You can tell when a tornado is coming. You want to watch it, but you know doing so won't leave you feeling the same."

"That so?"

"And you're from Texas," I said, lightening the mood. "So that feels extra fitting since that's tornado alley."

She nodded. "Tornado it is. So, you never finished telling me about that trip you took with your family—"

"Hey, we're going to go decorate the Jeep now. We need the keys," Carson said, interrupting our dance. I sighed, letting go of Maisie while glaring at him. *Really, bro? Right now?*

He stood there, annoyed and waiting.

Maisie picked up the hem of her dress with a polite curtsey. "I better go help Kaylee get out of her gown. She has this really cute outfit for the send-off."

"Thanks for the dance, tornado."

She flashed me a small smile. I stood there, watching her slender back move and hips sway. Hopefully, it was the last time I'd have to watch her walk away from me.

# Chapter Twelve

The wedding had been perfect. I'd had to fight back tears several times. Kaylee and Harley were so damn cute together. During the ceremony, the sun had set behind Harley's wide shoulders, making him almost glow. Watching him stare at Kaylee while he'd said his vows, I'd all but melted into a pile of mush on the dock. I was beyond happy for them.

With the rowdy bunch from Kaylee's side of the world mixed with all the Greek shenanigans from Harley's, the whole night was full of laughter. It was the perfect fusion of down-to-earth and playful, just like them.

When I wasn't preoccupied with Kaylee and Harley's love, I was trying my best to ignore the live wire between Dane and me. I could always sense where he was and when he was looking at me out of the corner of his eye. When we stood for photos, goose bumps erupted all over my arms because his breath feathered on my neck, his warm chest pressing against my back with how we were positioned. I was thankful everyone's eyes were on my best friend, otherwise I'd likely be called out for blushing.

Kaylee didn't toss her bouquet, and Harley didn't dig for a garter, but they did have lots of dancing and delicious food. They planted a tree, something about nurturing their love or some tree hugger shit. Then they staked a cool wooden sign next to the tree that served as a guest book, with everyone scrawling their best wishes on it with a silver Sharpie. When they left the celebration, we all blew bubbles as Harley and Kaylee ran toward her Jeep hand in hand.

Most of my anxiety had subsided now that the wedding was over and Kaylee was safely on her way to Boston with her now husband to catch a flight to Greece. I was whisked away with the other bridesmaids to sort out gifts and box up leftovers from the caterer. Out of my periphery at one point, I saw Dane escorting a granny to her car, but by the time I got to my hearse, he was nowhere in sight. All logic told me to go to Tilly's to get my cards before heading back to the cottage. I had been so busy all day, I hadn't made it there. But when I made my way to that part of town, I navigated to Dane's shop without even thinking about it.

His back lot was gated shut, so I parked in front. When I walked up to the front door, it was cracked. I didn't have his number, so I couldn't text him I was here, but I saw a light on so I figured he must be tinkering.

As I slid in, my eyes adjusted to the bright light coming from one industrial bulb hooked on the lifted hood of an old truck. It was enough to light my way through the small lobby and cluttered shop.

"Dane?"

Maybe he wasn't home yet? There were so many cars in his back lot, I didn't even scan it to see if his was parked there come to think of it. Maybe I could leave a Post-it for him to call me before I left town?

Weaving through vehicles, tool chests, and tires, I made my way to the staircase. The reasonable part of my brain told me this was borderline trespassing, maybe even stalking. The nosy part of me was greedy for any details or snooping opportunities. The latter part won over, shocker, and I found myself ascending the stairway up to his loft.

By the time I made it to the top, I was holding my breath as my pulse thrummed in my temples, giving me a slight headrush. I crept forward. It was even darker up here with just a half pony wall dividing it from the stairway landing. Windows facing Main Street let in weak light. I could make out a couch and a long bar comprising a U-shaped kitchen.

A short hallway was beyond the whirring refrigerator. Wanting to rule out Dane was here, I inched even closer. A tiny, insecure corner of my mind worried he was out with some townie or a girl from the wedding. Maybe Harley's hot cousin or something. Surely, he wouldn't be here. But the closer I got, the noise I thought was the fridge was actually . . . groaning?

I closed my eyes in a desperate attempt to hear better but was quickly met with a distinct crack of a mannish noise followed by something slick. I leaned in closer, careful not to bump the door with my shoulder. Staring down at the handle, I waited a couple of seconds to hear a woman or some dirty talk, but nothing came, just deeper breathing and more wet noises.

My hand grasped the cold handle and swung the door wide. On the other side, Dane lay sprawled out in the bed, ruthlessly pumping his cock.

His thick, *glorious*, reputation-worthy cock.

He jumped then threw his head back on the pillow in a throaty chuckle as he continued. "Come for the show, sweetheart?"

"What the fuck are you doing?" I spat, fighting to look away but unable to stop watching.

"What does it look like I'm doing? Trying to get you off my mind." His strokes were now looser, lazily gliding up and down. "You clearly don't mind the view."

The noises erupting between his palm and shaft sounded like a sinful symphony I wanted more of. If any other man were doing this, I'd be grossed out, but something about Dane's shamelessness made it that much hotter. It felt oddly voyeuristic, like a line I shouldn't cross. But oh god, did I want to cross that line. Seeing him mostly naked, sprawled out on his bed in the faint powdery blue glow of night made me want to latch my gaze on his groin until it was covered in his cum.

I dropped my purse off my shoulder and crawled into his bed. Without asking, I grabbed the band of his boxer briefs that were pushed down around his muscled thighs. He fought a smile, holding his dick while shifting his body to help me yank the fabric off his legs. I sat back on my heels, not touching him from where I remained on the corner of his bed.

"Keep pumping," I whispered wickedly.

"You'd like that?" He twisted his wrist as he covered the crown, slathering more pre-cum. "You want to sit your pretty little ass in my bed and boss me around, tornado?"

"Hand," I said sternly.

When he presented a calloused palm to me, I leaned forward, grabbing his wrist to spit in it. Flicking my eyes to his, I saw his jaw slack as he returned his hand to its rightful place.

"Oh, you're so nasty, baby. I love it." A new slant of desire lit his eyes, making his lids heavy.

"Show me what this cock can do. Prove it lives up to all the hype." I mockingly scanned his headboard with exaggeration. "I don't see any notches in your bedpost. How do you keep track of all the tourists you fuck in this bed?"

He growled in frustration.

"Doesn't matter. You won't want to fuck anyone else once you get this pussy," I murmured, moving the flowy dress around to spread my legs wider from where I kneeled. "*If* you get this pussy," I amended.

He jutted up his jaw as his strokes quickened. "Prove it to me." His eyes set on my breasts. I fleetingly wondered if he could see how hard my nipples were, if he could smell my arousal.

Steeling myself, I watched as his pulse beat in the ditch of his muscular neck, throbbing like something I wanted to lick. With each tug, his pecs bounced and shifted along with his abs, all the way down to the trimmed hair at the base of his cock. And oh god, his cock, it was . . . gorgeous. It wasn't obscenely long, or what I'd like to call a cervix crusher, but it was *more* than enough for me. It was so thick with a fat head and had a nice curve to it.

Staring at it, I thought about how much I wanted to feel it scraping the sensitive spots inside me as I slid down on it. My pussy clenched and my knees threatened to close together, the slight twitch catching Dane's attention, causing a knowing chuckle to husk out of him.

Trying to gain back control, I went on. "You don't have to show off for me, big guy. You can just let it blow."

He closed his eyes, steadying his breath. "It's not going to work."

"What's not going to work?"

His eyes opened in a darkened squint, his voice gravelly. "Teasing me into submission. I don't submit. And it's a damn shame you're trying to top me instead of just coming apart underneath me like the needy, little mess you are."

His words snapped my brain like a rubber band. "What if I like it on top?" I asked as I lunged over him, shifting all the layers of my dress to straddle him, bracing myself with a hand on either side of his face. With my proclamation, he stopped touching himself. I continued to kneel over him, fighting the urge to sit.

"Just give me the green light," he said as he brought his dry hand up to my chest, his finger tracing the trim of my dress as it strained against my boobs. "I could fuck you so good it would change the way you walk. But I promise I'll never push you until you're ready."

With his words, I lowered myself. The only thing between his shaft and my pussy was a pathetically sheer, seamless panty.

Both of us groaned, feeling my heat mixed with his slicked-up cock.

Fighting the urge to kiss him, I began to sway, feeling the rim of his head stroking my clit. "You can't touch me. You hear me? You're not allowed to touch anywhere this dress covers."

Fighting ragged breaths, he gritted his jaw. "But I could taste you. Dip a finger in your pussy for me."

*Dear god, this man is straight up nasty.*

He pinned me in place with his dominant words. Before I knew it, I was shifting my dress around to glide a hand under, concealing myself in the process. My middle finger slid against his cock as I dipped it inside myself, a little impressed but also alarmed at how wet I already was as I presented a glistening finger up to him.

He held my wrist and sucked as we continued to grind, his lashes fluttering with his heavy breath. "Fuck!" he hissed. "You taste so good. No wonder I can't stop thinking about you." He continued to tongue my finger, swirling around it in a way that mesmerized me and gave me way too many thoughts.

"I've been thinking about you, too," I confessed, hoping my softening energy opened us both up. I continued to ride him, grinding on him in slow circles, feeling my underwear completely soak. His eyes hungrily sparkled underneath me as he kissed my palm, letting it drop, urging me on. "I think about all the unspeakable things I'd like you to do to me. I want to ride this cock until my pussy aches."

"More," he said with a low voice. He was lasting a long time, all things considered.

"I want to ache because you fucked me so well. I want your hot cum dripping out of me."

"Yes," he whispered, my words pulling him under. His hand traveled to skim the sensitive skin of my back that was exposed. His touch was so tender for such a big guy.

I felt myself wanting to slide my underwear to the side and just fuck him already. One moment, one decision, one second and all this could be over. The hairline choice reminded me of another moment we'd had together, and all my walls went up as I leaned in to murmur my last blow. "And I want you to stop being such a fucking gentleman."

His nostrils flared as his abs constricted. He pushed me back slightly, so his hot load hit his stomach. It was the most vulnerable and virile thing I'd ever seen. Even his O-face was handsome. He moaned as he continued to spurt over and over again, the twitching of his dick making my core pulse with envy.

"Fuuuuck!" he hissed under his breath.

"Good god, that was way hotter than it should've been," I muttered, mostly to myself.

Instead of the tangy funk of cum, he smelled, well, still like cum but a bit muskier, with a headier funk to it I strangely didn't hate.

I watched in awe as he coasted down from his climax, his taut muscles easing. He looked soft but somehow strong, purely fuckable and huggable. His tattoos covered both arms and pecs, solar plexus, some along his sides, leaving his lower abs mostly bare only for the ink to start up again on his thighs clear down to the tops of his feet. I cursed the dim light preventing me from seeing all of them. Nonetheless, I was grateful for a stolen moment. One where he wasn't watching me for once.

When his eyes cracked open, his face pulled in a lazy smile before we both shared a little laugh.

"Not the burglar you expected, eh?" I freed him by getting off the bed as he expertly cupped his junk and strolled to the bathroom.

"I'm going to hop in the shower. You're welcome to hang out so we can actually, you know, talk."

I didn't even hide my gaze, watching his fine ass twitch with each step. But the second the water turned on, I slinked out of his place like a fucking coward.

Once inside the safety of my car, I looked at myself in the rearview mirror. Why was I running? Why couldn't I go back to his loft and fuck his brains out? Or simply talk.

*Because it wouldn't be that simple.*

He clearly had a pull on me. I would develop even deeper feelings, and then I'd want to wait around here in Maine, hoping he'd find a way to love me, to decide on me. Just like my mom had done for my biological father. Look where it had gotten her. I couldn't rot up here, even if I'd have my best friend. This was Kaylee's turf, not mine. I needed a place to call my own. But I couldn't help but wonder if the emptiness inside me as I drove away was worth the risk of waiting for someone like Dane to come around.

When I returned to the cottage, I took off my dress and caught a patch of something wet at the bottom. My bridesmaid dress had Dane's jizz on it. Needless to say, that was *not* the kind of party favor I thought I'd be taking home from my best friend's wedding, goddammit.

# Chapter Thirteen

# DANE

I rapped on the cottage door with a blueberry muffin and an iced Horny Hag drink for Maisie. Poe had said it was her favorite. But standing on the porch in this weird version of the morning after was beyond bizarre.

*Here are some carbs and coffee. Let's talk about how you watched me rub one out.*

This was a first for me. I'd never had a woman watch me jack off unless she was DJ diddling herself next to me in some kinky tandem masturbation fest. I'd also never had a woman dip while I was scrubbing my balls in the shower. Usually, I was the one who hinted it was time to go. What she'd done last night was so heartless and, well, strangely hot. It put another tally in the column of why Maisie was so damn attractive. I couldn't win against her, but I was determined to not outright lose.

When there wasn't an answer, I pushed the doorbell. Her hearse was in the driveway, so I knew she was there. I pulled out my phone to message her on the PadHopper app since I still didn't have her number.

**Me:** Answer the damn door.

**Maisie:** No.

**Me:** I have coffee.

**Maisie:** I'm not a coffee addict like Kaylee. That won't work on me.

**Me:** I mean, at this point, it's just bad manners.

**Maisie:** I've seen your taint. I think we're past social niceties.

**Me:** Say it taint so. You're really going to ignore me like this, tornado?

**Maisie:** Yeah. And by the way, this isn't very PadHopper Super Host of you.

Along with her text, she sent a screenshot of the fine print that stated a host cannot impede or harass a guest. She put a neon pink star next to the section which forbids excessive visits and visits before 9 am.

I sighed, placing the cup and muffin by the rocking chair. As I got close to the driveway, I heard her small voice. "Dane?"

Turning around, I saw her there on the front porch with tight, black Levi's with rips in all the right places, a cropped white T-shirt showing off a sliver of her tummy, and her brown leather cowgirl boots.

She held the cup under her chin, her doe eyes in full effect. "Thank you. You know, for not pushing me into something I wasn't ready for last night."

"It's the bare fucking minimum, Maze."

She shifted her weight from foot to foot. "Not every guy sees it that way." Her face twitched as she lifted her cup in a slight cheers.

I couldn't stop watching her. As I walked backward to my car, a piece of paper flapped in the wind under the windshield wiper on her hearse, catching my attention. I fought to rip it out. By the time I opened it, she was already by my side. Two simple words were typed out, large and in the center.

**Found you.**

"What does this mean?" I asked, showing her.

She read the words, her hand jerking away from the paper like it was about to bite her.

I stretched it to display it further. "Maisie, what does this mean?"

Her mouth formed a small line as she rolled her shoulders. "It must be an inside joke from some of the girls at the coffee shop."

"What do you mean?"

Moments like this, I was kicking myself in the ass for not having a porch camera at the cottage. If I did, I could just pull the footage.

She yanked the paper from my hand, turning to make her way back to the cottage. "Um, yeah, I dunno. This whole thing has been a fever dream."

"So you're just going to leave? Just like that?"

"Yeah, I'm sorry. I need to get going."

"What about last night? What about us?"

Then, at the threshold of my childhood home, she turned and murmured a sentence that never got easier to hear.

"There's no us, Dane. We were just a fling. I'm sorry, I have to go."

# Chapter Fourteen

I woke up to a selfie from Kaylee with Harley conked out on her shoulder on their way to Greece. Apparently, lumber daddy was hella claustrophobic. She'd had a plan to offer him half a Xanax once they got past TSA to soothe his nerves about being trapped on a plane. I guessed that plan had worked.

With her well on her way to her honeymoon, I felt silly being in Maine. Dane set the check out at the cottage to 11 o'clock, but I was already up and ready by 9 am. I was gnawing at my lip, taking in all the details of his family home when he swung by with coffee. I was too ashamed to face him. I mean, what kind of person bailed on someone after damn near grinding their way to a mutual orgasm?

Then he made the horrifying discovery of a note Boyd must've left for me. What creeper left a note on a stranger's car simply stating *found you*. Well, I guessed a creep for starters. But knowing he had tracked me down and took the effort to type it out, print it, and deliver it to me gave me major heebie-jeebies.

I folded the note with shaky hands, stuffing it into my small crossbody purse before wheeling my suitcase out to my car.

My plan was set. I would swing by Tilly's, get my cards, and then haul ass out of town, not even making a pit stop until I was low on gas. I had a hotel room reserved in Philly tonight, then two more days of travel to clear my head. After that, I'd have a clearer game plan on what to do with my life back in Texas. Some time spent on the open road would do me good.

Main Street was blocked off with cones, so I had to find a back road and park in the neighborhood behind Tilly's. Hustling, I marched up to the front door, only to find they weren't even open until 11 am on Sundays.

"Fuck!" I whimpered, checking my phone, confirming it wasn't even 10.

"Hey, Maisie!" A bright voice came from behind me.

I turned, shielding my eyes in the morning light. "Oh, hi, Azalea! What's all this for?" I asked, gesturing to the crowd forming on the street.

"It's a parade and festival for fiddlehead season."

"What the fuck is a fiddlehead?" I asked with a snort.

Azalea tucked a shiny strand of brown hair behind her ear with a smile. "It's a baby fern we fry up. Kinda tastes like asparagus but sweeter. They're about to go out of season."

"Y'all Mainers eat some weird shit. Bright red hot dogs, whoopie pies, ferns. At least in Texas, you know what part of the cow you're grilling."

"You have a point." She looked me up and down. "Hey, I saw you danced with Dane last night. You guys looked so cute together. That wasn't how he looks at other tourists. I can tell you that for damn sure."

I let out a deep sigh, bracing myself to lean against the sturdy door handle of Tilly's. "Azalea, I love ya, but you can't keep bringing this up. The last two times you were either drunk or in the midst of a menstrual cup removal."

She giggled bashfully. "I know, I know! But hear me out! I know I'm biased, as he was my first love. My first everything really, but he's a good guy. I don't even know why we stopped dating. I think one of us got mono or something stupid." A corner of her mouth lifted. "It wouldn't surprise me if only half the rumors are true."

I playfully rolled my eyes at her. "Half? That's giving him too much credit. Let's settle on two-thirds."

"You can't blame the guy for being an extrovert and dating a lot. It's just who he is."

She was right. That was just Dane— friendly and unashamed. I liked that. What you saw was what you got.

"I'm not trying to pressure you, but Kaylee says he attends almost every yoga and meditation class she holds at the community center, like he's on some self-discovery. Viviane at the bookstore has been complaining about finding books for the poor guy. I guess he's blazing through like five Western novels a week. He's home reading, not out raising hell. I don't want to sit here and preach that he's a changed man, but I really think you've inspired him."

"Good to know," I said, fighting the gnawing feeling in my stomach that he was probably just as lonely and tormented as I was.

She lifted a brow. "I saw him look at you for the first time at that engagement party. He lit up. Interrupted our conversation with Noah and everything. We all watched it. It was like a moth to a flame."

*Everyone witnessed Dane seeing me for the first time?*

"That night was kind of a blur," I mumbled.

But that was a lie. I remembered it all. Every smile, every joke, every prolonged, little touch.

The newfound information Azalea had given me and the delay Tilly's created was like a mirror being held up to my face, forcing me to see my shortsightedness.

I needed answers, dammit. Even if it was a final fuck or me explaining how he made me feel. I would be an idiot to leave here without saying my piece, even if the threatening note from Boyd was burning a hole in my purse. I had an hour to kill. I needed my I.D. and credit card to check into all my hotel rooms. It was as simple as that. It was a barrier to getting home at this point. Maybe fate wanted me to talk to Dane.

Azalea gestured up the street. "Noah snagged a spot for me to watch the parade with him up a little closer to Silver Springs. Want to join us?"

"I think I'll pass." I hugged her goodbye and before I knew it, my feet were clomping in the opposite direction, my hand flinging the door open at Dane's.

"Sorry, Lennie didn't lock the damn door. I'm closed on Sundays!" he yelled from somewhere inside.

I shut the door behind me. "Dane, it's me." I made my way past the lobby, into the dim shop just in time to see him twisting a bolt into a narrow spot under a truck that was lifted. His dexterous fingers moved with ease. A rush of heat erupted across my chest as I thought of other things his fingers could do with such skillful circular motion.

"What are you doing here?" he asked over his shoulder with a crumpled brow, killing my daydream.

I inched farther inside the shadowy shop. "I-I have some questions for you."

He sighed, stepping away from his work to hastily wash his hands. "What questions could you possibly have for me? I thought we were just some fling," he spat as he dried his hands before walking to stand in front of me.

He was in navy coveralls, the sleeves rolled up to his elbows, his tattoos on display. He was still heartbreakingly gorgeous, but the pained, guarded expression on his face was so foreign to me.

I dropped my purse and flung myself at him full force. "I'm sorry," I breathed.

He caught me, wrapping his arms around me in a bear hug, hauling me closer.

"I'm so sorry," I repeated, feeling my face pinch where I buried it against his chest.

He broke the hug to look at me, his large hands holding my face. The second our eyes locked, our mouths clashed in a fierce kiss.

I hadn't kissed him since the engagement party. The second his lips met mine, I questioned why I hadn't kissed him sooner. Everything around us might be confusing as hell, but *this*, this made perfect sense. Our lips brushing, our breaths mingling, our chests pressed tight. It was all a devotion to the unspeakable truth that we had something here, together.

The man knew what he was doing. He started out slow, letting me unravel and open up to him while holding my neck with one hand while the other clutched my lower back. His lips glided over mine, coaxing a little moan out of me before he teased my tongue with his.

I was completely lost in him already.

He tore off my jacket before he walked me backwards, pushing me against the wall, the air only slightly escaping my lungs before I gasped for other reasons as he hitched me up, my legs locking around his torso.

"I missed kissing you," I said breathlessly, feeling weightless as he held me. I ran my hands through his short hair, needing to feel as much of him as possible.

He covered me with more kisses in response. Pure desire and surrender flooded me, creating a buzz.

He whisked me to the hood of a bright red muscle car, the cool metal sending tingles up my spine as he laid me down, his brawny body covering me as he leaned over, never breaking the kiss. His hand slid under my ass, holding me closer to his body as we started a slow grind, every kiss, every grab hungrier and hungrier.

I frantically unzipped his coveralls, freeing his arms to reveal a white undershirt. "I need you," I said, admiring how his muscles moved under the thin fabric.

"Want you," he murmured as he kissed down my neck, his fingers traveling up my shirt, baring my stomach just in time for his lips to kiss the flesh. Flashbacks of the forest filled my mind. I couldn't be intimate with him at this angle, with him over me, seeing all of me. As weird as it was, I needed a shred of privacy during such an intimate act.

I pushed him back so I could jump off the hood.

"What are you doing?" He wiped his mouth. "I was just getting started."

"I need you in me." I pushed the coveralls lower, grabbing his cock out of his underwear only to take it with a bold pump.

He bit back a strangled groan as we both watched his length fully stiffen in my grasp as my other hand cupped his balls. Somewhere outside, I heard a whistle in the crowd for the parade. I was brought back to reality when his hands affectionately touched my shoulders, cueing that he wanted me to lie back, probably to eat me out, but I wasn't able to give him that. Instead, I let go of his dick long enough to shuck my pants down to my boots.

Bare-assed, I turned my back to him to press my chest against the hood of the car. "Please, please fuck me." It was rushed and needy, but I didn't care. I needed to fuck him to forget him. I just needed to feel him inside me in the hopes that I could get him out of me, out of my mind, my heart, my secret wishes.

His hand trailed down my backbone. "Maisie, baby."

I arched my back, but with my pants around my shins, I couldn't really spread my legs so I doubted he could see everything. Nonetheless, I had never been so bold, not even with Conner.

Dane's body lunged forward, cock first, pinning me to the car. It was then I noticed that the long oval windows dotting the tops of each garage door were the only things keeping us from the loud clanging of the parade just past the metal barrier. If someone was tall, they could peek in and watch us in the shadows. With the parade starting, more and more people were flooding the sidewalk, the tips of people's heads with the occasional face streaming by. I could hear the marching band dribbling up something resembling a beat, a rogue baby's shrill cry, and the ruffle of female laughter.

"Uh, fuck." I moaned, feeling his dick press into one of my cheeks as his arm snaked around me, his hand gently holding the front of my throat.

"Tell me you'll stay another night," he whispered in my ear.

"Fuck me!" I breathed.

He rolled his hips slightly, gliding his dick against me. "You want that? You want all these people a glimpse away from seeing you getting properly fucked over the hood of this car?"

"Yes," I hissed, closing my eyes, praying this was going to work.

"Tell me you'll stay," he repeated, his tone enticingly smooth and low. "One." *Thrust.* "More." *Thrust.* "Night."

I whimpered while shifting against him, feeling hot trails of pre-cum slather my ass.

Taking my silence as an answer, he pulled back, taking his cock and body heat with him. "I can't do this! You're such a mindfuck, Maisie!" He shoved his length back inside his coveralls, zipping them up.

I pulled up my pants, tears stinging my eyes. *Why am I like this? Why can't I be normal?* My voice broke when I spat, "I hate you!"

He picked up a red, tattered rag. "Just go!" He gestured to the door.

"Fine! I will. Go open Tinder and find your next fix!"

"I don't need Tinder! I have a fucking face!" he bellowed.

"Yes, a very punchable face! Oh god, you're fucking unbelievable!" I shrugged on my jacket and snatched up my purse. "You know what, for all these months, what happened in that forest haunted me. Now I see it was the biggest blessing. I didn't get trapped here with your bullshit!"

"I sleep just fine at night knowing I'm not a grade-A hypocrite like you, darlin'! You preach sex positivity, but you've done nothing but shame me. Then when you want to get fucked, you go about it in the most degrading way possible. Your friend is married. Congrats. Now get the fuck out of my town already!"

I skulked past him, unable to break eye contact, knowing it was likely the last time I'd see him. I pushed the door open to his shop, and the parade assaulted me with the harsh daylight and brash beats from the marching band. I shielded my eyes from the sun, determined to just wait in front of Tilly's for my cards before leaving.

For a small town, Pine Bluff really drew out a parade crowd. I waded through the sea of people at a painfully slow rate. Looking ahead, I saw Boyd leaning against a brick building, holding the straps of his bulletproof vest like he was hot shit. My blood ran cold and my heart crashed against my ribs as I slid behind a woman, hoping her height shielded me, but because of how painfully polite Mainers were, she allowed me more room. Her side-step created a perfect window for Boyd to spot me.

He kicked up from the wall, his jaw grinding in anticipation of his next pursuit. All the nerves on the back of my neck and down my spine prickled at the sight of the evil smirk on his face. His open threat from when he pulled me over rang in my head.

*You come into town acting like a fucking slut, you'll have to eventually deal with the consequences.*

Following my gut instinct, I smooshed myself further in the crowd, using their bodies as a defense, knowing damn well he wouldn't take me if it caused a scene. For once, I was grateful my hair was currently dark and not my usual pink. That would've been a dead giveaway. Instead, I blended in with the crowd, ducking and weaving, albeit impolitely, through the mass of spectators. I almost tripped over a wagon with a little toddler in it, gaining a side-eye from the mom when I grabbed her arm to steady myself.

Judging my options, I knew my car and Silver Springs were too far. In the other direction, all I could see was the two-story corner building painted white with a mural on the side stating Dane's Auto. It was like a beacon of safety. Safety that would surely come at a price.

*Just get to the door. You just need to make it to the door.* My intuition rang repeatedly as I roved closer, ready to pathetically barge inside, begging for sanctuary. When I pulled at the door I'd previously stormed out of, it was locked. I looked over my shoulder, clocking Boyd in the crowd about 30 yards away, his head on a swivel.

Bolting along the side of the building, I prayed both the back gated lot and door to his shop were open. A low rumbling morphed with the din of the parade. There Dane was, seated on his motorcycle, picking up the helmet. The bike was black-on-black, and, similar to Dane, it looked sexy, tough, and unpretentious.

His brows furrowed as I ran up to him.

"Please, help me!" I attempted to suck in a breath, fighting hyperventilation.

He stood up from his bike. "Maisie, what's wrong?"

"I need to hide. Please!" I pleaded, on the verge of hysterics.

"Then get on the bike."

"Please." I held the lapels of his leather jacket. "I'm begging you. Can I just hide in your shop until the parade is over?" I chanced a look over my shoulder to make sure the coast was still clear. I fought a sob turning back to him. "Boyd is after me. Please, he can't find me!"

Dane's eyes shot wide in horror as he put the helmet over my head.

"What the hell is your plan?" I asked, panic bleeding into my tone.

"Getting you the hell out of Dodge," he answered, belting the strap under my chin before sliding the face cover down. He pulled out sunglasses from his jacket as I stood there with too many thoughts in my head. Scowling, he looked at my patched denim jacket and tried to tuck some of my hair peeking out of the helmet. When that didn't work, he shucked off his leather jacket, helping me into it and popping the collar.

Taking a seat on the bike, he instructed, "Keep your shoulders close to your ears to hide as much of you as possible. If he stops us, don't say a fucking word, do you hear me?"

I nodded, sliding in behind him, wrapping my arms around his solid body. With a stomp of his foot and the twist of his wrist, the bike roared to life. If I wasn't already shaking, the power of the motor would've made my entire body tremble. Two seconds prior, I'd felt helpless, but now I felt unstoppable with this much power between my legs and my body pressed against Dane's dense back.

He paused at the gate, calculating his route. The side road I'd run up led to a neighborhood that was butted up against one of the bluffs, essentially creating a dead end. The other way was Main Street, clogged with festivities.

Boldly turning, Dane rolled toward the crowded sidewalk, revving in quick bursts as if to politely make his request to pass known. People parted slowly as he inched closer, gaining some annoyed looks. In the crowd, Boyd stumbled closer to us, his baton already drawn. His eyes tracked us, like he was trying to figure out if I was on the back of the bike. I could see it all painted on his face—hunger for power, straight-up suspicion, jealousy of Dane, and density in thought.

Dane continued merging on Main Street, audaciously weaving around the parade floats in the process as I clutched his body close, squeezing my eyes shut, while his bike howled through Pine Bluff, taking us far from Boyd and into the unknown in more ways than one.

# Chapter Fifteen

# DANE

In the past 24 hours, I'd been a breath away from fucking Maisie twice. I'd also watched my best friend get married. And now, I had the woman I'd vowed to hate clutching me on the back of my motorcycle as we fled from a cop. It was safe to say, life was throwing me a curveball.

After fighting with her and saying what I'd thought was my final goodbye, I'd needed a long drive to wrangle in my rage. I'd never forget the fearful look in her eyes when she'd run up to me behind my shop. I'd heard her say, *Boyd is after me*, and that was all it'd taken. I'd gone into defense mode.

Maisie was fearless. If she was scared, there was a reason.

We hauled ass down the freeway, Pine Bluff at least a half hour in our wake. I took an exit, feeling her inner thighs releasing on my legs, her body pulling off my back. I didn't want to admit that I already missed the sensation of her being that close, that vulnerable. All wrapped up in me.

I coasted to the rest stop, parking it to signal we needed to talk. Her little hands braced my shoulders as she got off my bike. I closed my eyes, steeling myself to not give into her sway, the hold she had on me. Not even an hour ago, we'd been at each other's throats. She'd bent herself over the car, begging me to fuck her, not giving me the dignity to look her in the eyes when I did it.

*Fuck. No.*

Even I had my standards.

I took off my sunglasses as she took off her helmet. "Thanks for the rescue." She slid out of my jacket, holding it up for me to take.

"Care to tell me what the fuck is going on?" I asked, shrugging it on.

She gnawed at her bottom lip, shifting her weight from foot to foot while she looked around the rest area.

"He didn't follow us here. You're safe with me."

She continued to eye our surroundings.

"He left the note on your car, huh?"

Her eyebrows pinched as her upper lip pulled in a way that looked like she was holding in a sob. "Can we just head back? I don't think I'm ready to talk about it."

"No."

"What do you mean?"

I crossed my arms, hearing my leather jacket creak. "You wanted a rescue. It came at a cost."

"You can't hold me hostage!"

"I'm not. You said you needed to hide." I gestured to the highway. "Hide out with me. Let's have an adventure."

"No."

"Maisie . . . ," I chided.

"There's a clear power imbalance here. You have the transportation, lay of the land, and overall brute strength."

"Brute strength?" I echoed skeptically.

"Yes, you and I both know it. You know I'm in a precarious situation and now you're pressuring me into something I don't want to do." She gave me an offended, little sniff. "It's quite rude, actually."

"Oh, so now you believe in manners when it doesn't involve my taint?" I asked, causing her to snicker.

After a few moments, she whispered, "I hate that."

"What?"

"That you can still make me laugh."

I gazed at her, trying to gauge if she was really softening. We were in this invisible duel. I reached out, taking her hand in mine, my thumb sweeping over her knuckles. "I will keep you safe. Let's go."

"We already went. We're damn near to New Hampshire."

"Let's keep going. Stay the course. You've been flipping and flopping on me for days."

With her free hand, she clawed at her roots in anguish. "I'm sorry. I don't mean to. There's just so much happening and I'm juggling everything."

I fought the urge to wrap her in my arms. I had to hold my own line. "Maybe you just need to calm the fuck down and let someone else worry about things for a bit."

"You really want to run away with me?" she asked, completely incredulous.

I let go of her hand as I took a step back, needing my own space to remain unaffected. "Yeah, see where the wind takes us. We have a lot in common. Maybe some time on the road will help us clear our heads."

She tilted her chin. "What do we have in common?"

I ticked them off on my fingers. "We both want to be away from Pine Bluff. We both watched our best friends get married, and even though we're happy for them, it's emotionally exhausting and a big change."

"Mm-hmm."

"We both run our own businesses, so in theory, we can make our own schedules, but we just overwork instead. I'm a Leo, you're an Aries, so we both have chaotic fire sign tendencies." That one got her mouth to twitch. "And to be frank, I really want more time with you."

"More time with me? The girl you said was a mindfuck?"

"You are. That's why I want more time with you."

She slumped her shoulders. "What about what I want?"

Opening my arms wide, I shot back, "I'm all ears, tornado."

She tucked a whisp of hair behind her ear and checked her phone. "This is a bad idea."

# Chapter Sixteen

The day clouded over, making everything dull and gray. Dane and I stood near his bike at the rest stop. His piercing green eyes pinned me as I stiffened in indecision.

As much as I didn't want to admit it, I really liked Dane. I wanted his attention, but I couldn't figure out how to show up in front of him. I was so damn insecure around him, all talk, no game, and he knew it. And god, that was so humiliating.

Now with him all but kidnapping me and pressuring me on this road trip, I felt a reckoning coming that I wasn't ready for.

"You broke me in that forest." I sucked in a sob that had unexpectedly tried to follow that sentence.

The muscles of his jaw feathered as he worked it, gritting back whatever words he wanted to say. The rest stop was in a valley on a slight hill, with highways on either side of us. It was like the whole world was moving by, but we were frozen together. He put his hands on his hips and walked around me in a small circle. The wind picked up, blowing my hair around. I held it back from my face, committed to watching him.

I used his silence as a cue to keep talking. "We were about to hook up and I was beneath you between those two trees. I took off my top, and you laughed at me. Like, full-on laughed at me. I get it, I have small boobs, but—"

"Are you serious?" he finally growled, turning to face me.

"That's what happened!"

"That is *not* what happened, and you know it," he said, his nostrils flaring. Sucking a breath, he gestured toward me. "When you took off your top, I noticed your armpit hair was dyed hot pink to match your hair. It was fucking funny, so I laughed. You flipped out."

"You think my body is funny?"

"I think neon pink body hair on anyone is. If the tables were turned, you'd laugh too."

I crossed my arms. "I dye my armpit hair pink to ward off douchebags. If a guy isn't down with some body hair, I don't want him." I purposefully looked him up and down, feeling defensive. "It's safe to say it works."

"Oh, come on!" he yelled, arms flailing. "It was kooky and cute and, I don't know, unexpected. Just like the girl I was falling so hard for. It was hilarious. I had to laugh! It was like finding a fucking troll doll under your shirt. There was absolutely no way to avoid it."

I rolled my eyes.

He continued, "Oh, and let's not forget what happened the second after. There you were, underneath me with your lacy bra and neon pink armpit hair. I chuckled because it was funny, big fucking deal. I was totally down to keep going because I'm a grown-ass man who doesn't give a fuck about body hair."

"Well then why didn't you explain that!"

"I was too busy. Because the second I took off my shirt, you eyed my chest tattoo and asked, 'Who's that?' like you were completely disgusted."

I held up a flat hand. "It's a very realistic tattoo. He was looking right at me, dude!"

He stepped closer to me, glowering. A prickle of fear ran up my spine. "It is my father," he said, seething.

"Right, but it's a bit weird to have a portrait of your dad on your pec. Like, clearly you didn't think that through."

"Oh, don't worry, darlin'. I'll never forget you saying, 'When girls say they want a daddy in the bedroom, they don't mean your dead dad on your chest staring back at them.' That shit is going to live rent free in my head until the day I die," he roared, pointing to his temple.

I chewed the inside of my cheek. I barely recalled saying that part. I'd been in such a humiliated haze, it'd clouded my thoughts.

"Low. Fucking. Blow, Maisie. Low *fucking* blow," he spat.

"Dane . . . I'm . . ." I shook my head, not sure how to even apologize.

"How dare you mock his memory!" He angrily pointing to the ground. "How dare you judge how I remember my father. And to make matters worse, you kicked me in the fucking chest, so I fell backwards while you grabbed your top and chucked a pinecone at me. Like I was taking advantage of you."

"I'm so sorry. I've lived half my life with my foot in my mouth. I've always been insecure about my boobs. I had just healed from getting my breast implants taken out so when you laughed, my mind immediately went to that."

"I was loving everything I was seeing." He gestured up and down my body. "Pink hair, perky tits, it was all keeping my attention. That's why I was so confused. Then you launched into that shit with my dad and it stung even worse."

Even though I was outside, the metaphorical walls were closing in on me. "I am so sorry." Tears stung my eyes. "I fucked up. I grew up with a mean mom, so I feel like I know how to say the cruelest things because it was the only way I knew how to defend myself against her." I sniffed. "And I think I was subconsciously jealous you knew your dad and had a good relationship with him." My voice quaked. "I'm not saying that's okay. I just think that's what ha—" A sob gushed up my throat. "Happened."

He took one step toward me and then two steps back. "Don't do the crying thing."

"I can't help it!" I dabbed my eyes, feeling like the meanest, shittiest person on earth.

"I'm serious. I've been wanting to get this off my chest for almost a year, and I am righteously angry at you, but if you're crying, something in me takes over."

His own sentence was interrupted by my sniffles. "Please, I'm so sorry. I don't want to make this all about me. You're right to be angry. I crossed the line and made assumptions."

Taking a calculated risk, I snaked my hand underneath his shirt to rest my palm on his bare pec, the one I knew had the tattoo of his father. "I am so sorry for what I said. I hope someday you can forgive me. I forget all the time about my armpit hair because I've been dyeing it off and on since college as a joke. Honestly, no one has laughed at it before. Either they ignore it or it's a deal breaker. It's not an excuse, but I hope you can see how I misread the situation. I thought it was my boobs. I was so nervous for someone to see me without implants for the first time after my surgery."

He covered my hand on his chest. His heartbeat thrummed under my palm. "I believe you."

I'd never connected the dots that he could be laughing at that. Even if I had, I still thought the moment would've been ruined with what I'd said about his tattoo. I had to face the reality that no matter what happened in the forest, I probably would've intentionally messed it up because I was so damn insecure and I hadn't slept with anyone since Conner.

I sucked in some air. "My chest has always been my biggest insecurity, and I worried I wasn't as pretty as the other girls you've been with."

"It's not like that, I promise you. You don't have to impress me, Maze. I was already sold." His shoulders slumped, his mouth drooping, like my confession had wounded him.

"How can I make this better? I know I hurt you. I *want* to make this better."

"I need some time with you." His Adam's apple worked up and down his throat. "That's how you could make this better. I don't say that to guilt you, but you confuse me so damn much. Yet at the same time, I feel like I've known you forever. You drive me fucking crazy."

"I feel the same way."

His thumb rubbed my hand that was still on his chest. "We just get each other. That's why we get on each other's nerves so damn much. I need more time to figure it all out and really see you clearly. Away from Pine Bluff and our friends. Now that we've unpacked the forest thing, maybe it won't feel like this huge elephant in the room."

I nodded, transfixed by his quiet power. I didn't know many people who would forgive someone so easily. I guessed that was the perk of Dane—nothing had to be a big deal. At times, it was infuriating, but in moments like this, I thought he was on to something.

We stood there in front of each other in loaded silence. I went on my tippy toes to wrap my arms around his neck. His forearms locked around my waist, holding me closer. "I'll run away with you," I whispered.

"Just keep going until we can breathe a little easier."

The wind picked up, swaying us. "Until we can breathe."

# Chapter Seventeen

# DANE

Things were starting to click into place. I wished she would've told me what was bothering her clear back in autumn. We could've lived without so much torment. Knowing she thought I'd been laughing at her was eating away at me. I still remembered that moment, watching her yank off her shirt, her breasts jiggling above the seam of her bra about to spill over, her small frame below me all soft and ready for more.

I'd loved the way her hair had been all mussed and her lips had been pillowy from our kisses. We'd talked for hours, and she'd fisted my shirt and pulled me into the forest. From there, it had been all stumbles and laughter and hungry grabs and kisses. I'd held her close to me, just enjoying the solid make-out session. Maisie was one hell of a kisser, and her confidence was refreshing. She'd been bold but had let me take the lead, a delicate balance only some women could pull off.

She was the one who'd asked if I had a condom.

She was the one who'd wanted the vacation hookup.

But once it had gotten down to it, she'd completely submitted to me, which was so attractive. The way our bodies had pressed together, the little sounds of impatience coming out of her mouth, I couldn't forget that autumn evening even if I tried.

Coming back to reality, I looked over my shoulder, forgetting she was wearing my helmet so I couldn't see her stunning face. I wanted those lips all swollen again. We were in this precarious spot, clarity just within my reach. It was beyond physical. I needed more time with her almost to justify to myself why I had been obsessing over her.

A part of me wished I could fall out of infatuation. That wasn't happening anytime soon. Another part of me kept reminding myself to not get totally whipped. I had to retain some level of control here. She was bound to leave me again. I couldn't just let her run rampant through my heart.

If this was a fling, I'd have to treat it that way, but I needed answers, nonetheless.

Deep into Vermont, we pulled over. Maisie's bladder was just as tiny as the rest of her. I knew girls had a pee a lot, but this was next level. We both went to the bathroom, and as she returned, I was leaning against my motorcycle, locking my phone after finalizing our plans.

"Cool bike, by the way," she said, pointing at a wheel. "Is it a Harley?"

"Nah, it's a Bonneville Triumph. Fun fact though, do you know what they called a Harley back in the day?"

"No, what?"

"A Milwaukee vibrator." I wiggled my eyebrows suggestively.

She rolled her eyes with a chuckle. "I'll remember that."

"Ready to hunker down for the night?" I asked, offering a granola bar and bottle of water I got from the vending machine for her.

She bit into the bar. "Yeah, I have a hotel reserved tonight in Philly. How far is that from here?"

"Too far. Five, six hours."

"I don't think I can be on the bike much longer. My legs are sore from riding."

I cocked an eyebrow, letting her double entendre marinate in the sexual tension.

"I have a tow guy named Bear. I already gave him a heads-up not to tow your hearse if someone calls about it."

"Thank you."

"And I got us a room at a hotel nearby. I'm warning you, it's not super nice, but on such short notice, it's our best shot."

"Let me guess, they only had one room available?"

I hadn't even thought to check. I wanted her by me. It was the most natural instinct. I committed to the façade and lied. "Yep," I said, popping the P.

She sipped some water, looking around at the cloudy afternoon. "We don't even have toothbrushes or clothing."

As it stood, I didn't think we'd be needing much clothing.

"There's a shopping center nearby," I offered. "Are you one of those prissy girls who wash new clothes before wearing them?"

"Yes," she whispered, screwing the cap on the bottle.

"Can you tough it out for me, baby girl?"

Her face softened at the mention of *baby girl*. Duly noted. I'd call her that if I kept getting that doe-eyed look on her.

"I can tough it out. Yeah."

I grasped her shoulders in my hands with a playful shake. "Relax. Boyd is a coward. He wouldn't follow us. Outside of Pine Bluff, he doesn't have any power. I got you."

"Right. I think I'll feel better once I get some sleep."

Of course, she hadn't been sleeping well with her road trip here. How could she? She'd been traveling alone, and I was sure staying at my cottage hadn't been easy. On top of all that, she'd been dealing with Boyd and helping with a wedding. She must be exhausted.

I pointed to the pathetic granola bar. "How 'bout once we get settled, you get a little shut eye. I'll run some errands, get you toothpaste and all that, and then I'll bring the greasiest Chinese food I can find back to the room."

"That's so domestic of you." She pursed her lips for a moment. "I'll even give you my fortune cookie."

"You've got yourself a deal."

The hotel was nestled against a woodsy hill on the outskirts of a peaceful town. It was a wide two-story building made to look like a log cabin, but it clearly wasn't. All the rooms faced a cheesy atrium that had a taxidermy deer overlooking a small pond that had seen better days. Decades of lemony furniture polish and cigarette smoke were almost smooshed by the ubiquitous clean vanilla smell all hotels used to fumigate their lobbies.

When I checked in, Maisie stood by me, maybe even unnecessarily close. I kinda loved having her side tucked up against mine. It was this weird mix of her being feisty but also drawn to me. I was glad I wasn't the only one fighting the pull.

The lady at the front desk looked too eager to be at work. Like maybe she was being threatened with a gun to her back behind the desk somewhere or someone had really filled up her bottle of happy pills. Her black, curly hair was pushed back with a thin headband that looked like it was pinching her head. Maybe that was why. With each head movement, tuffs of curls would jiggle.

Pulling up our reservation, she clapped her hands together. "Okay, Mr. and Mrs. MacCloyd, we have one room for one night with one king-size bed." She held up a pointer finger each time she said the word "one." "I do have it noted here that you're newlyweds. Congratulations!"

Maisie opened her mouth to correct her, but I wrapped my arm around her lower back, holding her close. "We're loving married life so far, aren't we, honey?"

Her eyes shot wide for a split second before a glint took over as she rubbed my chest. "You're so right. I am so glad we decided to honeymoon in . . ." She looked around the hotel.

"Bridgepoint, Vermont." I squeezed her closer with a sappy smile. "We just got married on a whale watching tour off the coast of Maine. My little lady here loves whales. But we couldn't do SeaWorld. It makes her cry. Isn't that right?"

Maisie squeaked out an affirmative noise. "Say, do you have maybe a room with two queens? Sometimes Daney here hogs the bed," she asked with a little snicker, layering on her Southern charm.

*Daney?*

The woman fidgeted with the mouse, picking it up and dropping it on the pad as she frantically clicked it. Her hair swung behind her as her buggy eyes searched the screen. "I'm so sorry, we don't."

"It's like the beginning of a bad porno," Maisie mumbled under her breath. I squeezed one of her butt cheeks, causing another squeak. "One king is fine. Thank you so much for looking into that," she amended in a louder tone.

"Do you want a coupon for the buffet across the street?"

"Hell no!" we both said in horror, snapping our heads to look at each other. Finally, something we both agreed on. The woman let out a nervous titter of laughter while sliding our key cards across the counter.

The suite itself was outdated but clean, with maroon accents. Once in the privacy of the room, Maisie flung off her purse and jacket on the bed. "Really, dude? Are you, like, some pathological liar? Why would you tell them we're on our honeymoon?"

"Just to piss you off, darlin'!" I said, grabbing the bin with cheap Champagne, chocolates, and fruit. I plucked out a banana, suggestively offering it to her.

She snatched it out of my hand and chucked it in the waste basket. "Be so fucking for real with me!"

I stepped closer to where she stood between the bed and the armoire with the TV. "What? Did you like being called Mrs. MacCloyd a bit too much?"

"Oh please!" She skimmed past me in outrage.

"It's funny! It doesn't harm anyone. I'm sure the fruit was left over from their sketchy continental breakfast."

She sank on the bed, glowering at me. "Why would you lie?"

I pulled the banana out of the empty bag in the garbage can and unpeeled it to eat. I hated wasting food. "I've done a lot worse."

Her eye twitched as she folded her arms over her chest. "Like what?"

"Don't worry about it," I said between bites.

"Has that ever really worked on anyone?"

"Yes, people who aren't suspicious as fuck."

"Have you hurt children?"

"God no. I'd hurt people who hurt children." Holding up my free hand, I ticked off the list on each finger. "You don't fuck with kids, women, or old people." I chomped into the banana, adding, "Or pets." I folded up the peel. "I'm gonna get going. Get some rest."

# Chapter Eighteen

# DANE

I had a feeling she would be asleep when I got back, so I took my time. I called Lennie to tell him I'd be out for part of the week, then I made sure to gas up the bike. I ran some other errands and ordered the food to pick up later.

Once I got in the store, I realized I had no clue what to get Maisie clothing wise. It invited a whole new batch of ideas inside my head. Would it be presumptuous to get her more than for just one day? What about panties and a bra?

I chuckled, deciding to have fun with it. That was usually my answer in life.

Luckily, I always kept an olive-colored rucksack in a compartment on my bike. I crammed the shopping bags inside it and strapped it in on my back for the drive back to the hotel. When I walked inside our room, I jolted Maisie awake, causing her to shriek in terror. The noise alone made my heart ache.

"It's just me," I soothed, plopping the rucksack and food on the dresser before darting to the bed to soothe her. I rubbed her back while watching her clasp her chest, catching a breath.

"Sorry, the beeping of the lock and how heavy the door was just kinda, wow." She sat up wearily.

"You've been through a lot, haven't you?" I asked.

She nodded. "Yeah, it's been quite the trip." She lifted her chin. "But it's not anything I can't handle."

"Damn straight. Here, let's get some food in you."

Both of us sat across from each other on the bed, cross-legged. I presented the paper bag of food. I didn't think to get paper plates, so we ate right from the cartons with chopsticks. Maisie damn near squealed when I presented egg rolls to her.

*Call her baby girl and get her egg rolls more often. Duly noted.*

I watched her eat, feeling slightly victorious that I could provide her with a little bubble of peace, even if it was fleeting. Clearing my throat, I asked, "Can I ask what he did this time?"

"Boyd?"

"Yeah, you were really scared back there."

She bit open a packet of soy sauce and expertly drizzled it in the hollowed-out end of the egg roll, letting the dark juice permeate the flaky shell. "I think he tried to spike my drink."

"That doesn't surprise me one bit."

She eyed me warily. "I'm concerned that doesn't shock you."

"He's slimy. Something about him always rubbed me the wrong way. Plus, he openly cheats on his wife, which I find degrading."

She continued to nibble on her egg roll. "That's messed up."

"Was this at the bachelorette party?" I asked.

"Yep, before you got there. I didn't see the bartender pour the drink. He just came out of nowhere with it and it was cloudy. I said no. I just had a feeling it was roofied. I'm really aware of that. I had my drink spiked in college. Luckily, Kaylee was paying attention and caught the guy trying to manhandle me out of the bar. I was slumped over and barely able to keep my eyes open. She went full Viking woman and smashed his head into a brick wall."

"Go, moose killer," I said in amusement. "Sorry that happened to you, though." I tried to stave off the protective flare that surged in my chest by chomping down on some cashew chicken.

"Thank you. It made me feel powerless. Just a few more seconds of her turning her head in a different direction could've resulted in god knows what."

I swallowed, pointing at her with my chopsticks. "I noticed you were drinking Thursday. Was it because Kaylee was with you?"

"Yeah, I only feel safe doing it if I know she's around. When it happened in college, the police down in Florida didn't do shit about it. So when I found out it was a cop trying to drug me up here in Maine, it just lit a fire under my ass. I filed a report with the state police about his conduct."

"As you should."

She twirled some noodles pensively. "After the rehearsal dinner, he pulled me over and I got mouthy with him. He asked where I was staying, and I lied. He was taking forever to write a ticket because he was lurking on me. He found out about Pretty Kitty and made sure to let me know I was a pervert and he wanted me out of his town."

I snorted. "That's ironic."

"And he gave me a ticket for driving without a license because I didn't have it on me. Since I was using an out of state driver's license, Tilly's kept both my I.D. and credit card when I opened my tab. Which reminds me." She groaned. "I still don't have my cards. I was on my way to Tilly's when the whole parade thing happened."

"So you were somewhere in southern Maine, with no I.D. or car and a cop on your tail."

"Well, when you put it like that." Her mouth jerked with a sheepish smile.

"So this is why you were so dodgy this morning? I mean, things ended weirdly between us last night but—"

"It wasn't all you," she interrupted. "I wanted to get out of town, even before I saw the note. Then when you found it, I knew I had to haul ass, even if it meant skipping the chance to work it out with you."

I was horrified he'd left her the note and harassed her, but I'd be lying if I didn't admit that I was relieved that was her main motive.

"Maisie, sweetheart, why didn't you tell me the night he pulled you over? I would've stayed at the cottage with you."

"I wanted to handle it myself," she whispered.

I curled my hand to run my knuckles along her jaw. "I've got you."

She leaned into my touch. "Thank you, but I've got myself."

I cupped her face, cocking an eyebrow.

"Okay, you've got me, too," she amended, scootching closer to me on the bed so our knees touched.

I could handle Boyd. Was it annoying he'd scared her? Yes, but I was relieved that was all she was worried about.

"Leave it to you to get in this much trouble at a wedding, tornado."

"Hush!" She shoved at my chest. Her gaze flicked down to her lap then back up to mine. "Can I ask you some tough questions now?"

I picked up the last egg roll with my chopsticks. "Shoot."

"What happened to your family?"

"Shit, you weren't kidding." I racked my brain on how to make sense of it.

"I know you mentioned both your parents died, and your sister, Jamie."

"Good memory. So, um, yeah, my mom was the first to go. She had breast cancer and passed away before I was even out of high school."

Her hand rested on my knee. "I'm sorry."

"Yeah, it was pretty tough. We were all really close. She was a damn good mother. She was so fun. Like, there was always something to do, a party to throw, an adventure to go on. She definitely made my childhood magical. And my dad—" I felt a grin warm my face. "He was crazy about her."

"That's so cute."

"It was. Needless to say, my sister didn't handle my mom's passing well. She, um"—I choked back the sting of guilt in my throat—"started drinking and partying to cope. I wasn't keeping an eye on her. One night, she was driving and crashed on a bridge. The impact killed her. She was barely 20."

Her brow furrowed. "Oh my goodness, that's so young."

"Yeah, I'll be honest, I kind of felt like an idiot when I first met you and assumed you were drinking. I shouldn't do that. Especially after what happened with Jamie. You'd think someone I love dying because of drunk driving would make me more aware of sobriety."

She squeezed my leg. "You had no way of knowing I was wary about that. Or that my mom's an alcoholic. You didn't do anything wrong."

I nodded, unable to accept what she was saying.

"What about your dad?"

"He died a couple years ago. He was shoveling snow in front of the cottage and had a heart attack. I was at the shop." I worked up enough courage to say the rest. "No one found him. When I came home, he was . . . cold."

I stared at the wall in front of me, and bursts of color soared in my periphery as I wrangled in my panic. Sometimes, I'd still see his stony face in my mind when it snowed. Talking about it also brought up memories.

Maisie sweetly brushing her hand up and down my leg brought me back to the moment. Her eyes locked with mine. "I'm sorry you lost them. That's so hard."

"Thank you. It was tough. Maybe it's just wishful thinking, but I swear sometimes I can feel them. Jamie loved basketball and Girl Scout cookies. I always try to buy a couple boxes when I can."

"Thin mints?"

I shook my head, feeling lighter. "Nah, she liked Samoa cookies best."

"What reminds you of your dad?"

"The shop. It was his. Frank's Auto."

"Was it your grandfather's before that?"

"Oh, no, um . . ." I searched my memory for an appropriate answer. "My grandfather died really young. He didn't even live in Pine Bluff; he was from Boston. My dad was a transplant. My mom, on the other hand, was born and raised in Maine."

"That's cool."

I pointed to her nails. "Did you go to the salon three doors down from my shop with Kaylee to get your nails done before the wedding?"

"Yes." She splayed out her hand.

"That was my mom's salon. She cut hair."

"Wait." Her hand skimmed the scissor tattoo just under my elbow. "Oh, so is this tattoo to remember your mom?"

No one ever asked what my tattoos meant. The way she instantly made sense of it made my chest tighten. She saw me. She got me.

"Yes. And the roses are for Jamie. She loved white roses. My mom taught her how to grow them in the garden at the cottage."

"This is a really sweet way to remember them." Maisie reverently brushed the long lines of the scissors with a pensive little hum.

"That reminds me, I got something for you while I was in town." I got up from the bed to fetch a sack.

"Patrica's Beauty Supply?" she said with a creased brow, standing up.

Grabbing a tube of hot pink hair dye and scissors, I held both up like trophies. "I figured you might want to cut your hair now that the wedding is over. You mentioned before you like to do it yourself, so I figured I'd grab the stuff for it. The lady at the store included clippers, bleach, and a cape. She said you'd know what to do. If not, we can find a salon somewhere tomorrow."

"Dane," she breathed. "You did this for me?"

"Well yeah," I said, placing the items back in the bag. "I wanted you to feel like yourself again."

She leapt at me for a hug. "Let's do it!"

She snatched the bag and scurried into the bathroom. I made myself useful and threw out the food containers outside. When I came back, she had put on the cape and was playing music on her phone.

"Are you just going to watch me?" she asked, looking at me behind her in the mirror.

"Yeah, if you don't mind."

A loaded silence filled the small bathroom as I leaned against the doorframe. She busied herself with mixing the bleach in the bowl, but I could've sworn a flush crept up her neck and on her cheeks.

As she clipped her hair up into sections, she asked me more about my family. I told her all about my mom's salon and how my dad had gone in for a weekly haircut to flirt with her until she'd agreed to date him. And how I'd had to hang out there after school when I'd been little, so I'd grown up around a lot of women. That established her theory of why I like women so much. I guessed she wasn't wrong.

Then she asked about the cottage and my mom's style. I told her all about how my mom would go antiquing all over New England. She'd be hours away from home and call my dad, playing all innocent to ask him to meet her at an estate sale with his truck to haul furniture home. He'd always grumble about it, but we'd all known he loved it. Eventually, he'd just gone with her.

As I told her about growing up in Pine Bluff, I watched as layer by layer, Maisie came back to herself. Not only was her hair visibly lightning, but so was the proverbial load off her shoulders. Watching her process was hypnotic. I couldn't help but laugh when she squeezed her bleached hair into a mohawk. She kept flaring her nostrils and making goofy voices.

I snatched the brush with bleach and playfully lifted her arm up, forcing the cape to gather by her shoulder.

"What are you doing?" she asked.

"We're going to dye your armpit hair. Get everything matching."

She threw her head back with a snort, letting me continue to hold her arm and peek inside the sleeve of her shirt.

"I shaved for the special occasion!"

"You always keep me guessing. Anything else you want pretty in pink?" I flicked a glance down her body.

"My kitty is already pretty."

"I was talking about leg hair, but fair enough."

She swatted me and snatched the brush from my grip. "What about you?"

Laughing, I bolted as she chased me around the hotel room like a bleached, gooped up, mohawked maniac. I ran from one corner to the other, then eventually shielded myself behind the curtains. She hopped up on the bed like a ninja, all but crawling the wall to reach me.

"Maisie! Don't you dare!" I grasped her wrist.

"I think a pink streak would suit you! It would make you look extra tough on that motorcycle." She hopped on the lounge chair, standing on the arm to tower over me.

"I will leave your ass here!"

"No! Not in Vermont!" She snorted.

Seeing an advantage, I tackled her, hugging her legs to my chest to ensure the top part of her was well above me as the most addictive giggle erupted from her. As I ran, she squirmed and put up a good fight. I plopped her on the ground with a smack of her ass. "Get in the shower and wash it off, woman!"

"You just want me naked," she said over her shoulder with a coy smile.

Neither confirming nor denying, I plucked the clothes I'd gotten for myself out of the bags, handing her the rest before pulling the door shut behind me.

The hair-dye demon had been wrangled . . . for now.

# Chapter Nineteen

    I stood in the hotel bathroom, watching the pink dye run down the drain around my feet. I felt like I was floating, like I could finally breathe and be myself now that I was done being a maid of honor. I was still on the run, but the only thing I was interested in was running into Dane's arms. I wanted to crash into him and discover everything we'd buried last year. Being near him was magnetic, and I couldn't deny how I felt any longer.

    For once, I didn't have a game plan and I didn't really mind. I was so used to being in charge, taking the lead, and calling the shots. I wanted to let Dane lead me, see what kind of man he was and if he was up to snuff.

    While he was away, I'd canceled the hotels I'd booked for the way home, knowing there was no way I was going to reach them now. I'd checked my email to see if anyone from the police department had responded. No such luck. Dom hadn't texted me back either, so I guessed no news was good news. He was busy running Pretty Kitty while I was away.

    I toweled off and used the blow dryer. Dane had bought himself some pomade that I used. It was Crew and smelled amazing. He'd also snagged a teeny bottle of face lotion and a package of makeup wipes, which was more than most guys would think of. Luckily, I had my make-up staples in my purse if I felt like putting any on tomorrow.

He'd picked out the most ridiculous outfits for me, like a short, white, floral sundress, which I was sure was for some nasty fantasy he had, a giant oversize black shirt and hot-pink cotton booty shorts, a black lacy bra, which was eerily close to my size, some cheeky panties, and a red hooker thong. Not suggestive at all.

"Is your goal to make me look like a fucking porn star?" I shouted, stringing the thong between my hands.

A low chuckle came from the room. "Pick your poison. You gave up control, now you get to live with the consequences."

His point of me giving up control sent a thrill through me. I had. I really had. I didn't know if it was the moment I'd gotten on his bike or how I let him take the lead once we'd settled, but I had. And it felt so damn good. I didn't realize how much I'd needed that. I was used to being a boss at work and a bold wild child with Kaylee. Before that, I'd gotten really good grades in college to keep my scholarships and grants. And even before all that, I'd been in charge of myself while my mom had drunk and fucked her way through most of Austin. If it wasn't for my mom dating a softball coach when I'd been in middle school, I would've never had an extracurricular hobby.

I picked the shorts and shirt. Looking at myself in the mirror one last time, I was unable to fight my grin.

"Are you ready for the grand reveal?" I asked, flinging the door open and gliding out into the room like I was in some Miss America pageant. "Ta-da!"

The room was dim with just one lamp on next to the bed. Dane's eyes crinkled in a smile, one of the first genuine ones I'd seen on him since we'd arrived. "There's my girl."

*His girl.* I didn't hate it. Letting the giddy feeling sweep me away, I did a little twirl to really give him his money's worth.

"C'mere," he said, snatching my waist to pull me onto his lap from where he sat at the foot of the bed.

Wrapping my arms around his neck, I let my body greedily settle onto him, my core smooshing against him along with my breasts. This close, he could probably feel I wasn't wearing a bra. If not, he would soon with the way he swept his hands up and down my back and along my sides.

"I like being this close," I admitted.

His hand traveled to touch my newly pink, coiffed hair. "I like you this close too. You're so beautiful, Maisie. I've never seen anyone like you in my life."

I playfully scoffed, rolling my eyes.

"No, it's true. You look like a damn faerie. You have such a pretty face. It's stuck with me. I see it when I close my eyes at night." He swallowed hard, his eyes roaming mine as his hand delicately touched my cheeks then my forehead, moving to my nose. "These eyes, this little swoop nose, these lips." His fingertips traced my mouth. I leaned in closer, giving him permission.

His lips melded into mine, his hands grasping my waist, both of us instantly lost in the kiss. I broke it to trail my mouth over his stubbled jaw. "You know, you're not bad-looking yourself." I scored my nails through his scalp, causing a groan to creak out of him. "You've stuck with me, too. These smoky green eyes and your smile. And this dent right here." I ran just the tip of my tongue over his chin before feathering a gentle kiss.

"Maisie," he whispered, half tortured, half swept away. He grabbed my hips to shift me directly on his bulge.

"You feel so good against me," I said, rocking slightly while I reached to pull off his shirt. Before I could, he flipped us, situating himself over me.

"Did I say you could take off my shirt, tornado?" he whispered into a kiss before biting my bottom lip. We moved together, sliding our lips and bodies against one another. With each roll and skim, another layer of my defense wore off, revealing nothing but pure desire.

I broke the kiss, needing to take a breath, not realizing I'd poked the bear. Being the dumbass I was, I continued to reach for the fabric at his waist.

He grabbed both of my hands and pinned them above my head with a low grumble that went straight to my pussy. From there, he nuzzled my neck. "What's off-limits?"

"Hm?" I said stupidly, lost in the way his hands floated down my ribs.

"What's. Off. Limits? I want to respect your boundaries."

I really was in over my head. "I'll let you know if you push up against any."

He shook his head, clearly not loving my vague answer.

The truth was, I really didn't know anymore. I was so horny, he could probably talk me into damn near anything. I focused on the ceiling to give him a decent answer. "Um, no butt stuff. You can finish anywhere but my face." I shook my head. "I hate that."

"Good." He lifted my shirt slightly, exposing my stomach. "I've wanted to lick these since the moment I saw them," he murmured before dragging his tongue against my hip bones. I wiggled in anticipation, causing him to hold a hip down to playfully nip.

"Dane, please, let me touch you."

"No." He continued to kiss up my stomach and across my ribs before latching his gaze with mine. With a nod from me, he pushed up my black shirt, exposing my breasts to the cool air.

"Don't worry, I've healed. You can do whatever." My sentence trailed off as his hands went to my ribs as he cradled me, placing a gentle kiss on each nipple. My scars were on the very bottom of my nipples, mostly camouflaged.

"Jesus Christ, Maisie. Look at you. You're perfect. Never feel insecure about your body, especially around me."

I swept my thumbs up his cheekbones as he settled his torso against my core, my legs open and framing him. "I don't want you to think I'm shallow because I had implants. Or that I'm fickle because I took them out."

"How are fake boobs any different from my tattoos? It's something you do to your body to make you feel more comfortable in it."

"I guess so," I said, trying to fight noticing how with each word muttered by him, air would drift over the sensitive skin.

"But it sounds like yours were making you sick. You were given this body to feel good. Do you feel better without them?"

"Yes."

"Good, because all I want is for you to feel good." With his vow, he lowered his mouth back to my breast, swirling one nipple with the tip of his tongue. A little gasp escaped me. He feathered his tongue back and forth across the peak, causing me to hold my breath.

"Please, please don't stop."

His other hand hungrily grabbed the other, the callouses scraping across my tender flesh as he squeezed and rubbed a thumb across the nipple. I loved that he was testing how rough I liked it, seeing how much I could take. Still covering the other breast with his mouth, he sucked and nibbled until my nipple was completely erect and covered in his spit. "I can feel how wet you're getting."

"Yeah." I sighed, lost in the feeling.

"I bet other parts of you are just as sensitive as these perfect tits."

I nodded, lifting my hips to grind against him, all but dragging my pussy against his belt in desperation.

"You're going to show me," he said.

"I will," I promised, completely lightheaded, hoping I was moments away from finally getting him inside me, from being filled with Dane and drained of all dread. Something about him being a part of me felt like a solution, a plea to the universe. I needed to experience having him.

He popped off my tits, kissing each nipple then nuzzling between them before working lower. When he reached the band of my shorts, I lifted my bum, helping him take them off. He sucked in a breath as my mound was exposed. I could tell he already liked what he saw. And in my full moment of brazen glory, I spread my legs wider, planting a foot on either side of where he knelt in front of me on the bed.

"Oh baby," he murmured, touching my calves while staring at my center. His reverential tone made me want to smile but I fought it. "This." He trailed off, lost in thought. "This is the prettiest pussy I've ever seen."

I gently touched myself, running my fingers over my lips. "There's a reason I called my shop Pretty Kitty."

"It's all making sense," he said, eyes still locked between my legs as he backed off the bed, literally falling to his knees. I knew he just needed to look at it a little longer. I'd had this reaction before.

There was a very mature part of me that knew all bodies were beautiful, but on the flipside, there was a tiny part of me that loved knowing I had an extra pretty pussy. Nothing on earth had made me feel as powerful than spreading my legs and watching a man fall to his knees in devotion.

*If you want to see God, let me spread my legs.*

I knew the portal between a woman's legs was what men had first prayed about. Right up there with rain for crops, protection from wild beasts, and air in their lungs. We birthed civilizations, bled without dying, and could receive endless orgasms. Talk about power. It was validating to remind men of this undisputable truth. As long as I had one of *these*, I could get as many of *those* as I wanted.

Taking a ragged breath, he shifted his shoulders, still transfixed as he lunged for his leather jacket that was on the back of the desk chair. I crunched up to watch him in confusion as he presented a silky black drawstring pouch from the inside pocket.

"You're going to show me how wet and beautiful you can get."

Opening the bag, he revealed a pink, pearlescent sex toy. My favorite one of all time and the best seller at my store. *How did he know?*

"Oh my god! Did you steal that from my car?"

He clicked it on with a pleased chuckle. "Yep," he said simply with zero shame.

"Dane! You stole a clit sucker from me?"

"It's not really stealing if I give it back to you. Consider it investing in the future." He flashed me a sexy smile.

I flopped back on the bed, fighting a laugh, too horny to deal with this. "Oh my god, and you've had it in your coat for days? Just waiting?"

"Pussy preparedness. What did you expect? Besides, you should be impressed I got away with it. It's all charged and clean, I promise."

"What about you? You still have your clothes on."

He pressed the toy to his palm, deciding to change the setting. "You already watched me come. It's your turn." He offered it with a darkened look. "Now show me how you like it."

I froze in confusion.

Reading the side of the toy, he looked up at me. "It says Satisfyer. Hopefully it lives up to its name. If it doesn't, I sure will."

"But I . . . Shouldn't we just fuck?" I was in torture seeing the man I wanted next to the single thing that had brought me countless orgasms. Sure, it was my loyal pussy pleaser, but couldn't a girl just crave some good old-fashioned cock?

No longer patient, he wrapped my hand around the toy as he pressed it against my core. "I'm earning your trust. You're earning this dick."

"Fuck." I whimpered, throwing my head back, feeling my lips spread around the toy, my clit nestled in the middle. The pulsing beat thumped against my sensitive nerves, my toes instantly curling.

"Ah yeah," he urged, his voice deep with desire. "Run it through your lips like that, let me hear how slick it is against you."

I shifted my hips, rocking against our hands and the toy. "Please, please just fuck me. I promise I'll make it so good for you."

I craved the weight of him on me. The sound of his wild undoing. I wanted to smell his sweat, feel our bodies connected. This wasn't enough.

"You're doing so well on your own. Look how pretty you are all sprawled out for me. Fuck, you're getting so wet." Standing up, he lifted his chin. "Don't you dare stop." Seconds later, he slid a towel underneath me, kneeling before me once more to kiss up my inner thighs. I tilted my pelvis, hoping to feel his mouth. He pulled away but continued to lazily trace patterns up my inner thighs and over my hip bones, across my breasts, heightening every pulse of the toy against me.

A familiar pull of tingling formed low in my body. I blinked, focusing my breath in order to make my orgasm more intense.

"That's it. You're doing so well breathing it all in. Are you going to come apart for me? Earn this cock, yeah?"

Before I could answer or argue, my body trembled, my pussy clenching nothing as an orgasm ripped through me. I covered my face with my free hand and attempted to lift the toy away from myself, but Dane clutched it firmly, shifting it to pulse at my entrance.

"Now look at me when you come this time." His demand clear, he moved the toy back up to my clit.

I didn't want to admit it, but now that I was doing all this alone, I was feeling a little shy, exposed. "I need your dick in me. Or a finger. Something, anything," I begged.

His lips twitched as he bit back what I could only guess was a smirk. "Earn it." His other hand covered my breast with an encouraging squeeze. "Come for me again. Let me see how pretty you are when you lose yourself." He was really getting off on this.

I urged our hands to push the toy harder against my clit, letting another orgasm shudder my body seconds later. "Fuck," I cried out, body twitching, legs shaky.

Dane took the gadget, plopping it next to me as his hands skimmed my chest, tummy, and hips. "God, you're beautiful."

"I can't come anymore. I'm too . . . It's too . . ."

"I know." He kissed up my torso, covering me with my shirt as he lay down beside me, pulling me against his chest. Once I was surrounded by his warmth, the night got blurry after that. I grew tired, knowing I had to crash for a quick nap before cleaning up. I murmured this was normal and to go on without me. I hadn't come that hard in weeks. I'd been so busy with the road trip and the wedding.

I heard him showering and brushing his teeth. He wandered out and came back with bottled water. While he was doing that, I cleaned myself up and got in bed, forming a wall of pillows between us.

Dane grunted, getting under the covers. "What the fuck?"

"It's a barrier."

"I can't hold you?"

"You didn't give me any dick! You're earning my trust. I'm earning your dick. Both call for a pillow barrier."

Flicking off his lamp, he let out a chuckle. "You're something else."

# Chapter Twenty

Melon-colored sunlight streamed through the dinky hotel drapes like a spotlight on my face. I was down to my boxer briefs, and Maisie clung to me like a koala, my morning wood pressing into the side of her shin. The dawn sparkled on her fuchsia hair and the tiny golden hoop through her nostril. Seeing her beautiful face soft with sleep made my heart squeeze in fondness. I loved her wild side, but I craved more of her sweetness. The idea of waking up to her on my chest more often was, well, appealing.

If she cracked her eyes open, she'd be face-to-face, literally, with the notorious tattoo of my dad. Wanting to avoid another blow to my ego, I rested my hand on my pec, hoping it looked nonchalant. The slight movement made her stir in her sleep and clutch me closer.

*Needy girl.*

I liked that about Maisie. She needed my protection and understanding. She needed my discretion and dick. I liked that. So few people in my life had asked things from me, and when they had, I'd really fucked it up. I'd mastered fucking up things at this point.

A familiar ache settled in my chest and without thinking, I brushed Maisie's forehead with a worried kiss.

"Huh?" she said, groggily lifting her head. "Dane? Oh god!" She immediately lowered her leg to avoid my boner.

"You obliterated the pillow wall around 3 am." I kissed her forehead again. "Sounded like you were having a nightmare. Something about birds."

She ran her hand through her hair, realizing it was short, and with a whimper, she tucked herself back into my chest. "I forgot where I was."

"You're safe," I said, squeezing her slightly. "This is cute." I held up her hand up to inspect a delicate ring on her thumb comprised of daisies.

"Thank you. It's a friendship ring Kaylee and I got together in San Francisco. The daisies are a nod to the hippies, you know, flower power." She flashed me a peace sign.

"Tell me more." I kissed the back of her hand as she dished all about the trip they'd taken. She was wearing her big shirt and shorts, but I kinda wished we were both naked. I wanted to feel her against me in so many ways. The level of self-control I'd exhibited last night was monk level. I was proud of myself, even if no one else was.

*Manwhore my ass.*

The conversation meandered back to Kaylee and Harley and how weird it was that our best friends had married each other.

"Does Kaylee know you're with me?" I asked.

"No, I didn't want to bother her on her honeymoon. They're supposed to be unplugged. You know, fucking each other's brains out." She looked up at me. "Does Harley know you're with me?"

"No, I don't even know if they made it to Greece safely. Har is a closed book. I'm in the dark most of the time. It was a fucking miracle he told me about Kaylee to begin with."

"I don't want to lie to them. I'm not Rosie," she said dryly.

My body shook her with silent laughter.

"What?" she asked.

"I watched the whole thing unfold last year, but I only had pieces of the puzzle. I thought it was so fucking weird Rosie and Kaylee played nice after their love triangle."

Maisie bolted straight up in the bed to turn to look at me. "I know, right?"

"It's unnatural. I'm not saying there needed to be a catfight, but it was so *after school special* of them to get along. Like a *Saved by the Bell* episode or something." She bobbed her head in enthusiasm, clearly loving the dirt, so I went on. "They kept trying to set me up with Rosie, but I could tell she was seeing someone else. I low-key thought she went back to that creep in Boston who cheated on them to begin with."

"No!" She gasped. "Tyler? You though Rosie went back to Tyler?"

"Yeah, I figured she was ducking out with him again and didn't want to tell Kaylee because it would fuck up her portion of the business. I mean, that makes sense, right?"

"It does. Wow."

"I didn't say anything because I didn't want to hurt Kaylee. But I was wrong. I figured out it was Carson but didn't give a shit at that point. I was dating this tourist last summer and it kinda fucked me up. I didn't have time to worry about other people's drama."

"Why do you do that?" she asked.

"Do what?"

"Act like it's some affliction that you have to date all the tourists. I mean, wouldn't it be easier to be honest with yourself?"

I leaned back in the bed, away from her. "You think I date because I don't want to settle down?"

"Um, yeah. Isn't that the whole point? The women you date are just visiting Pine Bluff. When their summer vacation is over or their seasonal job has ended, they pack up and leave. Zero commitment."

"You honestly think I like being left every summer? After spending weeks, sometimes months with a woman, hoping she stays?"

She shrugged, fiddling with her thumb ring. "I mean, someone might stay."

"No one stays."

A loaded silence punched the air between us. Finally, Maisie looked up with big, naïve eyes. "Maybe instead of others staying, you need to leave?"

"I can't."

She scoffed. "Why not?"

"I have to work for myself. My shop is all I have."

"I'm sure another garage would love a mechanic like you."

"I can't work for anyone but myself. You're just going to have to take my word for it. Speaking of businesses, when are you going to tell Kaylee something is up with Pretty Kitty?"

Her mouth gaped then wavered halfway shut. "How did you know?"

It was my turn to shrug. "Lucky guess. I figured if it was business as usual, you wouldn't be blazing through town with a hearse filled with vibrators." We both chuckled. "Was that the last of your inventory?"

She pulled her knees to her chest, bracing her forearms on her shins. "It's not like that. I'm actually getting offers to be acquired by investors. I'm trying to decide on how to proceed."

"A chain of Pretty Kitties?" I teased.

"Yeah, turns out sexually repressed Republicans really love adult videos and BDSM. Are we shocked?"

"No. But why are you ashamed to tell Kaylee? That's great news."

"She has that antiestablishment streak to her; you know, *fuck the man* and corporate greed and all. I mean, look at her parents. I'm pretty sure her birth certificate has pressed flowers on it and was signed by a shaman at some drum circle."

*God, she was witty.*

"You're not wrong, but she doesn't have to agree with what you do with your business."

She fiddled with the edge of the sheets. "I know, but she helped me open it."

"What if you gave her a cut?"

"I was already going to do that, but it's more than just money."

"What if you loop her in with your new plans? Make her feel included again."

"That's just it. I don't know what to do with myself. But it's a really good offer. I'm supposed to be in Seattle to meet the investors at the end of June."

"What if you helped her out with Silver Springs? Return the favor? You could stay at my cottage for free."

"Oh god, you're shameless, aren't you? I can't believe you just threw that out there." She turned her head toward the window.

"Why would I be ashamed?"

"Because you want me in Pine Bluff."

"Again, what's so shameful about that?"

Her gaze flitted back to me with a stern stare. "Wouldn't you feel like you're entrapping me?"

"No, it would be a fresh start." I trailed my knuckles up her shin. "With people who care about you."

"It would be a trap. The town would never feel like mine. It would be Kaylee's, or yours. Hell, if we want to get technical about it, it would be Harley that brought me there."

I pulled my hand away to rub my scruff. "Wow, you have zero intention of doing this, don't you?"

"What *is* this?"

"Never mind, tornado. We can play it how you feel it."

"Did you just quote Fleetwood Mac?"

I tilted my head, letting my neck crack. "Unintentionally, yes."

She twisted her thumb ring around with her pointer finger. "My whole road trip was for me to get away from it all. Sort my thoughts, come up with a plan. How would following you back solve anything?"

"It was just an offer."

"I'm sorry. I'm not close to feeling like I even know you."

"Maisie, be real," I chided, dipping my chin, sick of her act.

She let out a nervous hum, lifting her pink eyebrows.

"You know me, and I know you. The second we met, that part was undeniable. Listen, I don't believe in all this woo-woo stuff you and Kaylee do, but I believe in the basics, and without it sounding cliché, I think we both know this isn't our first lifetime bumping into each other."

She snorted. "Oh my god, did you just call me your soulmate?"

I locked my eyes on her, letting the moment be whatever it would be. My truth was one of my best assets—I knew that. "I think it's safe to say you feel familiar. And maybe a part of this is why it's so jarring to be around each other. It's intense, don't you agree?"

"Yes," she whispered, dropping her legs from where she shielded her chest.

"And we have some things to explore."

She continued to stare at me, really taking me in. "Who knows what we're going to find in each other."

"Well, aside from you always being on the verge of bolting, I like what I'm finding so far."

"I like what I'm finding so far," she echoed. "I just . . ."

"You're cagey. I get it."

Her stomach gurgled loud enough to hear. "And bordering on hangry," she offered, zapping our reverie with practicality.

I got up from the bed, picking her up like a bride just because I could. She giggled and wrapped her arms around my neck. "Are you a waffle or pancake person?"

She kissed my cheek. "I don't discriminate when it comes to breakfast food."

"One more tally on the board of why I like you."

# Chapter Twenty-One

Dane sawed into a meaty omelet across from me, the cheap plastic table jiggling a little under the weight of his pressure. Since we were in Vermont, home of the crunchy granola type people, it had been interesting tracking down a greasy diner for breakfast. About 20 minutes from our motel was Babe's Diner, which held on to the rooster-themed kitchens of the 90s. A woman, I assumed Babe, donned compression socks, Keds, and a lumpy green sweater hanging off her as she shuffled around, pouring coffee.

"Refill?" she asked.

"Might as well," Dane and I said in unison, snapping our heads to gawk at each other the second it happened.

Babe chuckled while pouring. "How long have you guys been together?"

"Feels like lifetimes," Dane said with a wink, knowing it would make me both blush and suppress an eyeroll.

"You guys are sure cute together. It's fun to see a couple laughing and actually talking. Most people just sit across from each other on their phones." She flashed a knowing glance at me, relaying *girl, he's a keeper.*

"Thank you, ma'am."

"Are we paying together or separately?"

"Together," Dane answered before I could.

Once Babe was out of sight, I leaned forward with an indignant huff. "For the love of God, let me pay for something." Even though my credit card was at Tilly's, I still had my debit card and some cash with me.

"No, that's not how I roll," he said flatly, turning his attention back to his omelet. He was wearing a charcoal shirt today, with a tiny Adidas logo over one of his pecs, the sleeves strained on his biceps. It must've been something he'd snagged for himself at the store. I was wearing the baggy shirt I'd slept in and my jeans from yesterday. It was too cold for the sundress. Wherever we ended up, I prayed it had a washing machine.

He had some mysterious plan which made me feel at ease but also anxious. A weird limbo only Dane had concocted in my body. On a very real level, I knew I was physically protected by him, but on another, I worried how this was all going to play out.

"Let's play two truths and a lie," I offered, trying to keep the energy light.

"Okay, you go first," he said.

I drizzled more syrup on my plate. "Hmm, okay. I've never faked an orgasm. I've never been to New York. And Halloween is my favorite holiday."

Dane tilted his head in consideration, pursing his lips. "Hmm, I can see you as a spooky person, so I bet Halloween is your favorite. And I'm sure you've been to New York, so I guess you're lying about faking it."

I made a buzzer noise in my throat. "Wrong!"

"Oh really? You've never faked it?" He brought his coffee up to his lips for a sip.

"Nope, I don't believe in participation trophies for penetration."

He damn near choked on his coffee, fighting to not spray me in the face with it. "Dear god, woman! Warn me!"

I wiggled in my seat, pleased my zinger had landed. I liked shocking people, especially him. "I've never been to New York. Your turn."

"Let's see. My last meal would be tacos, I'm scared of clowns, and my parents almost named me Jeremy."

"I feel like the taco thing is a lie."

"You're right. My last meal would be meatloaf with mashed potatoes."

"Meatloaf?"

"I'm a simple man. What would be your last meal?"

I wanted to tease him some more for earnestly picking meatloaf but decided to move on. "Easy. A crawfish boil from H-E-B and a cold Big Red."

"What's H-E-B?"

"It's like a grocery store down in Texas, but better. You really need to experience it in person to understand it. In the summers, they have vendors out front that make tamales and other treats, but the crawfish boils are heavenly. They have corn and potatoes along with the crawfish, and it's always super spicy. They sell it in this bag that you dump out on the table, and you get to dig into it like some barbarian. It's so satisfying. I dream of it."

He gave me a lopsided smile. "And a Big Red?"

"It's an upgraded cream soda."

"Even better than your beloved Diet Coke?"

"Hands down."

"Good to know. Speaking of food, I think this is delicious" he said, pointing to his plate with his fork.

"Places like this are underrated."

"I have this idea 'bout combining somewhere to eat with a shop for oil changes."

I delicately bit into a piece of bacon. "Tell me more."

"Everyone who drops off their car to me usually walks over to Tilly's Tavern to wait until I have news for them.

Sometimes, the women go get their nails or hair done at the salon. So I've always thought I could use that pattern in behavior and create a novelty experience."

"Like 'hey, get your oil changed and a manicure' kinda thing?"

"Exactly. Or a haircut. As a dude, I have to get a haircut like every three weeks. It's a bitch. But if you combine two errands, it's almost like you're doing a favor for them." He took a sip of his coffee with a squint. "But you need a haircut more often than an oil change, so I never figured out how to tackle that problem."

"But you do need to eat every day, so that would be an easier sell." I drummed my fingers on my lip in consideration. "Fill'er up!" I exclaimed, pointing my finger in the air.

"Huh?"

"You know, when people talk about filling up a tank with fuel, they say, 'fill her up'. Fill'er up. You fill up yourself with food, and you fill up the car with oil and whatever windshield fluid thingies you sell people on."

He gulped and grinned. "You don't know jack shit about cars, do you?"

"Nope! Good thing I'm getting frisky with a mechanic."

That made him wiggle his eyebrows and chomp a piece of sausage off his fork. "Fill'er up." He nodded. "I like it. You could serve burgers, milkshakes, onion rings. You know, play into that whole retro Americana thing."

"Right, like that mural on the side of your shop," I said, dragging a chunk of my French toast through syrup before taking a bite.

On the exposed exterior wall visible from Main Street, there was a cool vintage-looking mural that had a bunch of muscle cars parked at a drive-in movie. It was a fucking masterpiece. I could only imagine Dane had a touch of nostalgia by requesting it.

"Do you know who painted that?" he asked.

"No, who?"

"Carson," he said with a pained groan and another bite.

"The guy's fucking scary. I've gotten one word out of him." I held up a finger. "One!"

"Well, you did compare him and Harley to Burt and Earnie from *Sesame Street* at the stag party."

We both threw our heads back in laughter, achieving side-eyes from others in the diner.

"I was so hammered. I barely remember that!" Gaining composure, I asked, "Where's the lie?"

He pointed to his face with his fork. "It's the brows, right? So fucking serious." Squaring his shoulders with a glance out the window, he went on, "But I feel bad. I kind of ruined his life."

"Kind of?"

"I spread rumors that he kills whatever woman he loves."

I damn near gagged on my food. Kaylee had never told me this much dirt about Rosie and Carson. She'd known I hadn't wanted to hear about Rosie because I hadn't had a good feeling about her. But now I had to know. "Jesus Christ, why would you say that?"

"He was dating my sister when she died. I accused him of not watching out for her. I was barely out of high school and away from Pine Bluff when it happened. I blamed him for her death. It was just easier to project on him, I guess." He shifted in his seat. "I'm not saying it's okay. I guess I just didn't know where to direct my rage. Then my dad died a couple years later, and I just felt more alone."

"Anyone would."

"Anyways, my big mouth kinda ruined his reputation in town for a while. I told everyone he was responsible for killing Jamie, and then the other girl him and Harley dated had that freak accident and passed away, which really fueled my theory. It was immature, but he always treated me like a stupid kid, so it was my way to push back."

"Did you apologize?"

"As best I could. I helped him out when everything went down with the Rosie nightmare. Even pushed Boyd away because his dumbass was trying to arrest Carson. I'll never forget the fear in Carson's face when I drove them away from town to save her."

Horror whipped through my nerves at the mention of Boyd.

"Anyways, I think Carson and I are good now. I apologized in front of the whole town, owned up to my bullshit." His wide shoulders lifted as he cut into his omelet once more. "We're back to tolerating each other."

Distracting both of us, I pivoted to the next question on my mind. "Why were you away from Pine Bluff when your sister died? Did you go to college or something?"

He straightened, sitting back from the table. "Uh, nah, college isn't really my thing. I'm more street smart than book smart. I've been reading more though. I've been getting really into Westerns. I'm sure you're sick of people glamorizing the West, huh?"

He was definitely avoiding my question, but I guessed I'd let him.

"You're not going to believe me, but my mom and dad met at a rodeo," I offered.

"No shit?"

"She was a buckle bunny, fucked her way through the rodeo circuit. Said there wasn't much else to do in Texas back in the day. What's weird is she still romanticizes what happened with my dad. She gets this wistful look in her eyes and goes off about how he was some handsome cowboy from Mexico. She knew just enough Spanish to flirt with him. I guess body language did the rest. I was conceived in some crummy hotel off I-35 just outside of Austin. Glamorous, huh?"

"One time is all it takes."

"Yep."

"So then what?" he asked.

"That was it. She didn't even get his last name or phone number. He was gone when she woke up. She was 23 years old, and all that Baptist guilt made her go forward with the pregnancy." I made a sweeping gesture at myself with my fork. "And here I am, 30 years later! The beautiful mistake."

Dane almost cringed at my statement, not letting my self-deprecation lighten the mood. "You're beautiful, and you're not a mistake."

I lifted a single shoulder. "If you say so."

"I'm sure your dad would've been involved if he knew about you. Did you ever do one of those DNA tests to find him?"

"All the DNA in the world couldn't convince me I was wanted."

His brows furrowed in silence.

"My mom made it very clear she wanted more of my dad, less of me. He was the one that got away, and seeing my face every day reminded her of that."

"So you're half Latina?"

"Yep, for all I know. My mom is white. I think that was also part of the problem. My grandparents are racists pieces of shit. So not only was I a lovechild, but I was also somehow even less desirable because I wasn't this pristine white baby born into wedlock like my grandparents would've liked."

"That's disgusting," Dane said vehemently.

"Yeah, my mom has two sisters, and they both got married and had babies. All my other cousins are white. I was the outlier. And they'll never admit it, but they treated me differently. I got more hand-me-downs and the worst seat at family dinners. My grandpa wouldn't put me on his lap, and my grandma didn't give me any heirlooms when I eloped. Things like that."

"So you've always felt like an outsider?"

"A little bit, in my family at least. I've always had friends. I knew I had to patchwork my own community. I had a softball coach that really showed up for me in middle school." I felt a smile tug at my face. "And things got a lot easier once I met Kaylee. She was also a misfit."

"I remember you telling me about living with her grandma while you guys went to college in Florida. That's so random but wholesome."

I'd told him that clear back in September when we'd first met. He remembered, which was flattering.

"Did I ever mention my mom hates Kaylee? I find it funny. I went no contact with her after my divorce. I haven't regretted it."

"What was the final straw?"

I leaned forward conspiratorially. "I had an abortion."

His eyes shot wide for a second.

"Listen, my ex was trying to trap me with a baby. I had my reasons."

He leaned forward, too, joining me. "I respect your choice. I just wasn't expecting that. What did he do?"

I looked around the diner, ensuring we were mostly alone. The next group of patrons were three booths over, so I felt safe to continue. "He stealthed me."

His eyes danced upward as he searched his memory. "I don't think I've heard of that."

"When I wasn't looking, he slipped the condom off. All stealthily. He didn't even admit it until a month later."

"As in . . ."

"I was late."

His nostrils flared ever so slightly. "Maisie, that's rape."

"I know." All I could do was let out a sad laugh. "He didn't see it that way. He acted like the second we got married, he gained access to my body, like he owned me or something. He would bitch and moan about wearing condoms. I remember he would whine, 'What's the perk of getting hitched if I don't get to fuck you raw?' Like the marriage certificate canceled out my autonomy. Plus, I really needed condoms as a backup plan because I was trying out all different kinds of birth control medication, thinking they were making me sick, when really it was my breast implants."

He leaned in even farther, his tone nothing short of fervent. "Even if you were into the whole sex part, doing that without you knowing is wrong. You know that, right? He took the choice away from you."

"I know. At the time, I beat myself up for not catching it. I showered right after so I really couldn't tell." I fought a panicked sensation, recalling the dreaded moment I'd taken a pregnancy test alone and almost blacked out.

He grabbed my hand. "You trusted someone who you thought loved you. You were in a very vulnerable situation. There's no reason that should've even been on your mind."

I blinked back unexpected tears. "Yeah, I know."

"He sounds like a real dick."

"He was. When I told him what I was doing, he called me a whore and wouldn't even go with me to the doctor. Thank God for Kaylee. She went with me, let me stay at her place. Her mom, who is a nurse, checked in on me and brought me food and flowers. I was just so mad that my own husband wasn't there for me. I couldn't stop thinking about how he directly caused me all that pain. He made the choice, but I suffered the consequences."

"It's not fair. I'm so sorry." He squeezed my hand.

I looked down at my fork covered in syrup, recalling that entire cloud of time. "A couple days later, when Kaylee knew he was going to be at the ranch all day, she pulled up with an ice-cold Diet Coke for me along with a U-Haul and some of the high school football players she'd roped into helping. Within a matter of hours, she moved me out and into her place, no questions asked."

"Moose killer knows how to move without notice. I've seen it in action." We both chuckled, thinking about Kaylee and her loose cannon antics. "So that's when you filed for divorce?"

"Yeah, that was the final straw for me. I told my mom what happened, and she picked his side, called me an abomination.

I hung up on her, never looked back. It's been almost three years. I wouldn't reserve the word cunt for that many women, but I will say with my full chest that *my mom is a fucking cunt.*"

Dane nodded. "I mean, even if she didn't agree with your choice, she had to know that living with a man like that wasn't safe for you, let alone a child."

I squeezed his hand one more time before pulling away to sit back up. "Anyways, now that you know all my trauma, would you like to get the check?"

"Mm-hmm," he said, pulling out his wallet. "And Maisie . . ."

"Yeah?"

"This doesn't change how I feel about you."

"I'm glad."

After he threw a couple of bills on the table, he stood up and knocked on it.

"Why do you do that?" I asked in mild amusement.

He looked at the table in confusion. "Do what?"

"Knock on the table. You did that at the rehearsal dinner as well. Each time you're done with your meal, you knock on the table when you stand up to leave."

His lips twitched so quickly, I barely caught it, but I was so obsessed with him that I noticed everything at this point. "Guess it's subconscious." He placed his hand on my lower back as we walked out. "How do you feel about cheesy roadside attractions?"

# Chapter Twenty-Two

DANE

I hadn't even intended on learning about Maisie's past at breakfast, but my plans for today couldn't be more fitting. I'd known there was a reason behind her guard and tendency to assume the worst about someone, namely me. If my mom and spouse had betrayed me like that, I would probably show that much mistrust, too.

We used the rucksack to hold all our stuff and Maisie wore it on her back, which was comical because it was almost as big as she was. I enjoyed having her on my bike though. She was super handsy, which wasn't a hardship for me at all. At red lights, she'd rub my shoulders or sneak her hands up under my jacket to trace her nails against the bare skin of my back. At one point, she reached around me and started rubbing closer and closer to my groin. If it weren't for a school bus pulling up alongside us, I'd have no clue how that would've ended. Having her cling to me was quickly becoming my new addiction. I wanted more and more of it.

After breakfast, I took her to the Ben & Jerry's Museum for a tour because that was just what you did when you were in Vermont. Plus, girls loved ice cream. I fought getting a hard-on watching her lick and moan while eating her cone. After that, we meandered to a roadside attraction that was a giant King Kong statue holding a vintage VW Beetle. We took dorky selfies in front of it, and she texted them to me, which meant I finally got her fucking number. It had just taken a wedding, crashing a parade, several orgasms, and crossing state lines for fuck's sake.

After that, I drove her to an industrial part of a small town, praying my bike didn't get stolen where I parked it. This next adventure was either going to be hit or miss.

"Just Beat It?" she said, reading the sign mounted on the warehouse. "Is this like a Michael Jackson thing?"

I took the rucksack from her, holding it in one hand and reaching for hers with my other. "No, it's a rage room."

"What the hell is that?"

"Haven't you seen them online? You get all suited up and destroy a bunch of junk. You know, let the rage out."

"Oh, fuck yeah, count me in!" Her eyes went wild with the potential of destruction.

"Come on, my little tornado."

While checking in at the front desk, instrumental music with a deep bass hummed in the warehouse with occasional prompts of someone murmuring, "Who hurt you?" and "Feel the rage, feel it all." Out of context, it would've been psychotic, but I could see how it subconsciously put you in the mania needed to get going.

My phone buzzed with a call. "Sorry, I need to answer this," I said, stepping away from the counter.

"Lennie, what's up?"

"Where the hell are you, boss?"

"At the intersection of *mind your business* and *get fucked*," I shot back.

I heard a crunching, like he was cupping his hand around the landline of the shop. "The fuzz are here sniffing around, man. You gotta warn a brother!"

Unable to take my eyes off Maisie, I watched as she continued small talk with the teenage boy working.

"What do you mean?"

"Boyd was just here, with his fancy big-boy pants, asking me where you were and if I knew how long you'd be out of town."

"What did you tell him?"

"I didn't say shit. I don't talk to cops. I just stood there not saying anything. He kept trying to weasel something out of me, got all up in my face, little twerp. I finally had to stink him out by making my favorite sandwich. He was so sure you had that little gal with you. I get the feeling he was looking for her."

"Maisie?" I asked, causing her to swing her head my way. I held up a hand in apology.

"Yeah, is that who you're with?"

"Lennie, I don't have to tell you shit."

"Why would he be looking for her?"

I cleared my throat. "I'm not sure. Listen, if he shows up again, just explain you're too busy to talk."

"Will do."

"Sorry to leave you with short notice."

I could hear his smile over the phone. "No worries, you deserve some fun. It's summer."

I ended the call and walked back to Maisie.

"Everything okay?" she asked with a bright voice, taking my hand.

"Um, yeah, just Lennie asking about shop stuff," I lied. I didn't want to stress her out. As long as she was by my side, no harm would ever come to her. I'd make sure of that.

The room assigned to us had a high ceiling with rough particle boards as walls and smooth concrete flooring. Various stumps of wood and stacked tires had outdated electronics teetering on them along with a crate full of glass bottles and other breakable goods.

We joked and teased each other, getting into the heavy-duty coveralls, helmets, and work gloves. I knew two types came to a place like this: those who wanted the novelty of it and the people who *actually* needed to obliterate inanimate objects to get their anger out. Maisie was a sleeping storm. I just needed to wait it out for her to get going. She was full of latent, righteous rage that needed to be funneled somewhere. She deserved that much.

I lined up some bottles on a table, offering her a baseball bat with a nod of encouragement. When that didn't work, I hit one myself. The pop was loud as it exploded against the bat and then again on the wall. When I handed her the bat again, she took it, her pink eyebrows pinched.

"You got this, baby girl. Let some steam out. Make these bottles your bitch."

Straightening her back, she wrapped her gloved hands around the bat like a pro. The glass shattered into pieces on her first swing. Shriek after shriek, she hit each bottle, smashing them against the wall.

And just as I'd suspected, what started as playful morphed into impromptu therapy. Each of her swings got harder, more purposeful. Sensing she liked the challenge of target practice, I positioned myself accordingly. "Here! Hit this!" I yelled with a toss of a light bulb in the air.

She swung and missed, which pissed her off even more.

"Try again!" I tossed a brown beer bottle with a ripped label up in the air.

Her mouth went into a fine line with her calculated swing. The bottle cracked against her bat and sprinkled around the room.

"Good hit!"

She wiggled her butt before adjusting her stance. "Thank you! I play softball. Now pull!"

I threw another bottle. Whack.

"Pull!"

After about five rounds, I started getting creative with objects. She liked hitting the mugs and plates, but not the old

VHS tapes. When she was done with target shots, she grabbed a long-handled rubber mallet with a giggle. I never thought someone twerking with a mallet could be hot, but I stood corrected. With a high-pitched screech, she belted into an old printer, plastic bursting all around us. I flinched as bits hit my face shield as her battle cry echoed in the room.

I hung back as Maisie continued to obliterate the printer, lasering in on smashing every bit of it then moving on to an old tube TV, hitting the middle of it like a bullseye before stomping on the pieces in her cowgirl boots. It was the cutest fury imaginable.

"C'mon, join me!"

"You keep going," I said. "I'm gonna search for more stuff."

I wasn't scared of her rage. It was a part of her. A needed part of her society didn't allow her to show. Rage was just as pure as joy or curiosity. It needed to be observed, so instead, I stood witness, trying my best to appear neutral. To look busy, I started digging the hook of a hammer into a tire while watching her.

The guy at the front desk must've been gauging her reaction because the lights morphed into more reddish than white-hued, along with louder beats with the music.

"Who hurt you?" The music rumbled along with the prompt like a tidal wave.

"Fuck!" she screamed, wailing on the remnants of the printer and TV. "Fuck, fuck, fuck!" A strangled noise skittered out her throat as she went full apeshit on the shambles, moving to an old stove, dinging the sides of it, ripping out the coils on the burners, then plucking out the knobs. "You bastard!" She pushed it over with a heave, watching it topple.

She picked up the baseball bat once more, cracking down swing after swing, shattering everything within five feet of her.

"I hate you!" she shouted. Her screams morphed into sobs, but she continued her destruction, eventually falling to her knees and tugging her helmet off.

"Cover your ears," she murmured.

Tugging off my gloves and helmet, I did.

Deep within her body, she let out a more guttural, ferocious scream, the force of it quivering her jaw. She freed a hand from her glove to wipe at the corner of her eyes then straightened her shoulders with an upcast glance at the ceiling. I could've sworn she was praying, so I let her be, staying silent across the room.

With one last sniffle, she got to her feet and took off her other glove. Before she could even ask, I was there, wrapping her in my arms. "I've got you."

She let out a long sigh. "I needed that."

"Glad it helped."

She swayed me in the hug. "Oh my goodness, this is like a high. I feel so much better."

"Sometimes, it's therapeutic to just feel the anger."

She stepped out of the hug. "Are you insinuating I need therapy?"

"Well, everyone does, but—"

"What do you mean?"

I ducked my chin. *Isn't this obvious?* "Therapy is for everyone. I think at a certain point in someone's life, you should unpack all your shit with an unbiased person."

"You go to therapy?" Her tone was outright incredulous.

I shrugged. "I mean, yeah. Since I'm self-employed, I don't have stellar insurance, but Maxine set me up with one of her colleagues. Her name is Joyce. I work on her car in exchange for sessions."

"How often?"

"Once a month? I used to go more when the grief was fresh. I'm in a good spot now. Birthdays and holidays are tough. You never really forget someone like that, you know? There will always be a hole in my chest for the family I've lost, but I like to think I can fill it just a little with new people. You know, new experiences and chances for memories." I gestured to the mess we just made. "Like this, I'll never forget what we just did."

"I'm filling up a part of your heart?"

I cupped her face, running a thumb down her jaw. "Yes," I whispered. "Yes, Maisie, you are definitely filling up a part of my heart."

She lifted to her tip toes, silently requesting a kiss. I covered her lips with mine, loving how she wrapped her arms around my neck and pressed her chest into mine, a little sigh escaping her mouth once we were close. We swayed with the kiss, getting lost in it. Even with destruction all around us paired with the maddening bass line of the music, the world faded into a little pocket of just Maisie and me.

She broke the kiss with a playful peck on each of my cheeks. "Thank you."

"You had fun?"

"Absolutely! Ice cream and violence, who knew that was my ideal date?"

"What else would you like to do with our time together?"

"I have this idea, but I dunno. It's probably too out there." She fiddled with the snaps on her coveralls, suddenly bashful.

"Tell me, what is it?"

Her forehead wrinkled as her warm eyes melted me in my spot. "Baby, do you think you could maybe take me to the ocean?"

We hauled ass to the coast, the four-hour drive zipping by in a blur of possessive, little touches and hilly highways lined with trees. She asked if we were going to New Hampshire. I forgot people outside of New England didn't know that New

Hampshire only had about eighteen miles of beach and we made fun of them for it.

Since it was late May and tourist season was ramping up, I knew better than to take us to one of the tourist traps here in Maine, like Old Orchard Beach, Kennebunkport, Rockland, and Bar Harbor. Instead, I pitched us to a small coastal town called Dry Creek Harbor. It was an old port town that was now mostly retired people and summer homes. It was always a solid bet if you were a local. The beaches were quiet, if not a little sleepy, but you could usually find a lobster fisherman at dusk to buy from straight from the dock.

On PadHopper, I found a little salt-washed cottage right on the beach. It was outdated, with cedar shakes on the side now bleached gray from decades of salt brine. When we entered, we came in through the kitchen door and were immediately met with the churning ocean out the window over the farmhouse sink. The wooden floors were warped from years of humidity and little feet shuffling. A small table with two chairs was pushed up against the wall, and on the other side was a quaint sitting room big enough for one small couch, an old gas stove, and an armchair with books on a bowed shelf above it. Through the kitchen was the single bedroom with the bathroom attached. Everything had coastal charm, with soft blues, fake hydrangeas in milk jugs, and white, thin curtains. The bed had spindled walnut posts with a kitchen chair beside it acting like a nightstand with a glass-based lamp.

"It's perfect," she said in awe.

I sniffed the air that was a little musty in my opinion. "I wouldn't say perfect, but—"

"No, it's perfect!" she proclaimed. "I'm happy you found it."

I nudged her playfully with my elbow before walking farther into the bedroom. "The perks of being with a PadHopper Super Host." She snickered at my lame joke as I opened the window next to the bed, inviting salty air to flood where we'd be sleeping. "Oh, and there was a reason I picked this place. Check the end of the hallway."

I waited in silence, knowing she was about to find the stacked washer and dryer. "Sweet baby Jesus! Lord knows we needed more clothing options."

We spent the next hour getting our shit together. We threw in laundry and went to a local market for a salad kit, some fruit, granola bars, string cheese, and some things for dinner. We couldn't keep surviving off diner food.

Walking through the aisles with Maisie was, well, nice. It was the most normal thing we'd done together. We'd been either part of a wedding party, fleeing from cops, on the brink of frustrated sex, or smashing ovens. Seeing her in a mundane situation gave me a deeper appreciation of her. She carried herself in a friendly, lighthearted manner.

When we went through the checkout, she weaseled past me and paid with her debit card before I could get to the machine. I acted nonchalant but made sure to flash her a stern look. All she did was stick out her tongue before picking up the bag she'd have to hold between us on the drive back.

Once we got back to the cottage, we went for a sunset walk on the beach hand in hand like some Hallmark movie. I even cracked a joke about it, which she appreciated. Our conversation meandered to funny childhood memories, bitching about our businesses, and our favorite conspiracy theories. We both believed Princess Diana was murdered and something was sketchy about Antarctica. She thought the Denver airport had bad vibes and that Avril Lavinge had died years ago and some body double was out there pretending to be her. I wasn't sold on the latter.

She mentioned she saw a pool hall on the outskirts of town, closer to one of the colleges, so I decided we'd go there for an impromptu date. Much to my surprise, she put on the floral sundress I'd gotten her. It had little pink flowers to match her hair. She accentuated her lips with a sparkly gloss. It made them even more enticing, and I wanted to see the color smeared by the end of the night.

The billiard hall was as dim as it was loud. Clashes of balls getting shot across the tables thundered, creating a nonstop echo. Low murmurs of laughter and conversations filled the spaces between each boom. Walking in, I knew I had a target on my back. For starters, we'd rolled up to the joint on my bike. The rumble of it alone had caught people's attention even though I'd been driving safely.

Secondly, Maisie was on my arm. She was the type of woman you saw and wondered what her life story must be. And it wasn't just her pink hair and confident strut. From her jewelry to her clothing, even the way she held her mouth in a smirk made you wonder what she'd seen and what could possibly be hidden underneath her playful demeanor. As a guy, it was intoxicating. Nothing was sexier than a playful woman. I would be lying if I didn't admit I felt like hot shit having her as a date.

As we walked past a pack of men, she squeezed my forearm, all but resting one of her boobs on it. I leaned in and kissed her temple before whispering, "They're all looking at you, tornado. Are you going to stir up the whole place?"

"Depends on how I feel," she said with a playful wink. "And how badly you behave."

I grabbed her ass in response, earning a sexy giggle.

At the bar, I ordered Diet Cokes for both of us. I was sure the last thing she wanted to do was drink. She was vulnerable. Even with me. I couldn't exclude myself as a threat to her. That was her decision to make. All I could do was show up and prove time and time again that all I wanted was safety for her, to be that hideout.

We snagged a high-top table. A couple rounds into darts, they put on "Night Moves" by Bob Seger, one of my favorite songs. I sang along in a low hum.

Hearing it with a dart in hand, Maisie jumped up and down. "Ohmygawd, you love this song, too?"

"Yes, put the weapon down, darlin'. It's time to dance." With an adorable squeak, she flung the dart at the board, barely making it. "Such accuracy!"

She took my hand, waltzing out onto the dance floor in her cowgirl boots. "Are you going to spin me around this place?"

"Damn straight."

"Perfect, then afterwards, will you show me how to play pool?"

"Sure thing," I said, dipping her only to fling her back up and over into my other arm. "Anything you want."

The song morphed into some bro-country song by Luke Bryan. I grabbed her hips, swaying with her to the chorus she knew every word of. She beamed up at me, touching my jaw affectionately before complimenting me on my dancing skills. I liked that she didn't mind me openly manhandling her.

The place had been bustling when we'd first arrived but was dwindling down, as you'd expect on a weeknight. This worked to our advantage because we were able to get our own room with a pool table at the end of the hall filled with sports memorabilia lining the walls.

"Okay, so, you grab a pole, which is known as a cue." I went to the rack, fetching us each one.

"I love grabbing poles," she said with a mischievous wiggle of her eyebrows. To prove her point, she suggestively ran her hand up and down the one I gave her before fully snatching it from me.

"I bet you do. And we both know you like busting balls, so now is your time to shine."

I racked the pool balls, centering them on the table. From there, I explained the game and showed her my techniques and how to not scrape the green felt on the table. Even though we were across from each other, with each shot of the ball, we inched closer, resulting in the most cliché move of me covering her body from behind while we shared a stick for a shot.

Together, we leaned over, holding our breaths while we zeroed in on a ball and hit our blow.

Each shot, she made the cutest satisfied squeal. When the 8-ball hit the pocket, she demanded a kiss.

"Okay, how 'bout a bet?" she asked. "If you win, you get to tie me to that bed tonight."

"With what?"

She tipped her head to the side, her warm eyes pensively searching the ceiling for solutions. "We'll get creative. I'm sure we can find something."

I skimmed her clavicle with the tip of my cue, causing one of her sundress straps to fall off her shoulder. She let out a girlish gasp, hamming it up. "And if you win?" I asked.

"Then I get to tie *you* to the bedpost." She slid the strap back up with a devious look.

*God, she's so fun.*

Ignoring the clear advantage I had, all I could do was raise my eyebrows. "Sure thing."

We reset the balls on the table, and she assumed position in front of me again, this time wiggling her butt against my groin.

"You're not going to want to do that," I warned.

"What? This?" she said, arching against me further.

"Mm-hmm," I whispered against her ear. "Listen, I know there's a joke about blue balls and some hard wood, but I don't have a lot of blood in my brain to make it." I thrust against her slowly, caging her with my arms as we both stretched over the table.

"Dane," she said breathlessly. Grabbing one of my forearms, she ground her ass against me.

"Yeah, baby?"

She bit her bottom lip as my breath fanned against her ear. "Can I tell you a secret?"

"Sure, anything."

"I'm wearing *the* most uncomfortable underwear."

"Can I see?" I abandoned the cue, letting it clank on the green felt. I stood up, freeing her. Before she could even fully turn around, I grabbed her by the hips and hoisted her on the edge of the pool table. She held my shoulders and eyed the doorway behind me, ensuring my body would block anyone walking by. And with a sexy, little smile, she opened her knees.

My hand tickled up her thigh, teasing her. Then I moved boldly up, expecting to run into lace or satin. But what I found was Maisie's warm pussy waiting for me. I brushed my thumb along the edge of one of her lips, causing us both to groan.

"Sorry, I forgot to mention I *was* wearing the most uncomfortable underwear. But I fixed the problem."

"Now we have a new one."

She braced herself with one arm on the pool table, and her other hand reached to stroke me over my pants. "And what's that?"

"You're drenched with no end in sight."

"You could help me with my predicament."

I kissed her until we were both breathless then kept my lips close to hers as I whispered, "Just thinking of how good you taste makes my mouth water."

"It should. I promise, nothing will ever taste as good as I do."

Her confidence boiled my restraint. I knew I shouldn't finger her because my hands were probably disgusting from playing pool. But I still had eyes. Eyes that needed just a peek of what was waiting for me. I guided her back onto the table, letting my hand drop from her neck to her breasts. I palmed one then dragged my hand down to pluck up the hem of her dress.

With a debaucherously dangerous idea, I grabbed the wooden cue and put it behind her knees, hoisting her legs up so I could trail kisses there to taunt her for driving me crazy. Her feminine scent wafted to me, making me almost shudder in need.

I kissed her shins, then her knees. Her sexy laugh filled the space between loud cracks of balls being hit by people in other rooms. My mouth trailed up her inner thighs as I lifted the stick, causing her dress and knees to hitch higher, finally exposing her glistening flesh to the air.

"What the fuck are you doing?" a harsh voice barked behind us.

With a yelp, Maisie rolled to her side with the cue still stuck under her knees. It snagged on the lights above the table, causing them to swing around.

I shielded her, helping her down. "Sorry, man, we . . . uh . . ." I wiped the drool from the corner of my mouth, not able to stitch together much logic.

"You can't fuck on our table!"

On pure adrenaline, I grabbed Maisie's hand and ran, pushing the cue against the guy's chest as we passed him.

"I'm calling the cops! This is some weird, kinky, indecent exposure shit!"

"You're lucky you got a glimpse, buddy!" she shot back.

A quiet murmur rippled around as we raced to the door, grabbing the helmet and our coats off the rack roughly in the process. The night air felt like freedom as we beelined to my bike. I kicked it to start as she strapped on the helmet with a cackle before I ripped away as fast as I could control the torc.

As we made our way to the seaside cottage, the single headlight from my bike was like a spotlight competing with the moon glimmering on the water alongside the road. Maisie held me tight, and I couldn't wipe the grin off my face. I could barely park and sit the helmet down before scooping her back up and hitching her across my body, loving how she locked her legs around my waist.

"That was close," she said, wrapping her arms around my neck.

"Good thing we make a good team."

She distracted me by kissing my ear as I fought the door, throwing the keys on the counter before hoisting her next to the kitchen sink. We took turns kicking off our shoes and throwing off our jackets, making quick work of washing our hands with a lighthearted laugh, both of us barely drying them between frenzied kisses.

With a wild glint in her eyes, she tugged off my shirt. "Dane, baby, you can show off with foreplay later. I just need your cock in me now." With her breathy plea, she unbuckled my belt, unzipping my zipper right before I lifted her from the counter, whisking her away. In a feverish rush of kisses, we clashed around the kitchen, resulting in me pinning her against the wall, jiggling some of the antiques displayed on a shelf, causing seashells to tumble to the floor. Hooking an arm around my neck, she gathered her dress around her waist with her free hand, helping me set my sights. I notched my cock against her slick heat and we both moaned, but with just my tip inside her, she flinched with a hiss of pain.

"Fuck it, I'm a showoff and I want to do this properly," I said, abandoning that plan as I charged to the bed. The moon lit up the fluttering curtains, casting a silvery glow through the open window. I dropped my girl on the mattress, watching her become illuminated as well, her eyes twinkling.

"God, you're so strong. I love it," she said as I tore off the rest of my clothing. "I want you to take it. It's all yours," she said, kneeling on the bed, squirming out of her sundress.

I'd known she'd be wiggling out of that sundress eventually. Seeing it right in front of me snapped some primal instinct. "Get on your hands and knees." I had some questions I wanted answered.

With zero hesitation, she assumed the position, exposing her bare ass. Her curves were subtle but beautiful. I ran my hand down her spine, admiring her toned back. "I love these dimples right here."

She hummed in appreciation as I kissed each one low on her back before I moved lower, and just as I suspected, right where her leg creased to her cute ass cheek, she had a small tattoo that simply stated *lucky you* in cursive.

"Tell me what this says," I said, rubbing my hand up her right hip.

She looked back at me smugly. "It says 'lucky you.'"

"Appropriate." I waited for her to chuckle. Right when she did, I smacked her ass.

"Yes," she hissed, melting to her elbows, ass up. "Aw, fuck yes."

"If you keep acting like this, you're going to have my cum all over your ass." I leaned in, licking the tattoo before nipping her cheek. "All over this tattoo."

"Prove it."

I rolled her back over, loving how she giggled like a little faerie beneath me, short pink hair already mussed, perky nipples begging to be licked, tan skin flawless in the low light.

She smoothed her hands over my chest, pulling me down for a kiss. Our tongues brushed and stroked. The kiss got messier and needier as I ground my dick against her silky skin. I nuzzled her neck, letting my mouth rove to one of her breasts. Flicking my tongue against a nipple, I incited a hiss of pleasure from her as she held the back of my head.

"I love how sensitive your tits are." I pushed both of them together, tracing my tongue from nipple to nipple, increasing the pace as they hardened.

"Jesus Christ," she whispered.

I continued, swirling and flicking until she squirmed, clawing at my shoulders. I squeezed a mound, pulling off it to release her coppery bud with a loud pop, my spit glazing her flesh. She chanced a glance down, making little sounds of pleasure as I repeated it on her other breast.

"Your hands are so rough," she whispered.

"I'm sorry. Am I hurting you?"

"No, it feels—" She interrupted herself by biting her bottom lip while I rolled her nipple. "It feels strangely good."

"Promise you'll let me know if I hurt you?" I knew my hands were rough from work, and if I wasn't careful, I was sure my weight could crush her.

"I promise," she said, widening her legs, urging me on.

I kissed down her torso. Even her belly button was cute. God, what was wrong with me? I never thought a belly button could be adorable, but hers was. It was small, perfectly round, and shallow.

"Show me how bad you want it," I said.

She reached down between my face and her center to spread her pussy for me.

"More."

I watched as she ran her finger through her center, bringing the moisture across her lips and clit before slowly rubbing it. "Please, please put one of those rough fingers inside me. Just the thought of it is driving me fucking crazy," she gritted out.

I had so much built-up desire, my teeth almost ached. No longer able to fight it, I groaned, sliding my middle finger into her palm up, letting her suck me in.

A breath hitched in her throat. "Wait, start with one then move up to two."

"This is only one of my fingers, sweetheart."

"Oh god!" She covered her face with her free hand, tilting her hips even more as I curled my finger. "Oh god!" she repeated for what I suspected was a different reason. And with that, I dropped my head, finishing what I'd started in the pool hall.

# Chapter Twenty-Three

The rasp of Dane's stubble grazed my inner thighs. His finger curled inside me as he lowered his sinful mouth to my center.

*Oh, fuck.*

He let out a groan. "I will never stop eating this pussy. Do you understand?" he said with a heavy-lidded blink. "You're fucking perfect."

"Yes," I breathed as he rubbed deep inside me, making everything liquify.

He returned his mouth to my core and continued, slow and bold, confident in his approach. And for good reason. Dane knew how to eat a pussy. He responded to every touch, every whimper, seamlessly reading my mind and body. The man was dialed into me.

I ran my fingers roughly through his hair. "Your mouth feels so good on me. I love what you're doing."

"Prove it. Play with your tits for me."

Obeying, I brushed my hands over my chest. The pressure of him watching me get off last night and then the tease on the pool table mixed with the quick escape lit my nervous system on fire. I was aching for relief.

Never had I craved a man to watch me come like I did Dane. Now that he had seen me come apart last night, it was oddly freeing. I was emboldened. Usually, I teetered on the fine line between making sure my guy was happy and also ensuring I got off or at least had a good time myself. But with Dane, that wasn't even a worry. I was shameless. Desperate. Vulnerable.

I closed my eyes, smooshing my boobs together before letting them bounce apart, inciting a growl against my pussy as he worked his finger and tongue, pushing me to the edge before letting me crash. I felt myself soak his face as an orgasm surged inside me. His mouth retreated but he kept stroking, curling his finger. "I'm adding a second, take a deep breath," he said. "I can tell you're so hungry for it, aren't you?"

"Mm-hmm."

He slid a second finger inside, and my body expanded to welcome him. I hadn't had a dick or fingers inside me since my divorce. Even the products I'd tested out for my store didn't have the same effect because I had control over them. Having my pleasure in someone else's hands had a certain thrill to it.

"Aren't you glad you waited for this? For me to tease this pussy properly?"

Before I could answer, I felt the distinct pressure of him hitting that extra sensitive spot inside me. My body clenched and pulsed against his hand, wetting it even more with a gushing noise sounding off between us.

Dane muttered something under his breath that I didn't catch because I was suspended in bliss as one orgasm after another crashed over me, his green eyes blazing with lust as they darted around my body and back up to mine. Underneath him, I was a mewling mess, pleasure crashing over and over again until I was moaning, shaking, and soaking his palm.

But his hand never left me. Veins trailed down his arms, bulging slightly each time he moved his fingers inside me. In the moonlight, he looked so powerful and virile, his muscles and tattoos glowing. My legs were draped over his thick thighs, but I got the perfect view of his ragged breath as it constricted his abs, clear down to where they cut in a V-shape above his groin.

Almost everything below my waist went numb with too much sensation as my core thumped like my heart had fallen down my body. Dane had simply out-fucked me already. I got to my elbows, trying to back away from his hand and scoot myself up on the pillows with no luck. His hand chased me, never leaving my core.

"Don't run from it, beautiful. I can go all night."

"I don't doubt it," I said, brushing his hand out of me. "I need you in me though." I pushed him to recline on the bed, his back up against the headboard as I straddled his thighs, seizing that thick cock of his.

I delved my hand to my pussy, earning a groan from Dane as he watched me slather his length with my own nectar, my boobs jiggling with each tug.

I wiggled closer to his groin, mentally gauging if it was bigger than the other guys' I'd been with.

"Are you fucking sizing up my dick?"

"It's not personal. It's a little intimidating, okay?" I failed to hide my giggle. "I feel like I'm about to mount it. I'm scared it won't fit."

He affectionately scattered little touches over my cheek, shoulders, and breasts. "Of course it will. Baby, we were made for this." Grabbing my hips, he mumbled, "Now get over it and get on it." With a sexy laugh, he held me up, piercing my entrance and causing a moan to break in the back of my throat as, inch by inch, I sank down.

"Oh my god!" I mouthed, shifting my hips to get used to him.

With a hungry look, he lifted me by the hips then sat me down on it once more.

"Jesus," I breathed, still adjusting, palms flat on his pecs.

He wrapped his arms around the small of my back, keeping me close as he rocked himself deeper inside me. "Just as I thought, perfect."

I kissed him as I encircled my arms around his neck and continued to grind and rock with him, still a little shocked but positively hooked already.

Sex with Dane was like the first hour at a beach on a summer day: warm, addictive, and bright, with just enough simple goodness to cast away any worry. Accepting the bliss was fleeting—I took in every little sensation. The softness of his lips on mine, the rough, calloused hands now gripping my ass, the low, mannish noises rumbling his chest, and his solid pecs brushing against my aching nipples with each movement.

I had to break our kiss when I came again, my pussy throbbing on his dick. "Oh god!" I clung to him, resting my forehead on his shoulder.

"Fuck," he breathed. "You feel so damn good. The way you're gripping me." He groaned, trying to slow me down. But I was a woman determined. With my legs still trembling on either side of his meaty thighs, I continued to ride him like the cock-hungry little slut I was.

With a frustrated grunt, he rolled me on my back, managing to stay inside me in the process as we tussled in the bed. "I say when we come."

I clasped him tighter with my center.

With my taunt, he unceremoniously pulled from me, leaving me hollow and impatient. Before I could even whine about it, he picked up my leg, kissing the inside of my ankle before pushing it high to where my knee was by my shoulder. And with it, he plunged back into me once more, hitting deep before returning to his shallow thrusts. The different angle caused a stronger sensation. I cried out, fisting the bedding to keep myself in place.

With a smug look, he leaned in close, still holding my ankle. "You're in over your head, kinda like this leg of yours."

*Lord, have mercy.*

In that moment, I knew I had to let him take over. I brought my hands up to sweetly hold his face as I nodded in surrender. "I'm yours."

Sensing my retreat, he draped my leg over his shoulder, a tender look softening his face as I hooked my other leg around his firm ass.

"I'll come with you," I whispered. "I've never done that, but I'll try."

"We'll do it together. Just feel with me." He kept his rhythm, eyes searching mine in the silvery night, the waves matching our rolling torment.

A part of me knew this was absurd. Couples didn't often climax at the same time, let alone on their first time together. But something about the way our bodies moved, the way our breaths mingled gave me hope that maybe we could. I couldn't tell where I started and he ended. It was intoxicatingly intangible.

I continued to undulate beneath him, letting my guard down while all the pleasure seeped into my body. I loved how he'd steal glances down at where we joined, his breathing deepening.

He touched the side of my face, tenderly relaying what he couldn't say. I nodded, coaxing him to follow me into the release. And in one of the most vulnerable moments of my life, I locked eyes with Dane as we both came undone.

He stayed inside me, rolling me on top of him with a deep hum. My pussy squeezed in the aftermath of all the orgasms, surely dripping cum all over him. But I didn't care. All I could pay attention to was the beating of his heart against my ear, his scent all around me, just like his arms.

"God, baby, that was incredible," he whispered with an affectionate graze up the nape of my neck.

Still catching my breath, I turned my head to coyly smile at him.

"Do you trust me now?" he asked.

"Yes. I've never come with someone before."

He kissed the top of my head. "Like I said, we were made to do this together."

"I agree. Together."

I hoped he knew I wasn't just talking about sex, but traveling, life, laughing; hell, even eating with Dane was better than eating alone. He had so quickly woven his way into my life like a wildflower, taking root under the concrete of my lonely existence, blooming a fondness I wasn't ready for.

Time morphed as our breaths slowed, my head rush ceasing as the distinct flush of sex erupted on my skin.

"I can't wait to go again." I sighed.

"Me either."

I nuzzled his chest for a bit, taking in all his yummy pheromones while we came down from the high. Then a distinct tightening filled my core. "Dane?"

"Yeah."

"Are you getting hard again?"

"Yeah."

I mumbled about refractory time while I sat myself up to straddle him. "Wait, don't you need a minute?"

All he did in response was jut up his jaw as he clutched my hips with a thrust.

I fought to keep my balance. "Oh dear god, now I know why you're so popular—"

He stopped me mid-sentence, shushing me with a finger held to my lips. "Do you hear that? The sound of my cum getting pounded back into your perfect pussy?"

"Fuck, you're nasty!"

His pecs twitched as he reached to squeeze my tits. "Good, don't forget what I've done to you."

"Oh god." My eyes all but rolled to the back of my head as I swayed on top of him, feeling my clit sliding against the soaked base of his cock. "I won't."

"You want it from behind, don't you?"

My eyes shot wide at the offer. "Yes!" He flipped me over on all fours, smacking my ass before sliding in. "Again!" I pleaded, needing a bit of pain to fight how overloaded I felt.

He smacked the other cheek, causing me to clench his cock on impact.

"More!"

"Earn it."

Being a brat, I dropped my shoulders to the bed, reaching between my knees to grab his nuts. It was a risky move, but it earned a beastly groan from Dane as I continued to hold him, forcing him to fuck me close.

One of his calloused hands floated down my back before he raked his fingers through my short hair, tugging it slightly.

Yes. Finally. *Fuck!*

The moved caused me to release him to brace myself on the bed. I cried out his name with pleas repeatedly, the sound a little louder with each thrust as he damn near knocked the wind out of me. Something about him putting me in my place freed up my mind, forcing me to exist purely in the moment as buck after buck, he undid me.

Still cock-deep inside me, he lunged past my head, fisting a pillow with a growl and dragging it underneath my hip bones. My pelvis tilted as he settled his weight on me. His stubble scraped my shoulder blade as he leaned in to kiss my neck. Between the scruff and his hot breath on my sensitive ear, I felt my pussy pool with need and all the hairs on the back of my neck and forearms prick up. My eyes fluttered at the sensation, and if it weren't for his hips pinning my ass in place, my body would definitely be wiggling in overstimulation.

He tongued my ear then nipped at the lobe. "Close your legs for me, baby girl."

I brought my legs in closer, my pelvis still tilted with the pillow underneath me on the bed. With the movement, the trunk of his thick cock and pubic hair tickled my sensitive ass cheeks. I could feel my core clench with need for movement as his giant body covered me from tippy toes all the way up to my shoulders. I was engulfed by this man, loving every fucking second of it.

I sucked in a breath as he delved into me deeper. A wet eruption between us made him groan in reverence as he pulled out slightly, only to push back in. From behind, he was hitting way deeper than I expected.

"Ah fuck, you're so huge." I breathed, trying to adjust to the new sensation of being stretched and pushed harder than ever before.

"You're so perfect." He plunged in and out. "This pussy is perfect. And all mine."

I nodded, moving with him. The pressure of the pillow and his weight on either side of me made everything more noticeable, but a couple thrusts in, he knocked my knees even closer together while keeping his legs outside of mine.

"Oh fuck!" I cried. With my legs straight out, it was like every nerve ending was firing off as his gorgeous cock dragged against every surface of my sex. I buried my face in the pillow, muffling my screams.

His arm snaked around the front of me, his large hand cradling my neck and jaw. "No, I want to hear you." He continued to pump into me, holding my throat to keep me off the bed. "I want everyone on this whole damn beach to hear what a lucky bastard I am."

I didn't have enough brain cells to string together a thought, let alone coherent sentences. But the noises he was eliciting from me were nothing short of animalistic. With each thrust, my ass acted like a little speed bump. Low, low on his abdomen hit over and over, rubbing our juices with sinful smacks. His warm muscles and body hair scraping against my back put me into some kinda haze, only plummeting when I felt him dripping sweat on my lower back. All sensations blurred—a thrust, a trickle of sweat, my pussy hungrily taking his cock as he fucked me into the bed. I was enveloped by everything Dane and wanted to drown in him.

"Please let me come, please, please!" I pleaded.

He trapped me further by bending one of his knees, gaining more leverage to fuck me deeper. And with it he leaned to one side of me, still holding my neck as he began to whisper the filthiest things in my ear.

"No one knows we're here together, but you won't be able to deny that you've had my DNA dripping out of you."

"Yes!" I cried.

"Who makes you feel this"—*thrust*—"good?"

"You! Only you have—" My proclamation broke as my orgasm flooded, my body slacking in his embrace. If it wasn't for his grip around my throat, my head would've collapsed.

He slowed his movements. "So fucking good."

"Let me up," I said breathily as I got to my knees with him still inside me. I touched where I stretched over him and twisted to show him how I sucked his cum from our first round off my fingers.

He drew in a fighting breath. "Soon, that will be my cock in your mouth, not your fingers."

"Lucky you," I taunted.

With my words, he pulled out of me, covering my tattoo in his release before we collapsed together on the bed.

# Chapter Twenty-Four

# DANE

Maisie downed the glass of water I'd gotten her after we'd cleaned up. She handed it back to me, wiping her mouth with the back of her hand, a bashful smile making her look suddenly innocent. We had gone two rounds and I still wanted more. I could spend the rest of my life pressed against her, hearing her cry out my name.

All I could think the whole time was this had been worth the wait. It had been worth all the torment and obsession. It hadn't even been the sensations of mind-numbingly good sex, but rather the look in her eyes when we'd fallen apart together. She was feisty and fun, with an undercurrent of pure madness.

Getting under the covers, still naked, she turned toward me, the ocean loyally thundering outside the window just behind her. I wanted to memorize this moment, to keep it with me forever. I traced her cheekbone, down her jaw, over her lips.

"What are you thinking?" she asked, scootching closer.

"That this has been worth it."

"What part?"

I blinked slowly, struggling to stay awake. "Fighting with each other, all those months apart, the trip, now this." I gestured at us in bed together. "Even if it's just for a short time, it's been nice to know all that pain wasn't for nothing. Having a night like this confirms it's all been worth it."

She rested her hand over my heart. "You're worth it," she said earnestly.

I wanted to believe her, but at that moment, I honestly didn't. I thought it was because I knew this was fleeting. So I couldn't help it when a sad half-laugh escaped me.

She patted my chest. "No, I mean it."

"I love how you came to that conclusion after you slept with me," I jested, hoping to diffuse any awkwardness.

She remained in her conviction. "Why do you do that?"

"Do what?"

"You don't let me compliment you. It's kinda confusing. You're the most confident, insecure person I know." She gnawed her bottom lip. "Aside from myself, of course."

I remained silent.

She delicately traced her nails over my bicep, roving over my shoulder, tickling in a comforting way. "No, but for real, why don't you think you're worth it?"

A sting filled my throat as I stared at the ocean just past her. When I felt I could speak with a steady tone, I answered, "I guess so many people have left me, after a while I just came to the conclusion I wasn't worth staying for."

Her face pinched in discomfort. "Dane," she whispered.

"It's true. I don't need your pity. It's just a fact I've had to accept."

"Is that why you only date tourists?"

"What do you mean?"

"I know you dated Azalea in high school, but beyond that, everyone says you just date the women in town on vacation or with seasonal jobs. Do you think you subconsciously pick them because you know they'll leave?"

I pulled some of the covers higher up on my body. "Are you trying to psychoanalyze me?"

"No, I'm just connecting the dots. Think about it."

This version of pillow talk wasn't what I'd had in mind. Forget the fact that we'd just had full-on sex, this moment was real exposure.

"I guess I just kinda stopped believing in love when I watched my dad lose my mom. Then when he died, I watched their love story disappear." I took a breath to analyze my own answer, adding, "As corny as that sounds."

"It's not corny." She looked at me with kind eyes, her fingertips tracing my cheekbone. "So because of that loss, you don't think you're allowed companionship?"

I'd never thought of it like that. I guessed I'd been on autopilot, trying to survive.

"I just don't think it's in the cards for me, so I take what I can get, when I can get it."

My chest tightened. This was getting too deep. Of course, leave it to Maisie to draw something out of me I wasn't ready to face. She was the queen of that.

"But their love story didn't die. You're proof of that," she whispered, tracing my lips. "It can live on."

I snorted, grabbing her hand and holding it to kiss her knuckles. "Yeah, an empty cottage and a lonely son trying to keep an auto shop afloat. I'm sure that's what they had in mind. You're sweet to say that though."

I turned her over, wrapping her up as the little spoon. We both grew quiet, the waves pulling us under into sleep without answers.

The song "Gunpowder & Lead" by Miranda Lambert bleated in the frigid morning air, causing me to jerk against Maisie beside me in the bed.

"What in the hillbilly bullshit is this?" I groaned, turning away from her and covering the side of my head with a pillow.

"Sorry!" She stretched to snatch her phone off the floor. "Hey, beeeetch!" she croaked with forced enthusiasm.

Kaylee's voice filled the call. "Hey, girl! Aw, you look so pretty with your pink hair back. Before I forget, look at this freaking view!"

"How gorgeous! Tell me everything! How's Greece?"

Undetected, I faked being asleep as Kaylee told her all about Harley's claustrophobia on their flight, her jet lag, and their seaside villa.

"Harley keeps talking in Greek. It's so fucking hot. I mean, who knew ordering food could be sexy? But I stand corrected."

"Harley? Oh, you mean your husband!" Maisie said, eliciting a girlish squeal from both of them. Sobering, she added, "I'm so glad you're having fun."

"I am! We're having the time of our lives. It's so nice to get away and be all alone." A pause filled the call. "Are you topless under those sheets? You don't sleep naked. Wait, where the fuck are you?"

Taking my cue, I rolled over, wrapping my arm around Maisie with a shit-eating grin. "Hey, moose killer."

Her jaw dropped along with her phone as she raced around shrieking, eventually pulling the phone back up, this time with Harley next to her.

"We leave you alone for two days!" He held up two fingers with a laugh. "Two fucking days!"

Kaylee threw her head back in a cackle. "I won!"

Harley shook his head, staring at us pensively, still smiling.

"You won?" Maisie asked.

"Yeah, we placed a bet. Harley said one day. I said two."

I couldn't help but ask, "What did you win?"

Harley and Kaylee exchanged mischievous smiles.

"Oh god!" Maisie said, catching the hint that it was something dirty. "Ignore us. You guys are on your freaking honeymoon! Go have fun!"

"Wait," Harley said. "Where are you guys, though?"

"We're in Dry Creek Harbor. We took my bike for a little trip."

He nodded in recognition.

A smile spread on Kaylee's face. "Wait, Maisie, you're riding a Harley in Maine? I thought that was my job?"

Maisie shook her head, rolling her lips to hide a smile.

"It's a Bonneville Triumph," I said, annoyed she'd think I'd drive a Harley Davidson.

Maisie turned to whisper, "It's an inside joke, baby," as Kaylee forced Harley to hold the phone while she started singing about "getting the D from Mr. D" as she gyrated and spanked the air. Maisie stuck out her tongue while shimmying her shoulders in an attempt to join her dancing.

"Wait!" Kaylee said mid-hump before snatching the phone back from Harley. "Will I be seeing you when we get back?" she asked with a wide-eyed look that lasted a millisecond. I was sure she was dying for a full report from Maisie.

An awkward gap slashed the air as Maisie purposefully avoided the sight of us in the corner of the video call. Shame bloomed within me. *What the fuck was I doing?*

"Um, probably not. I need to get back home."

"We're just having some fun before she leaves," I added, twisting the dagger in my own heart I didn't know was there.

Maisie played with her hair in silence.

"Don't let him talk you into playing poker, he cheats!" Harley said, lightening the mood.

"Hey now! It's not my fault I have good luck."

"You count cards!" he shot back.

"Thanks for the warning. You two love birds have fun together! And Kaylee, don't forget to put sunscreen on your tits!" She blew them kisses and let the phone fall to her chest when the call ended.

"Now they know," I offered.

"How do you feel about it?"

"Fine." I shrugged, suiting up with my typical armor of indifference. "You?"

"Fine. Totally fine." She beelined to the bathroom. When she opened the door with her hair tamed and minty breath, she returned to where I was. "I just have to get back to Texas eventually, you know? I've already been gone for a week."

"I get it. I shouldn't be away for long. I don't trust Lennie all alone." I held her waist from where I remained sitting at the edge of the bed, chiding myself for thinking it could be something more. "We'll make use of the time we do have."

I'd booked the seaside cottage for two nights, so tonight was our last one together. My stomach curled in unease as I thought about that. It was too soon, and I was also worried she viewed this as just a fling. Maybe I was swoony or childish, but I thought we were getting somewhere different. Somewhere deeper.

"Did I lose you?" she asked, jolting me from my reverie, her delicate hand rubbing the scruff on my jaw.

I swallowed the lump in my throat. "Not at all." A flash of orange on her wrist caught my attention. "This crystal bracelet is pretty. Did Kaylee give it to you?"

She cocked her head to the side, her posture relaxing. "Yeah, she did."

"I love it." I kissed the stones, keeping my eyes on hers.

A slant of warm sunlight streaked across the room behind her from the hallway while our bed remained tucked away in the shadows. It must've provided her with enough light, though, because her fingertips trailed over the black-and-gray portrait of my father. Her brows pinched as her fingers roamed the shoulder above it, causing her to peek over at my back.

"A crow." Her voice was barely intelligible.

The tattoo was holding up well, the black packed in with enough highlights and indigo to let it breathe. One of the best tattoo artists in Boston had done it for me years ago. He'd even used the piece in a magazine that had featured him. He'd positioned the crow to appear like it was flying across my shoulder blade, the edges of a wing unfurling on my trap muscle.

She continued to stroke it in awe. I'd had that happen before. It was hyperrealistic. If you stared at it long enough, you could swear the feathers were moving.

"I've always liked crows," I offered. "I think they're really misunderstood."

"I never noticed this one before," she said, finally raising her gaze back up to mine.

"Don't feel too bad. I have so many, I forget what's on me. It would probably take hours to really look at each one."

Her eyes simmered with an intensity I didn't quite understand, but I didn't have the time to figure it out because the next thing I knew, she pressed her smooth body to me, her tits damn near on either side of my chin. As my hands floated to cup her butt, all my worries vanished. Something about having her naked in my arms made me feel like everything was going to be okay. She settled onto my lap as we swayed together in a kiss, our touches getting bolder, my morning wood morphing into regular wood.

"Remember our bet last night?" she asked, her voice now husky.

I ran my hands up her silky curves. "Yeah, neither of us won, so where does that leave us?"

She hopped off me, her cute ass jiggling with each step as she hobbled into the kitchen.

A rush of pride filled me. "I told you I'd have you walking different!" I yelled.

"Hush!" she said. Coming back to the bedroom, she presented a black 8-ball with a smirk. "This was in my jacket."

"Maisie! Did you seriously steal that?"

"Checkmate!" she said, handing it to me.

An amused laugh escaped me. "That's not what you say when you win at pool. That's chess."

She shrugged, causing her breasts to bounce. "Don't care! I'm ready to claim my winnings. Are you down?"

She didn't have to ask me twice. I guessed my face gave it away because she made her way to the rucksack at the foot of the bed. Digging around inside it, she held up the thong I'd gotten her, pressing her lips together in consideration as she tossed it on the bed. She repeated the same action with her bra before throwing the satin black bag with her toy on the bed next to me.

"Lie back," she said, gesturing to me. To my surprise, when I did, she didn't put on the thong and bra, but instead straddled me, using the strappy fabric to loop around the bedpost then around my wrists, making impromptu restraints that weren't too tight. All I could do was smile watching her tie them up, loving how her boobs skimmed my face when she lunged to each side.

"We should gamble on things more often," I said, trying my best to get a nipple closer to my mouth but failing.

She moved to kiss my neck, licking my Adam's apple. "I couldn't agree more."

Without any hands, I quickly realized I had to depend on other parts of my body. Bending my leg, I pressed my erection against her. Just feeling her heat caused me to picture the most intimate sight of her in my mind. Hers was the prettiest pussy I'd ever seen in my life. And I'd seen my fair share. Not to be dramatic, but it had damn near taken my breath away. The color, the shape, the taste, the way it parted when she dragged her fingers through her center, god, all of it was just too perfect. I wanted to spend a lifetime nose deep, cock deep inside it, worshipping her.

"I miss the way you feel already," I murmured.

She hovered her mouth over mine. "The way I feel?"

"Yeah. So hot and perfect."

"You like the feel of me gripping you? Riding you?" she asked, pulling up from me to reach for the little black bag. "How 'bout a new sensation?"

"Untie my hands, I'd love to use it on you."

She shook her head, making a clicking noise with her tongue. "Now Dane, are you insinuating only women can enjoy sex toys?"

I rolled my head back on the pillow, knowing that was a jab from when I'd teased her in front of Viviane.

Turning on the toy, she held it to my wrist, letting it thump against my veins right below the restraint. From there, she dragged it over my arm, hitting the sensitive ditch of my elbow before trailing little kisses along the way to my neck, where she placed the toy on one side while kissing the other just under my ear. It felt nice, I guessed. The air pulsing tickled and her lips anywhere on my body would be welcomed, but it was the anticipation of where she'd be going next that piqued my interest.

"Want another friendly wager?" she whispered. Not sure of what else I could lose, I nodded, barely able to keep my eyes open. "I bet this could get my nipple harder than your mouth." She licked my bottom lip with her tease.

"Let's bet on it." I sealed the deal with a kiss.

With a pleased hum, she sat up, cupping her own breast while holding the Satisfyer to it. Seconds later, she released the erect bud, her coppery nipple stiff.

"Bring those titties to me," I grumbled, making her laugh and all but motorboat me. I nuzzled the unaffected one then swirled the tip of my tongue around her areola, inciting a hiss as I sucked it into my mouth. She braced herself on the headboard, encouraging me. I sucked and nibbled, flicking the tip as I eased myself off it to look at it.

"You won," she said with an airy laugh, kissing down my chest to try out the toy on my nipples. We shared a little smile when there wasn't much of an effect on me. Continuing her exploration, she licked my abs.

"What are you going to do with that mouth?" I asked.

Her eyelashes fluttered as she fought to remain unaffected by my dirty words. "I'm going to let you feel how soft other parts of me are."

She gently palmed my cock, settling between my legs. Something about her pale nails holding my dick as she feathered gentle kisses over the crown pinned me in desperation.

"Neck and nipples were lackluster, but what about here?" she said, placing the hollowed-out, circular head of the toy at the base of my dick, on the underside, near my balls. With her question, she licked up the length of me.

I choked back a noise. "Um, good, yeah, that's nice."

"Mmm, think you'll like this spot better," she murmured, swirling her little pink tongue over the tip before moving the toy to pulse right where the underside of my shaft met my crown.

*And now I get the big deal.*

Before I could even tell her how amazing it felt, she was tonguing my nuts, gently skimming her lips over them. Mixed with the pulse of the toy and the wetness of her mouth, I could barely stay in reality. I was floating out of my body, it felt so damn good. To make my torment even better, she pinned my cock between her lips and the toy, rubbing them up and down my shaft in simultaneous torture. It was almost too much.

"Maisie, baby," I breathed, wishing I could touch her, feeling completely out of control.

In the zone, she dropped the toy to stroke along with her mouth, her tongue dipping out to swirl around me after each of my moans. It was sloppy and brazen. Her warm eyes trapping me in place made it that much hotter. I'd gotten head plenty of times, and what made it good was when you could tell the woman was enjoying it as much as you. Maisie was. I could tell by her commitment and the way her free hand mindlessly grabbed one of my pecs, trailing down my abs before squeezing the side of my hip.

"You're cute with a mouth full of my cock."

She picked the toy back up to press it on my taint while she sucked. I shot her a wide-eyed look as it vibrated on the sensitive span of skin between my nuts and ass. This was a first, even for me, and it was . . . well . . . fucking incredible.

She let out a pleased chuckle and pressed the toy harder against me as she plunged back on my length. "Oh fuck!"

She clicked the gadget, making it thrum quicker and me see God in the process.

Noises heaved out of me I had never even heard as she bobbed and sucked, taking the rest of my sanity with her. I spilled into her, watching her continue to keep her lips locked around my shaft.

Letting out a satisfied hum, she clicked off the toy and released me from the restraints. All I could do was brush her shoulder lovingly, my mind gone.

"Checkmate," I breathed, making her giggle before she pranced off to the bathroom.

We got ready for the day and made breakfast. I caught her glowering at her phone while I washed a cutting board we used for fruit.

"Something wrong?" I asked.

"It's nothing." Her eyes stayed glued on the screen and her shoulders scrunched closer to her neck.

I dried my hands, turning to stand in front of her. "Tell me." I swept little touches over her, hoping she could feel my concern.

She locked her phone with a sigh, finally bringing her eyes up to meet mine. "It's just, I reported Boyd Friday and it's already Tuesday. No one has gotten back to me."

"That's a good point. It wasn't some casual allegation."

"Right. I mean"—her teeth worried her bottom lip—"maybe I need to be patient. I'm sure it goes through a chain of command; they investigate it before they do anything. I just figured someone would've called me by now. It's making me question if I overreacted."

I clasped her shoulders, each one easily filling up my palms. She really was a tiny woman. "You did the right thing. He needs to get his feet held to the fire."

"Yeah," she breathed.

"And as long as you're with me, nothing will happen. You're safe. I got you."

Her chin lifted with a defiant little scoff. "I've got myself."

We'd done this before, but I'd keep reminding her. All I had to do was cock an eyebrow and she grumbled, "And you've got me, too." A bashful smile melted her face as she curled into me for a hug.

Breathing her in, I knew I wanted to protect her until the day I died. Even though she was a flight risk, she had bared herself to me, told me everything. I appreciated how candid she had been about her mean mom and her abusive ex, her abortion and getting roofied in college, hell, even her business plans.

A wriggle of dread edged on the periphery of my conscious. *But you haven't told her everything, now, have you?*

I pushed it away, finding something lighter and fun.

"I saw a flyer for whale watching. You down?" I asked, hoping she picked up on the inside joke about my lie to the front desk lady at the hotel in Vermont.

Pulling up from my chest, she grinned impishly. "Sounds great, much better than SeaWorld."

An hour later, we stood in line together. "You'll love it, I promise. You can't even taste the potato," I said to Maisie.

"Potato donuts? So freaking random."

"Yeah, bet you didn't know we have potatoes here in Maine."

"No, I thought that was an Idaho thing."

"We have them too. Instead of flour, you can use mashed-up potatoes to make donuts. They come out fluffier. Just trust me." I spotted some souvenirs on the wall behind her. "Hey, did you want a patch for your jacket?"

She checked over her shoulder to figure out what I was referring to. "Oh, sure, yeah." Her options were the shape of Maine, a cartoon donut, a lobster, and a pine tree. She went with a pine tree. "To remind me of Pine Bluff," she said awkwardly.

I pointed to her patched shoulder. "So you've been to all these places?"

We shuffled ahead in line. "Um, no. This was actually my dad's jacket. It's the only thing he left behind with my mom. She found it the morning after, said it smelled like him, so she wore it for a while. I found it abandoned in the back of a closet when I was a teenager, kept it ever since."

I eyed the jacket with new reverence—the pale shearling lining, the W for Wrangler stitched on each breast pocket, and the stylish way it was a bit oversized on her.

"I made up this story." She shook her head with a wistful expression. "Maybe it's cheesy, but I like to think he collected all these patches while touring with the rodeo. It feels like having a part of his life with me."

"It makes sense. You're probably right." We inspected the patches together. "They're from all over the Southwest."

"This one is my favorite." She twisted and pointed to one on her right flank.

It was a saloon girl holding a rifle with a lasso at her feet. "Cody, Wyoming," I read out loud.

"Yep, I think she's a cutie." She patted the patch. "Anyways, maybe it's time I add my own story." She smiled at me, but it didn't reach her eyes.

I couldn't help but notice the all too familiar heavy feeling, the sensation of sinking that came when someone was about to leave me.

# Chapter Twenty-Five

Dane wasn't pulling away, but he was carefully neutral, picking the right conversations and questions. The day had clouded over once again, so not even sunshine was my company. He stood behind me while whale watching, bracing himself on the rail of the boat. I held on to his forearms, letting his strong frame steady me as I watched the midnight blue waves rise and fall.

Along with feeling exposed that he knew I was running from Boyd, something about our call with Kaylee and Harley this morning had irked me. I could twist Kaylee's tits for asking me if I was staying in Pine Bluff. She had really put me on the spot with that one. Plus, I didn't want Dane to think that was a possibility. I was relieved she knew about us, but her and Harley's playful gamble brought me back to reality—I was just a tourist to Dane. Something so predictable people bet on it.

I wondered if I was the first person he'd done this with. Did he take all the women to this cute, little coastal town? Did the lie of whale watching come so easily to him because he had done this before? Was I on a pre-planned date and didn't know it?

I racked my mind, going over all the things we had done. They'd flowed so seamlessly, one into another. Impromptu makeover, ice cream, rage room, dancing, and billiards. My front teeth dug into the inside of my lower lip. What if this was just one of the plots Dane followed to help a tourist loosen up? How had he planned everything so easily? My skin itched with the realization that I might be a gullible dumbass.

"Dane?" I whispered over the waves. The boat was crowded with lots of people, including some loud children, but we had found our own little pocket together toward the back.

"Yeah, baby girl?" His breath tickled my ear while he leaned in.

"Have you done this before?"

"Whale watching? Nah, not since I was a kid. Although, there's a puffin tour I've wanted to go on, but it sells out every year within seconds." He complained under his breath.

"Puffins?"

"Can't a guy like penguins?"

"Sure." I turned my head to look at him.

His eyes were kind but guarded. "Why do you ask?"

"I just wondered." I gave him a quick peck and turned my attention back to the sea, my own emotions churning like the waves.

He leaned down again, popping my reverie. "Get out of your head and be here with me."

I let out a humorless laugh. "How did you know I was all up in my head?"

"I know you." He kissed my temple and started humming a song I didn't recognize, but the vibration of it against my back calmed me down.

After we disembarked, we walked along a beach path with the last shreds of sunset. Dane spotted a fisherman pulling in and met him at the dock to buy some lobster straight from the cage. I was squeamish about how he was going to steam or stab it to death in the cottage to cook it, but I figured I better trust my Mainer man to know what he was doing. While he murdered the lobster, I excused myself to the front porch.

I checked some work reports and a text from my neighbor confirming she'd watered my houseplants. I had several feral texts from Kaylee, which made me smile.

**Kaylee: OMG YOU FUCKED DANE!**

**Kaylee: You'll have to tell me everything. You were glowing! And you guys are so cute together.**

**Kaylee: I just asked Harley. He agrees.**

**Kaylee: Okay, I guess you're too busy getting the D from Mr. D! This time difference is a real bitch. I hate being so far ahead of you in Greece. Anyways, when you pull yourself away from fucking him, please call me. We have to talk about it. I love and miss you!**

I hearted the messages, hoping I didn't wake her up.

**Me: I will tell you everything. Probably tomorrow while I'm driving and need the distraction. I love and miss you too! Make sure to put sunscreen on your titties.**

I didn't want to worry her on her honeymoon about my Dane drama or how Boyd stalking me had forced me to end up on this impromptu trip to begin with. Kaylee was a very loving friend, and I knew she'd prioritize me over her own honeymoon, so I had to deliver the news in a smart fashion. Thinking of her reminded me of Texas. Considering the rest of my journey back, I Googled Tilly's to call them about my cards. A guy named Bronn answered and promised he'd safeguard them until I returned tomorrow. Once I ended the call, the Google search stared me dead in the face. I mindlessly started typing out Dane's name, but stopped myself before I could press search. The squeeze low in my gut eased. I was being skeptical as fuck. Dane had been so kind and understanding to me, several times over. Lurking on him now felt gross.

It was a long-standing habit of mine to be mistrusting. I knew I was skeptical because my mom had made me that way. How could I trust anyone else if I couldn't trust my own mother? The sole nurturer assigned to me at birth. I often wondered how she'd held me as a baby. Had she looked down upon me with disgust? Had she snarled her lip when I'd begun to cry? Had we ever laughed? Played?

A burning rimmed my eyes as my breath shallowed.

The most nefarious thing about my mom was her passive criticizing. I'd never been pretty enough for her. She'd run her hands over my skin and point out freckles, scars, or imperfections instead of simply caressing me with loving kindness. When I'd laid my head in her lap as a child, she would inspect my ears, making sure I knew my earlobes weren't fit for hoops. Who knew even your ears could be wrong?

She'd interrupt my laughter to let me know my front teeth were a little bucked and I should've worn my retainer more often. If that wasn't enough to make me self-conscious, I'd been warned to not crack my knuckles because my fingers were already thin and it would be just a matter of time until arthritis knotted them with age. Oh, and let's not even start with the hair. It was too boyish and loud.

I could still hear her hatred echo in my mind.

*Maisie, why do you need so much attention to begin with?*

Being in front of my mother was like walking a wire. I'd lived on the edge of dread, knowing at any moment she'd say something that would shatter my self-esteem. I'd spent most of my life wishing I could figure out how to be enough for her, never questioning if maybe she wasn't enough for me. Kind enough, thoughtful enough, reliable enough.

When she'd looked at me, I hadn't been her child she loved with infinite selflessness. I'd been a mess to scan, to detect any flaw. I couldn't just be in front of her. I'd had to apologize, contrive, and hide. My sole existence had been of her making, yet I was a continual affliction she lamented. How dare I be so needy? So wild? If there was one thing I'd learned over the years, it was that I couldn't apologize my way into her heart. I couldn't win over someone who'd fundamentally never wanted me.

It wasn't until I'd gotten to college and surrounded myself with other women from all walks of life that I'd discovered how much I loved the feminine spirit. Drunk girls at parties had told me how beautiful I was. My boyfriends' moms would give me genuine compliments and invite me to lunch. Female professors would answer my questions without sarcasm.

My time away from my mother had weaved me into the woman I was. And most days, I genuinely liked myself, but ever since my ass had hit the Maine state line, I'd been second-guessing and falling back on old patterns of self-doubt, indecision, and feeling fatally flawed. Perhaps it was because all of this made me feel so out of control. It was bigger than me. My feelings for Dane, everything with Boyd, the chance to sell Pretty Kitty, Kaylee moving on into married life, it was all so much.

Clasping my hand over the bracelet Kaylee had given me, I sucked in a deep breath, letting the cool coastal air calm me. I needed to find my center, to fight for my own story. I couldn't let any doubt my mom had sown in my mind peek through.

My mom had made me feel lacking and unlovable, and now that Dane loved me, all my insecurities had bubbled up to the surface.

My head jerked at the thought as I doubled back on my own mental conclusion.

*Dane loved me?*

He'd certainly never said it, but it was obvious. I leaned forward to see him inside the kitchen, his gaze downcast as he scrubbed away at the sink. I realized at that moment that I loved him too. I wasn't really sure when it had happened. It wasn't a lightning bolt, but just a slow sizzle that notched higher with every hour spent together.

I wrapped my arms around myself as I mulled over the new realization.

I loved Dane. A lot. So much it kind of scared me.

But what was I going to do about it?

I snuck past him to put the dress he'd gotten me back on. I knew it meant a lot to him to see me wear it. I also fixed my hair that had been destroyed by the wind. Walking into the small kitchen, I caught Dane plating the lobster with potatoes and asparagus. I busied myself by searching for a lighter in the drawers, eventually finding one to light the taper candle on the table.

"Thanks for making dinner," I offered.

"My pleasure."

I stole a kiss before he pulled out my chair. He was back in the shirt he'd worn when we'd driven off that first day. It was plain white, but I loved how it stretched across his tattooed biceps, showing off the faint lines of his pecs and back muscles.

Dinner was delicious, and we chatted all about his passion for rebuilding and preserving vintage cars and trucks. He hated it when people painted them historically incorrect colors or, worse, when they named them something typical, like Betty.

"So the whole mechanic gig, you truly love it?" I asked.

"I do. My dad taught me everything I know. And I go to trainings to stay updated on all this new shit they're doing to cars." A smirk tugged at the corner of his mouth. "I know it sounds cheesy, but I like knowing I'm getting people back on the road, you know, enjoying their vacations and stuff. My dad took me fishing all the time growing up. I like to think I'm affording other little kids memories like that." His lips parted to flash his white smile. "But don't be fooled. I'm not noble. I charge out the ass for my hourly labor."

I snickered. "What's your biggest pet peeve?"

"When people bring in shitty parts they purchased on their own, expecting me to finish the job and somehow warrantee it."

"See, this is why you need to open Fill'er up. Then you can distract them with a burger or something," I joked.

"Something. I always have to be the bad cop. Lennie is too nice. He has all that peace and love hippie bullshit. It usually ends up costing me." He squeezed lemon over his lobster pensively. "Fill'er up isn't my only business idea."

I forked a stalk of asparagus, delicately chewing on it. "Spill."

"Night Owls. It would have to be in a bigger city, somewhere urban like near a hospital, but it would basically be a community for people who work swing or graveyard shifts, so the quiet hours would be flipped."

"Niche but brilliant!"

"Speaking of niche, here's one for ya, Down and Dirty. So basically, it's a cleaning service that does all the random things you never think to clean. I'm not talking baseboards and gutters, more like all the heat vents in your house."

This side of him was so cute. I must've been smiling at him like a fool because he wiped his mouth with his napkin bashfully. "What?"

"Nothing."

"When was the last time you cleaned the vent in your dryer? Not the lint one, but the one that goes up the wall and out of your house."

"Never, come to think of it."

He pointed at me with his fork. "See! That shit is a fire hazard. Oh! And I have an idea for a revenge business called Hate Mail. I'm pretty sure I'd need a lawyer to clear it, but wouldn't it be so funny to have a business where people pay you to send their enemies weird stuff like dead roses or dog shit?"

"We could even pair up with a private investigator to catch someone cheating and then attach pictures of the investigation to the bag of dog shit."

His eyes gleamed as he pointed at me with his fork. "That's even better!"

I bent my hands to make the shape of a box. "On our business card, we could write 'We're in the business of revenge.'"

"Yes!"

I silently swooned over the fact that I was saying "we" in regard to the future business plans, not "you." And he didn't correct me.

To hide my blush, I covered my mouth in my hand, scanning out the window to watch the waves. "That's such a pretty lighthouse," I said, nodding toward the island off the coast.

"Want to see it?"

I pulled my attention back to him. In the candlelight, he was indisputably gorgeous. His scruff had filled in day by day, resulting in a short beard. His smoky green eyes set on mine, making me feel naked.

"Yeah," I muttered apprehensively. How would we see it? We didn't have a boat.

He stood up from the table, knocking on it. "Do you have any of those bobby pin things from when your hair was longer?"

"Urm." I got up to search my purse in confusion as he cleaned up our dishes. I presented him with a single black bobby pin. His eyes darted around the kitchen, landing on the stack of papers the host had left us with information about the cottage, what to do in town, along with some take-out menus. They were held together with a paperclip Dane pulled away with a smirk.

"What the hell is your plan?" I asked as he unbent the paperclip then held the bobby pin to the flame of the candle, melting off the rubber tips.

"My girl wants to see the lighthouse." He blew out the candle dramatically. "I'm gonna show her the damn lighthouse."

He took my hand, ripping me out the door, leading me down to the dock. He looked around before boldly stepping into one of the ocean skimmers, holding up his hand for me to take.

"What the fuck are you doing? This isn't our boat!"

"Want to know who the most trusting people in the world are?"

I scoffed in bewilderment. "Who?"

"Rich, old people. Maine is full of 'em. Now get your cute ass in here." He grasped me by the ribs, all but hauling me inside.

I let out a giggle, steadying myself. "You're so bad!" I kinda loved it.

He unwrapped the ropes holding the boat to the dock then turned on the flashlight on his phone and gestured for me to aim it at the trolling motor in the back.

"How are you going to turn this thing on?"

He snuffed out air, clearly offended at my question. Not even answering me, he swung the plastic cover up to study the motor inside it, fiddling with it for a second before a low rumble sounded as it churned in the water.

I squealed. "Oh my gosh, you did it!"

Taking his phone back, he pocketed it. "It's almost like I work on motors for a living." With his proclamation, he slapped my ass.

I sat down next to him, feeling giddy and free as he guided us out of the harbor, skimming the waves as we neared the island with the lighthouse. Along with a milky white moon, the stars dappled the sapphire sky. It was as if I were at the edge of the world, everything around me new and blue.

I caught Dane watching me, his expression soft and hungry.

"What?" I asked, feeling shy.

"I love how you look at the world around you. You really try to see it, and it's so fun to watch you experience it all with a sense of wonder."

"Oh yeah?" I crossed my legs, holding my dress down in the breeze.

He nodded. "Your curiosity is infectious." Still manning the motor with one hand, he leaned over for a quick kiss. "And so are your kisses."

When we made it to the island, he roped the boat to the dock and helped me out. From what I could tell, no one was there. Standing proudly on top of a gentle slope, the crisp white lighthouse contrasted the indigo sky. It was at least three stories tall and wider than I'd imagined. Black iron and windows topped the structure, with metal siding coming to a point at the top. Behind the tower, a modest colonial home with black shutters and a red door was tucked away, surrounded by a short picket fence meant to detour guests but not block the view. According to the plaque, it served as a nautical museum now and was no longer inhabited. You even had to schedule a tour.

"So it just sits empty?" I asked in confusion.

"Yeah, now that everything is electronic, you don't really need a lightkeeper." He shrugged.

I staggered back from the house, taking in the details of the white, bumpy tower of the lighthouse, wondering how many centuries of sea spray and secrets coated its exterior. Something about its singular beacon in the night made it feel lonelier than I expected.

Dane held the side of my face tenderly, coaxing me to look at him. "Hey, don't be sad. It's a good thing. It was probably really miserable to live out here."

"Right. Plus, how cool is it that someone sacrificed their sanity to keep others safe? Pretty sweet if you ask me."

"Let's make up a story," he said, a dreaminess to his tone.

"A story?"

"Yeah, like what you did about your dad's jacket. We should make up a story of whoever lived here to make it less sad. I mean, usually it was family who passed the job down anyways."

I eyed the house. "Maybe it was a couple."

"See! Okay, maybe the guy was some retired pirate."

I snapped my fingers, catching the idea. "The girl was a working girl who fell in love with him."

"A pirate hooker?" he asked ruefully.

I snorted at the joke, wrapping my arms around his waist. "Exactly, a pirate hooker. Together, they lived here and knit nautical, striped sweaters."

"And wrote poetry." He turned to look up at the light. "About moths."

"There we go!"

"Want to see the light closer up?"

"How?"

"Follow me," he said, guiding me to the door at the bottom of the tower. He picked up the dangling padlock. "Can you believe it? It's a historic landmark and this is the only thing protecting it. A fucking padlock."

"Are you for real?"

"Yeah, that's how it is at most lighthouses." He turned on the flashlight on his phone again. I held it in silent agreement, aiming it at the lock as he picked it with the bobby pin and paperclip.

"Should I be concerned you're way too comfortable picking locks and stealing boats?" I asked as he pulled the mechanism open, slinging the door wide.

"Nah, I'm just ready for whatever adventure life presents." He flashed me a boyish grin and led me up the spiral staircase. At the top, I tried to catch my breath, unsure if it was because of running up the stairs or how Dane was making me feel.

I looked around at the observation space, grateful there was a couple feet between the light and windows so it didn't feel too cramped. The light in the middle swiveled in the night, its beam trudging through the waves and onto the land in a steady, hypnotic pattern. Lights littered the shore, the mainland feeling sleepy and far away.

"I'm sure if I were alone, this would be creepy."

He wrapped his arms around me from behind. "But you're with me."

"Yep, so everything feels okay. More than okay, really."

"I got you," he whispered, kissing the sensitive skin behind my ear.

I held his head, encouraging him to keep his mouth on my skin. His lips trailed over my shoulder, his fingers sweeping down the strap of my dress.

"Dane," I whispered, fading into lust, my nipples prickling. He saw them harden as well, his other hand reaching to cup one of my breasts while his thumb lazily traced my nipple, getting it even harder.

"I love being around you, Maze."

"I love being around you, too," I confessed.

His voice came out lower. "And I love being inside you."

"Yes," I exhaled. "I love you inside me as well."

I balled up my dress in my other hand, needing to expend some energy to not squirm as his scruff tickled the sensitive skin on my neck and shoulder. His hand covered mine at the bottom of my dress, both of us twisting the fabric as he licked and blew on my ear.

"I've been waiting all day for you to fill me up."

He turned me around, pushing me against the glass window. "Oh, I'll fill you up," he growled.

# Chapter Twenty-Six

# DANE

The light strobed against Maisie's tan skin, illuminating in tantalizing intervals. I pulled down the other strap of her sundress, letting the fabric barely cover her nipples. She gnawed on her bottom lip, watching me kiss her décolletage. She hastily undid my pants, pushing her hands up under my shirt to greedily touch my skin.

Giving in to what we both wanted, I slowly slid the dress down, exposing her tits to the cool summer night air.

"So gorgeous," I said, bending to tease them.

She nervously glanced out the windows surrounding us in the tower.

"What?" I murmured against the swell of her breast. "Are you nervous someone's going to see you here with me? All lit up like a sex-crazed goddess?"

"A little," she whispered, tracing the edge of my ear.

"Wait until they see what we do next." With my proclamation, I lifted her up, resting her on the rail below the window as her toned legs wrapped around me. I thrust against her as her giggle echoed around the tower. It was the sexiest thing I'd ever heard.

With one hand, she moved her red thong to the side, helping me rub my shaft against her center.

"Yes!" she hissed. "Aw, yes, just like that! Dear god, your cock looks so good sliding against me. Fuck me right here!"

We shifted together, helping my length to dip into her pussy. I braced my hand on the window next to her face, trying not to blow my load already. She was so warm and tight, and god it felt so good. Willing my legs to remain steady, I focused on rocking into her, letting her slide down my cock with each sway.

She rolled her head back against the glass, eyes closed. "Yes!" she whimpered. "Yes, just like that!"

I bucked harder. "You feel incredible."

"I—" She stopped herself from saying whatever it was.

I held her chin, forcing her to look at me, the light flashing against her cinnamon-colored eyes. "Tell me."

"I don't want to leave you," she said, voice thick.

"Don't." I covered her mouth with mine. Moving together quickly, each of us clearly wanted to transmute the intense feelings into something physical like an orgasm.

I cracked my eyes open to move her to my other arm, and in the process, something caught my eye. A subtle form in the beam tracing the grass surrounding the lighthouse on the island. It was us, our kinky outline cast all around.

"Check out our shadow," I said.

She turned, jaw dropping at the sight. Testing my theory, she raised a hand on the glass window, changing the outline on the ground. "It's weirdly beautiful," she said in awe.

"It's proof you're all around. That what we're doing here is beyond us."

Looking back at me, she kissed my chin then all over my face before bringing me in close to her body. The change of the angle made me come. She cried out, her pussy pulsing against me moments later, both of us shattering into the night.

The boat ride home was filled with orgasm-high smiles and grabby hands. It felt like my head and heart were bobbing along the waves, all common sense and logic escaping me.

Once inside the cottage, I lit the candle again and brought it in the room with us along with a warm rag to clean her up from what we'd done in the lighthouse. She watched me wipe her down, mewling in pleasure as I skimmed her aching clit with the rag, eventually dipping to replace it with my lips. She let out a shocked little laugh, tugging my hair as I slid my face side to side, opening her up to me as she fell back on the bed. Looping a leg over each shoulder, I went in for more.

One of my favorite things about being intimate with Maisie was once she opened her legs, she opened her mouth as well. She was vocal and didn't leave me in awkward silence. I loved the way she was always smattering on kisses and little moans of encouragement. Some women put on an act or were way too focused on looking pretty. I liked that Maisie advocated for her own pleasure and lost herself when she got it.

I hummed, taking in all her sweetness on my tongue.

"Mmm, you're like a human vibrator." She laughed at her own statement. "Get a finger inside me, please. You do it so well," she said, mussing with her own hair, freeing her own breast from her dress to roll her nipple.

"Do I?" I teased.

"Yes," she said breathily, "you do it so, *so* well."

I liked this side of her. When her guard was all down and she was just blunt, egoless.

I slid my middle finger inside her and was met with a happy gasp as I circled her clit with the pad of my thumb. I was used to working with my hands, but arguably this was way more fun than fixing a car.

She shifted her hips, silently steering me. When I felt her walls clamp down, I knew to keep the pace and pressure.

"Yes!" She hitched her voice high, the cords on her neck straining, legs wide. "Yes!"

"There you go, baby. Let it out for me."

Panting, she came hard, her face flushed, breasts heaving.

Recovering for only a second, she pulled me down on the bed, prowling over me like a tigress, yanking off my shirt and shoving down my pants to my knees. I kicked them off the rest of the way then held my cock, inviting her to get on it.

"I'm glad you're down for a second round," she said, shimmying onto me, touching her boobs to entice me.

"Yeah, you're a handful." I gripped her ass, thrusting in deeper, making her bounce. "Good thing I have two hands."

"Oh my god!" She sighed, love drunk. "You're so fuckable."

Her praise lit me up, along with seeing her toned torso bunch and move with each thrust. Her hip bones swiveled in her practiced motion of riding a cock. She was great at it. It made me want to show her a little something extra I had learned along the way.

"So are you. Look how you're riding this dick."

I caressed low on her abdomen and up her ribs. She shivered. "I love how rough your hands are from work. But they're always so soft with me."

That was my cue. I laid my hand palm flat against my torso and slid it down until my fingers were forked around the base of my dick in a V-shape, my pointer and middle on one side, my ring and pinky on the other. Instantly, Maisie's pussy lips dragged against my fingers, her clit gliding against my knuckles, the added texture surely helping.

Her eyes fluttered as she watched what I did. I couldn't help but fight the smirk.

"Oh," she said, her tone steeped in wonder as she continued to sway, her center pressing harder against my calloused hand. "Oh, that feels really good." When we moved faster, her face crumpled for a second. "Wait, move your hand higher."

I did, causing less direct contact with my knuckles on her clit. The slight adjustment made her moan and throw her head back, squeezing her little feet in overwhelm.

"How? When? It's so simple—" She interrupted herself with a loud cry.

"Eyes on me," I said, grabbing her chin with my free hand. "I want to see your pretty face when you come on my cock."

Panting, all she could do was kiss and rub my finger against her swollen mouth, her little gasps feathering on my skin.

"Yeah, grip this cock."

Her legs trembled as she continued to ride through an orgasm, her center pounding a lustful beat.

"That's my girl. Do it just like that."

She squeezed her core tighter, rolling up her pelvis in shallow, little swings, allowing me the raunchiest look at her glistening, stuffed pussy. One sight and I was fighting for my life.

"Baby," she whined, smacking my leg. "I need to tap out or have you toss me around."

"Gladly!"

I rolled us and hooked her delicate ankles on each of my shoulders and folded her like a sexy little pretzel while I shamelessly watched my cock pound her pussy until it was dripping with me.

Sated, we collapsed into a heap of messy, cummy, sweaty limbs, both of us staring insensibly at the ceiling.

"In-fucking-credible," she whispered, dragging a knuckle across my chest.

# Chapter Twenty-Seven

The dream of the crows came back. I hadn't had it since our first night in Vermont. I liked to think it was because Dane was subconsciously protecting me. When I'd seen his crow tattoo, it had felt even more like a sign.

I was supposed to be with him.

He was mine. I was his.

But the dream was different now. Everything vivid. The damp, cold earth. The dirty clay smell of the loamy forest mixed with the intoxicatingly crisp and distinct pine. The dusky twilight sky in hues of periwinkle, lilac, and blush. The distinct circle of black birds, racing above the branches.

Something new crept into my awareness: deep breathing. The rough feeling of canvas against my skin.

Cold panic crept into my veins, freezing me in place. A loud ting burst me out of my nightmare. Dane's arms protectively snaked around me in the late-morning light, holding me closer as he continued to sleep.

Another ting went off, and I realized it was my phone. I groaned, escaping his clutches while rubbing my eyes. My phone had ended up on the floor in last night's tryst. Unlocking it, I squinted at the text.

**Dom: You're fucking a felon.**

I yelped, sliding out of the bed to crouch over my phone.

**Dom: I dug up all this info and needed to wait for some record requests to come back.**

A picture came through, a baby-faced Dane pulling his best Blue Steel face in a mug shot. Then another one where he looked crestfallen with a black eye.
I peeked up over the edge of the bed, seeing the man I cared so much for in a new light. A shiver ran down my spine. I snatched Dane's white shirt and pulled it on as an impromptu nightgown.

**Me: Tell me everything.**

**Dom: He's nonviolent. Looks like he got caught over a decade ago with a fuck ton of weed, a gun that wasn't his, and a stolen car. He was transporting it across three different state lines—Massachusetts, New Hampshire, and Maine. He was barely 18.**

Court reports streamed in along with a news article talking about a drug circuit out of Boston around the same time as the arrest.

**Dom: They linked him to several stolen cars. He'd fix them up for other people in this elaborate theft ring. He was sentenced to 6 years and was released after 3 because of good behavior. Looks like he has some cousins in Boston who were involved. It was like a chop shop situation.**

**Dom: After he got out of prison, he stayed at an address in Boston that is unofficially linked to the Irish mob.**

**Me: Real funny.**

**Dom: I'm not fucking with you. Same address, same family name.**

Dom sent over a Reddit page talking about it, including a historical photo of several men sitting on the porch from the early 1900s. That particular segment of the mob in Boston allegedly disbanded in the 1960s, but I guessed old habits died hard.

I drew in a deep breath, peeking another glance at Dane. He was sprawled out, fast asleep on his back, his beefy arms sprawled wide. He looked so peaceful and innocent, his face relaxed with sleep.

**Me: Thanks, Dom. I'll be home in three days.**

**Dom: On the bright side, this felon is a fucking smokeshow. Look at that fucking V-cut right below his abs. Jesus Christ. I just know this fucker has 10 pounds of swinging dick and a bucket of balls.**

With his text, he sent several photos from tattoo conventions and ink magazines where Dane had been a model.

I let out a puffing little noise that was somewhere between a laugh and a sob, stirring Dane.

Reaching for the 8-ball on the stool next to the lamp, I rolled it across the bed hard enough to wake him.

# Chapter Twenty-Eight

"Huh?" I said groggily. Bleary-eyed, I picked up the cold 8-ball near my ribs. Maisie was kneeling on the floor, her head barely above the bed.

Her face was placid, but even in my post-sex sleepy stupor, I could sense her energy was restricted, about to snap.

"So, when were you going to tell me you're a fucking felon?"

And there it was. Her tone was vicious, her eyes in a furious squint.

"It was a long time ago."

She jumped to her feet. "Do you realize I'm running from a cop, being protected by a fucking criminal?!"

"Who better?" I said dryly.

"Sure, trap a girl, make her feel indebted to you, then tell her you're a felon."

"That's manipulative as fuck. Don't say that."

Her face screwed tight as I called her out on her twisted truth. "Dane! You lied to me!"

"Bullshit!" I stood up from the bed, feeling naked and defensive in more ways than one. "I never once lied to you."

"This is what you meant in Vermont, isn't it? I asked why you lied to the lady at the check-in desk, and you said you'd done worse. This is why you make the bed and keep everything tidy. Why you're weird about finishing your food and you knock on the table when you're done eating. Some weird ass prison habits."

I found a clean pair of underwear and pulled them up my legs. "Sounds like you pieced it all together, darlin'."

"This is why you can only work for yourself. You're a fucking felon, dude! No one will hire your ass!" She raked her hands through her hair, panic trembling her voice. "Oh my god, this is unbelievable. I'm such a fool!"

"I'm still the same guy."

Continuing on her train of thought, she pointed at me. "This is why you were away from Pine Bluff when your sister died. You were locked up!"

"Have you ever watched your mom die of cancer? Huh? Have you ever watched her lose chunks of her beautiful hair, the one thing that brought her joy? Listen, I know your mom is a complete cunt, but mine wasn't." My throat clogged with memories. "I miss her every fucking day, Maisie!" I yelled.

"What the hell does this have to do with your mom?" She tore off my white shirt and threw it at me.

"Who do you think the weed was for, huh?" I said, stepping closer. "This was before everyone caught up to logic and legalized it. Even with cancer, it was a bitch to get. The other pain meds didn't work. So I did what any loving son would and hooked her up with something that helped. It started off simple. My cousins down in Boston had a grower, I'd drive down there for the weekend, grab some, and bring it back."

She hooked her bra around her torso, sliding it around to loop through her arms. "And you needed to steal a car and a gun in the process?"

"They'd ask me to drive a car up to my dad and we'd fix it up at the shop and take it back down when I did another run for the pot. They'd give us a cut. I was fresh out of high school, and all my friends had left for college, and I was completely directionless. The medical bills were adding up, and I think my dad and I just turned a blind eye. We knew it was wrong, but we thought since we were keeping it in the family, it would be okay. We were cogs in the wheel."

She glared at me, silently yanking on the rest of her clothing.

"I was young and dumb. My mom passed away and I got cocky. I started selling to people around Portland on my way back to Pine Bluff. I was good with the people and built rapport. It got more frequent, and I think the officials at the tolls caught on. They'd see me every week in a different car. My dad was eaten up by grief, so he didn't have it in him to worry about me. One weekend, my uncle asked me to bring a rifle up to my dad for hunting season. I did, and that's when the bust happened at the border of New Hampshire. A trunk full of weed in a car that wasn't mine and a gun that wasn't registered to me under the back seat."

"Dane! Grand theft auto isn't a simple family business!"

"There you go again, being a complete hypocrite!"

"Hypocrite? How?"

"Oh, it was fun to break the law when it was something simple like cyberbullying Ted Cruz or being full-on pussy out on a public pool table."

"I doubt either of those would get me jail time."

"How 'bout stealing a boat or breaking and entering a historical monument to fuck each other's brains out? The second it's something less desirable or *icky*"—I mocked a girly tone—"then you get to judge the crime. Funny how that works."

"Oh yes, you're so noble. Listen, the weed thing I can look past, but chopping cars? Several? You're a thief!"

"I did what I did. I paid for it. That decision stole my youth. I didn't even get to say goodbye to my sister because I was fucking locked up. Do you know how hard that is? And I completely left my dad all alone to bury them in the same year.

He was all alone. Once I was out, I only got a couple years with him before he died. Don't you think I know my decision had consequences?"

She folded her arms over her chest. "Listen, I'm sorry you lost them, but I feel super unsafe now that I know you're a felon and didn't mention it. I told you some of my dark secrets. It feels like you kept this from me on purpose. I mean—"

"You feel unsafe around me? I'm an unsafe man?"

"Yes."

"You're putting me in the category of Boyd and your ex? Are you fucking for real?" I knew my question was loaded, but I didn't care. Not waiting for her to answer, I snatched my keys up. "Grab your shit."

"I want you to take me back to Pine Bluff."

"Yeah, I figured that much out, darlin'. It was obvious you were never going to fucking stay, and now this is just the perfect excuse to run away from this."

"This? What even is this?" she exclaimed.

I placed the 8-ball in her hand, covering her fingers to hold it. "This was the realist damn thing you've ever felt, and you're willing to throw it all away because you're scared."

# Chapter Twenty-Nine

Maisie

We gathered our things in the cottage in scathing silence. I fought a sob, pressing my chest against his wide shoulders as I wrapped my arms around him for the drive back. Our hearts were so close but now broken. Usually, when you broke up, you got to break away, but that wasn't the case.

We spent the bulk of the afternoon journeying back to Pine Bluff. Once we hit Main Street, I tapped his shoulder and asked him to drive to his shop instead of taking me to Tilly's.

We both got off the bike. I freed myself from the rucksack and helmet. "Can we talk, please? We've had time to cool off. I don't want to leave this way."

He walked to the back door of his shop. "What is there to talk about?"

I chased after him. "Dane, please."

He guided me inside, his lips in a thin line. It was empty since Lennie had gone home for the night. I hated that when I walked up the stairs, I imagined living there with him, maybe helping him with improving his business methods. I was good at that. Hell, I went to college for that.

Flicking on some lights, I could see what a sad, sterile bachelor pad it was. There was a simple leather couch, a scratched-up coffee table, a TV, and some weights. Then the kitchen, which only had two stools under the bar, and the hallway leading to his modest bedroom. Not much in regard to décor or homey touches.

The idea of Dane working full-time as a mechanic all week only to climb up to this sad loft above his business to avoid his cottage clawed at me with guilt. He deserved cuddles and fun dates with someone who actually cared about him, not just some flighty tourist. He deserved black-and-white pictures on the wall of him and his lover and cozy nights at home. He deserved someone who wanted to hear all about his day.

He'd made some mistakes when he was a young, dumb kid, and that shouldn't trap him here. I knew that. Prior to all this, I'd believed in prison reform and that the war on drugs was fundamentally unhelpful to our society because it was only one piece of the puzzle.

I shook my head and rubbed my temples, trying to make sense of everything clashing in my mind.

"Look, I'm nervous that you kept being a felon from me. We talked about so much for the days we were on the trip. You told me about other parts of your past, so it feels like you left it out intentionally."

"I did because I don't think it makes me a threat to society. Strange enough, I feel like it made me into a better man. I appreciate my life, even if you think it's pathetic." He made a sweeping gesture with his arm. "This is all I have and I'm happy about it most days. I just wish I had someone to share it with, and I didn't even realize that until I met you."

"Dane, I'm sorry you've had to live with this mess of feeling like you can only work for yourself and everyone leaves you, yet you can't leave here. Even if it's not with me, I truly want you to move on from this. You deserve a happier life. You deserve so much!"

"How can you say that but not want to be a part of it?"

I held up my hands in front of my chest. "I can't be with you. I can't stay here."

"Is it because Kaylee asked if you'd be hanging around in town when she got back? Are you ashamed of us?"

"No. If anything, I feel like I'm in a plug and play situation."

"Plug and play?" he asked in confusion.

I fiddled with the metal button on my jacket. "Yeah, how many tourists have you taken on whale watching cruises? Long walks on the beach." I rolled my eyes, waving to his oven. "Fresh lobster dinners."

"None," he said with an annoyed scowl.

"I don't really believe that. How did you plan everything so easily?"

"I problem solve for a living; it's all I do. Pivot, find the next approach. I also had months to think about all the things I'd like to do with you if I ever saw you again!" He leaned against the sink, rubbing his eyes. "Dear god, woman! What do I have to do to convince you?" His voice was so weary.

"To convince me what?"

"That I love you!"

I stepped back in shock.

"Because I do. I love you, Maisie. I don't know what else I can do to show you. I've tried to talk about it with you. I've tried to show you in so many different ways."

He had. I knew he had.

"I love you, too," I said. But even to my own ears, my voice was sad, small.

His eyes darted side to side. "You're showing it in a pretty weird way."

"I feel lied to, and on top of that, it's like you want me to be something I'm not. You want me to drop my whole life and fit into yours."

"No, I'm just trying to make this work." Tears glazed his eyes, a sob hitching in his throat. "I'm sick of not being enough for you!"

I winced, knowing the feeling. It was how I'd felt with my mom my whole life. A new roll of unease punched through my body.

"I'm sorry," I whispered. "I'm the problem."

"Don't give me that. The whole 'it's not you, it's me' bullshit. I deserve more than that."

"I can't stay here! I'm sorry, but I can't."

"Why? I don't get it. Kaylee is here. The town is mellow. You could even live at my cottage while we date. I can stay here to not crowd you."

"You don't get it! I can't pick up my entire life and move here. I need the sun. I need heat. I need wide, open spaces to feel free. I can't breathe here! It's too crowded with trees and expectations."

He folded his arms over his chest. "Expectations. That's a funny word for commitment."

"I'm not scared of commitment, but I don't think I can risk it. You treat everything like a fling, and you kept something really important from me. We had fun. There was a connection. We fell in love, but it just needs to be what it was."

"You know it's more than that." He stepped closer, his hands cradling my face.

"It will swallow me whole. You"—I shoved a finger in his chest—"will swallow me whole. I will be a shell of the woman you met."

"That's not how love works. We'll pour into each other. Make each other better."

All I could do was look up at him in silence.

He dropped his hands, backing away with a slow gulp as his eyes became glassier. "Maisie, please don't do this."

"Why can't you move to Texas with me?" I'd said it. I had finally fucking said it. Had I been thinking about it for months? Secretly, maybe, okay, totally yes, yes, I had. "I really don't think it will be that hard to find a job as a mechanic with a record."

"That's not it. You don't get it. I can't abandon my shop. It was my dad's. It's one of the last pieces I have of my family other than my last name."

"Is it worth it? Wouldn't your dad want you happy even if it means closing the shop?"

"You could just spend the summer in Pine Bluff. You're selling Pretty Kitty anyways. Couldn't you seal the deal remotely? Test things out here? If it doesn't work, then we can move on to other options. I'm not trying to sell my business; you are. You have more mobility."

"I can't."

"Tell me why."

Unshed tears blurred my vision. "Because I made a promise to myself that I wouldn't structure my entire life around a man. My mom did that. She was always looking for my dad, dragging me to every rodeo on the off chance she'd find him so she could throw me in front of him like evidence. Or she was hunting for another man to anchor to. She'd change her whole personality and reorient her entire life around a man who couldn't be bothered to remember my name."

"You're not anything like your mother."

I aggressively pointed at my own chest, my fingertip knocking my sternum. "But I am! I dropped almost everything and tried to fit in the box Conner wanted me in. I just broke out. You don't understand! All I have is my independence and it came at a great cost. I can't give it up."

"I don't want you to be anything you're not. I just want you to be mine."

"You can't mean that."

"I just want you," he reaffirmed.

"I want you, but I want to be myself. I keep running from you. I don't even know why you want me."

"I just know you're the one for me. You feel it too."

"I do," I murmured.

"If you're so hellbent on ruining my life, then you might as well give me an ounce of pleasure along with all this torture. Tell me you'll stay."

"Hellbent?"

"Yes."

"I'm hellbent?"

"Yes, and stubborn and maddening and a little too fucking pretty while you're at it. But here's some news for you." He pointed directly at my heart. "I'm hellbent on loving you."

He stared at me with soulful eyes, his deep breaths making his wide shoulders rise and fall.

I took my first step back, then another. With each one, his face would twitch in discomfort. Then, like ripping off a Band-Aid, I turned, racing down the stairs, blinking back tears.

My hands were tingling, so I shoved them in the pockets of my jacket and continued to book it to Tilly's. If I could just get my card and I.D. and get in my hearse, it would be the last hurdle. I'd be on the road, blaring my favorite break-up playlist, bawling my eyes out in peace.

I had a broken picker, and I'd picked the wrong one again. It was as simple as that.

He was a felon. He only knew flings. He was hellbent on staying in Maine.

I choked back a sob. It was already dusk. With all the adrenaline, I could probably drive well into the night, maybe find a hotel for late check-in a couple hours away. The seaside cottage flashed in my head and caused another cry to wheeze out of me. I dabbed my eyes, picking up my pace with Tilly's in sight.

I beelined to the bartender. His eyebrows were already raised in recognition as he opened his cash register and dug under the drawer, presenting my two cards with a nod. "One AmEx and a Texas license for a Maisie Quinn."

"Thank you!" I gasped, needing the good news.

"No problem." He slid the receipt to close out my tab across the bar with a chewed-up pen that said Barrett Towing with a roaring bear as the logo. I gnawed my lip, hoping my car was still where I'd parked it.

I made sure to tip him triple the amount of my bill since he'd safeguarded my shit and thanked him once more. Exiting Tilly's, I rounded the parking lot, making my way around the block to my hearse. Seeing her all shiny and safe, I wanted to bawl for other reasons besides just self-inflicted heartbreak. My keys were buried in my purse, unused for days. While digging, a loud swarm of crows flew over, settling on a tree way down the street. I eyed them, a chill settling over me.

*Get out now.*

With a frantic hand, I continued to dig in my purse, finding everything but my keys. I looked to my left, certain I heard footsteps. Then, with a buzzing noise behind me, all the muscles in my body tensed up like the worst charley horse of my life. I fell to the ground, and the cement grated my skin. As I tried to stand up, a whack on the back of my head jarred me.

The cawing faded. And just like the inky wing of a crow, blackness engulfed me, shrouding me in silence.

# Chapter Thirty

I froze as she left, her pink hair a streak down my stairs. I couldn't change her mind or make her see how we could be together. There was a voice in my head, maybe it was my dad's or maybe it was my mom's, but it was telling me I shouldn't have to beg someone to love me.

I bent over, my hands bracing my knees. I'd experienced loss and heartbreak before, but this was deeper, and it sliced right through me. I stayed there, trying to catch a breath. When I blinked, a tear fell from me, splashing on the hardwood floor. Then another and another.

I sniffled, standing up to crack both sides of my neck. She was gone, and I'd just have to deal with it. It was a risk I'd known I was taking the second I'd let her hop on my motorcycle.

I couldn't call Harley. Not only was he on his honeymoon, but it was the middle of the night in Greece. I didn't want to call Noah—he was too literal and optimistic.

I didn't want to read. I definitely didn't want to find another hookup. The idea of a woman who wasn't Maisie underneath me made me physically ill.

I guessed beer and pizza were in order, but I didn't want to be in public, so I decided to go to the store and bring it back for a *Breaking Bad* marathon while I watched the shapes and colors on the TV move while I really thought about what was on my mind.

Her.

Gone.

I wiped my face and pulled myself together, snatching the keys to my truck that I hadn't driven in over a week. I drove by Tilly's, pathetically glancing to see if she was inside with no luck. A hollow ache filled me by the time I made it to the outskirts of town when I realized she'd really left. She was probably roaring down I-95, blaring some Kelly Clarkson song.

While stuck at one of the only stoplights in town, trying to make a left-hand turn, I eyed all the cars at the intersection, silently praying one was her hearse. Chiding myself for being an idiot, I almost didn't catch a dark SUV flying through, a shock of pink hair lit up behind the back window for a split second.

My grief-stricken brain registered it was someone slumped over.

"Maisie!" I shouted.

With two cars in front of me and more blocking me from the right, I was stuck, helpless.

"Fucking shit!" I spat, eyeing Boyd's cop car hauling ass on Pine Ridge Road. I beat my hands on my wheel, feeling absolutely trapped in the gridlock of cars.

*Boyd has Maisie.*

My stomach churned, my spine tingling in terror. When the light turned green, I inched as close to the bumper of the car in front of me as I could, laying on my horn. As both cars inched through the intersection, I continued honking, urging them to veer to the side.

Flooring my truck, I raced in the direction he'd gone. The road was long and winding, leading to the forest surrounding the town. Several small parking lots speckled each trailhead, but I didn't know which one he'd stop at, and I didn't have time to check.

*Maisie, where are you?* I sent a plea to the universe, hoping on some level I could feel her. We were so connected at this point, I prayed I could.

Unable to pick up on anything, I gritted my jaw as I sped down the winding road. It was one thing to watch her leave. It was completely another to watch her unable to because Boyd had snatched her up. Rage singed my nerves, a metallic tinge seeping into my mouth.

He had Maisie. He had *my* Maisie.

She would've never gone with Boyd of her own accord. She wouldn't be slumped over in the back seat of his SUV unless he'd done something to her. Bile rose in my throat with the realization of what I might find.

Half a mile ahead, a large murder of crows flew in the bluish twilight of the sky, circling in the air like a spiral.

"Crows?" I spat the word in outrage.

Memories flickered of her having nightmares about birds in Vermont when she'd destroyed the pillow wall and cuddled me throughout the night. Then her reaction to my crow tattoo.

Crows.

With newfound determination, I stomped my gas pedal.

# Chapter Thirty-One

I woke up being hauled out of a vehicle by someone. Intense pressure filled my head, making it feel like it was about to explode. If that wasn't bad enough, I was seeing double everything, my vision blurry and not tracking as fast as I'd like.

"Who?" I whispered, trying to look up at the person carrying me. Realizing it was Boyd, I tried to scramble, but my body was so heavy, laden with incoordination. "No!" I yelled, pushing at his jaw, bopping his mouth.

"Be quiet," he grumbled, picking up his pace on the forest-lined trail.

"Fire!" I screamed. I sucked in as much air as I could, steeling to shriek again. "Fire! FIRE! There's a fire! Help!"

I knew to scream about a fire, not rape, because people cared more about property damage than a woman.

With a frustrated grunt, he dumped me on my feet, hauling me close to him while covering my mouth with the other hand. I stumbled so he jerked me closer, painfully grasping my breast, dragging me into the forest before throwing me down to the ground. My wrist stung as I tried to brace myself.

*Scream for a fire.*
*Act like you want it.*
*Tell him you're on your period.*
*Look him in the eye.*
*Scratch him to get DNA.*

All the stupid advice cycled through my head as I scrambled on the forest floor as he stood over me.

"I'm on my period. You don't want me. I promise."

His hands went to his belt to take out his gun. "Doesn't matter. That little cunt of yours will be bleeding once I rip it fucking you."

I clawed at the dirt, trying to get away, my vision going white in panic.

How could it end this way? Was he going to kill me first then rape me? Or the other way around?

Crows circled above us, their caws creating a building cacophony that echoed in my ears along with my drumming pulse.

He covered my mouth as he kneeled over me, pinning my bony hip bone to the earth with one of his knees, the cool dirt an icy companion in my horror. He lifted his gun under my chin, pushing it hard enough to incite a burn. "You were on the back of that bike with him, weren't you?"

I nodded without thinking.

"You fucked him, didn't you?" He lifted his hand with his question.

"Yes," I whispered.

With my admission, he reeled back, pistol-whipping me in the face. Blood erupted in my mouth as the metal clanged against my lip, knocking a tooth.

"Why couldn't you just fuck me like the little whore you are?" he roared, veins bulging on his forehead.

"Don't do this. Please don't do this! I'm saying no!" I pushed at his chest with my hands, causing my wrist to flare in pain, the rough canvas of his cop uniform scratching my palms. "No!"

He roughly seized my wrists, flinging them away. In the process, the bracelet Kaylee gave me snapped, beads slinging everywhere around us. My mouth gaped as white-hot pain shot up my arm, causing blood to gurgle in the back of my throat.

"You're going to lie back and take it. Or I'm going to go take this gun and empty it into Dane's stupid fucking head!"

His hand moved to my throat, squeezing enough to scare me. "Do you hear me?" He squeezed tighter, my vision getting spotty as I gulped down my own blood. "You embarrassed me that night at Tilly's. Now your scrawny ass is going to pay for it."

This was it. This was how I was going to die. Not peacefully in my bed but in this forest. Raped and murdered and left for the crows to pick out my lifeless eyes.

Unable to process my fate, I gasped in a breath. "I hate you!"

It was the only thing I wanted Boyd to know. It was the only thing I could muster from my brain.

I blinked back tears as he dropped his gun to reach down to unbuckle his belt. My entire body stiffened with the jangling of metal. My blood rushed to my head, bulging at my temples as I stared at the crows, unable to watch him trying to get an erection.

I thought of my stupid mom and Texas. I'd never see a sunset in Texas again. I'd never laugh with Kaylee over margaritas again. I'd never get to clutch Dane on a motorcycle ride again. None of it, ever again.

A light traveled across the tops of the trees. I followed it until it went across Boyd's face, the shadows of the branches lining his homely features.

"Get off her!" a deep voice barked in the night. Boyd turned to see who it was, but I already knew. More tears ran.

"This doesn't concern you!" Boyd yelled back.

He got to his feet, fisting the front of my jacket to yank me up. With my body stiff in shock, I crashed into him, unable to fight it when he put me in a headlock. A couple feet from us, the metal of Boyd's abandoned gun glinted on the forest floor.

"Leave her alone and I won't completely beat your ass," Dane growled, inching closer to us.

Boyd walked backwards, keeping his distance from Dane. I tried to scrunch, to sink lower on Boyd's chest to get away, but he yanked me back up, losing his balance, causing dirt to crumble beneath us as we slid deep into a ravine. I felt my clavicle snap on impact as he dragged me down with him, the grit of the rocks ripping up the front of me. Dirt filled up my mouth as it hung in silent screams.

A lantern flung past us, lighting up the forest in a ghoulish way where it landed. More dirt sprinkled down as Dane skidded toward us on the incline of the ravine. The air left my lungs as Boyd yanked me back up against his body, turning to shield us away from Dane. His heart hammered against my back. His hand painfully grasped my breast as his other arm snaked around my neck, headlocking me once more in the crook of his elbow.

I clawed at his arm, the sky getting darker before a loud, mannish roar erupted behind me.

Then something warm doused my entire head, drowning me.

# Chapter Thirty-Two

# DANE

I pounced down on Boyd, yanking his head back by his hair with one hand as I shoved my serrated hunting knife into the left side of his neck, feeling the grisly pop before the spray of blood from his artery exploded around my hand and down Maisie, showering her.

Her screams gurgled with his blood as I shoved the knife deeper as his body slacked, collapsing against me. I leaned back against the gully, still holding him while Maisie freed herself, crawling on her hands and knees.

I'd just killed a guy.

The forest curled around me, pale gray branches morphing like spindly fingers as they warped along with the dirt and sky. Everything swirled together in a kaleidoscope of unbridled rage and shock in my mind. My eyes jerked around, my mind forcing me to not look at what I had just done. But I knew. I could still feel his blood spurting on me, gushing like a garden hose with each pulse before it stopped.

The man in my arms was now dead. His life was over in one second. One pinch of metal against flesh.

A man who'd once been a little boy. A boy who'd gotten his first haircut from my mom at her salon. A kid I'd played little league with. A douche I'd eventually punched at homecoming when he'd tried to yank down Azalea's dress as a "joke."

A guy the whole town bemoaned but didn't do anything about because of social niceties. I guessed I wasn't nice because Chase Boyd was dead in my arms, but I felt no remorse.

Rapists didn't have feelings.

Rapists didn't deserve peace and a long life. They were scabs on society, only topped by people who fucked with children.

Yet, the strange mix of horror and relief caused me to freeze.

I'd taken a life.

My entire body shook as I focused on my breathing, trying to snap out of my murderous fog while Maisie curled in on herself in the fetal position, her guttural wails layering with the crows and a rustling from somewhere in the forest.

Footsteps thudded above me, causing me to look up only to see Noah with a headlamp on, shining it down at me.

Harley's work dog, Storm, let out a small woof, causing Noah to lean down to pat his head. "Yield. Good boy."

Noah's eyes scanned me in the ravine still holding Boyd in one arm, my other hand wrapped around the knife in his throat. Then he eyed Maisie who was a trembling mess, her face buried between her knees, dirt and blood staining almost every inch of her. He flitted his eyes back to mine, completely locked for a second, his mouth opening slightly while his brows scrunched. Something flipped in his mind, though, because he sucked in a breath, his eyes flat in a knowing way before they pulled from mine.

Swiveling his headlamp in another direction, talking to Storm once more, he declared, "This way, buddy."

The dog whined, sniffing the dirt, clearly knowing the problem. Noah tapped the dog's ribs. "Forward."

Storm sniffed in a different path, Noah following him, keeping up the charade of looking for something he had already found.

I lowered Boyd to the ground, positioning him on his side against the gully, unable to look in his blank eyes but not cruel enough to lay him flat on his face. From there, I went to Maisie, pulling her up and into my arms. "I've got you," I whispered, pushing her drenched hair back off her face.

"I peed a little." Her voice trembled as she swiped her mouth with a dirty hand.

I wrapped her in a hug, pulling her onto my lap, rocking us back and forth. "You're okay. I got you."

"Thank you," she whispered repeatedly, almost like a chant.

"You're safe. He's gone." I held up my hand to the side of her face so she wouldn't have to see his dead body.

"He . . ." Her voice quaked as she touched her mouth where her top canine tooth was now chipped. "He broke my tooth." She sniffed, looking down at herself drenched in blood. "My jacket!" She sobbed with the realization. "My dad's jacket is ruined. It's all ruined!"

I held her tighter, unsure what else to say. We stayed there, shaking and panting, clutching each other in silence.

"How did you find me?" she finally asked over my shoulder.

"The crows."

A new bout of sobs racked her body as she held me closer. "Dane! Oh, Dane." She buried her bloody face in the crook of my neck.

"We have to call someone," I whispered, fighting the dry heave from the iron smell of blood.

"We can't. They can't know you're here, that you did this." She pulled back, wide-eyed. I could tell she couldn't focus on my face. A churning in my stomach made me wonder what he'd done to her before I'd gotten there. "I'll take the fall. I'll say I had the knife." She pointed up the hill. "He had a gun. He was going to hurt you if I fought back." A cry pulled at her expression that was still full of terror.

"Hurt me? That's not what I'm worried about." I wiped away some dirt from her haunted face. "He hurt you, Maze. You can't take the fall for me. This was self-defense."

"Yes, I have to. You can't chance it."

I fought back my rush of feelings from knowing she'd take the fall for me, and so freely, without question.

I gathered a breath. "There's nothing to risk."

*You're worth every risk.*

The crows continued to circle us, creating their own incessant cyclone of cawing as I pulled out my phone.

"No! Dane!" she whined, a bite of desperation I'd never heard in her tone. "Please, please don't do this," she begged, fisting my shirt. "Let me call them. You drive off before someone sees you."

I wrapped her in my free arm, holding the phone to my ear with the other.

"911, what is your emergency?"

My mouth dried as Maisie's tears wet my neck. "Um, hi, this is Dane MacCloyd. I caught Officer Boyd trying to rape a woman in the forest and I, um, I killed him to protect her."

"You killed him?" the operator repeated, unable to hide the panicked tone.

I clutched the woman I loved tighter. "Yes."

# Chapter Thirty-Three

Maisie

The night after the incident was a blur of interviews and a sexual assault kit at the bigger hospital four towns over. The EMTs had to literally pull me off Dane. They wouldn't let him come with me to the hospital. I had a complete meltdown, screaming and crying because he was the only person I felt safe with.

I was transported by ambulance because they were worried about my heart since I'd been tased. They were also assessing my collarbone and wrist, along with a possible skull fracture and internal bleeding due to the assault. While they were loading me up, I insisted on someone searching for my purse either by my hearse or in Boyd's vehicle. It would have all the damning evidence I needed to keep Dane a free man.

After scans and examinations, they ruled out anything concerning my heart or internal bleeding. They confirmed a concussion, a hairline fracture to my clavicle, a sprained wrist, and a chipped canine tooth. They also found probes in my back from where he'd hit me with the Taser.

With my consent, pictures and samples were taken prior to cleaning me up and afterwards. I kept warning there would be

DNA from Dane on my skin, not just Boyd's. I squeezed my eyes shut, trying not to compare how differently each man had interacted with my body. One man's gentle kiss up my neck was another man's viselike grip.

I started zoning out and humming to myself while the sexual assault nurse examiner took pictures of my chipped tooth, split lip, and the blood vessels that ruptured in my eyes from him choking me. They also took pictures of the marks on my neck, around my breast, over my hip where he'd knelt on me, and all the scrapes on my skin from sliding down the ravine. Any evidence I could offer to prove this was self-defense and to save Dane, I would.

Along with the jacket, I'd lost my favorite cowgirl boots and the golden sun pendant Kaylee had given me. They were all coated in Boyd's blood and considered forensic evidence. I had already lost so much. It made me angry.

Afterwards, they gave me plain navy sweatpants and a gray shirt to wear. For some reason, that got me emotional. I was all alone. Kaylee was in Greece, completely unaware, and I had no clue where Dane was. I'd been assaulted and the love of my life had murdered someone, but there I was, all alone in borrowed clothes. It made everything feel too transient.

Everyone was clinically polite, but I could feel the undertones of pity. I didn't want them to pity me. All I could focus on was Dane. He'd killed a man. He'd stepped over a threshold you really couldn't come back from, even if it was in the name of self-defense.

An investigator named Chuck came into my hospital room. He wanted to get my statement while it was still fresh. Deep wrinkles creased his ruddy skin, and when he sat down, I got a whiff of wintergreen mints. He had my purse, thank God. I snapped into indifference, digging in my bag to show him the ticket and the creepy note. I told him the entire story, from the bachelorette party to the traffic ticket to finding the note and how Dane had gotten me out of town because I'd been scared of Boyd.

I provided screenshots of the texts to Kaylee along with the selfie I'd snapped when I'd been pulled over and the video I'd recorded. I also told him to find Rosie because she'd witnessed the whole exchange between Boyd and me and the sketchy drink offering.

Chuck knew about the complaint I'd filed about Boyd and tried to hide his regret that no one had contacted me. I thought he knew his team had dropped the ball on that one. He left me with his card and instructed me not to leave the state until he could corroborate details with others in the investigation. I was also not allowed to contact Dane until further notice.

By the time the medical examinations and interview were over, it was the middle of the night. I guessed I'd been up long enough to rule out any worry of a major concussion because a nurse brought me a surprisingly delicious burger and even better pain meds than I'd received earlier that night. They conked me out, but my dreams looped over and over in my head: Boyd pinning me to the ground, the crows, the primal scream of Dane behind us, the frightening splatter over me.

The next day was a blur of sleeping and additional scans. A crisis counselor came to my room, but I didn't have much to say. I wasn't sure if it was because of the meds or the shock. Probably both. I had guilt knowing most people in my position wouldn't receive this kind of care and that I was immensely privileged. It deepened as my mind drifted to Dane and what hell he was possibly in. Then the loop of flashbacks played in my mind once more.

By late afternoon, I was cleared to go. My sprained wrist was wrapped, and they were going to send me home with some pain meds for my clavicle. While I signed the discharge papers, a nurse explained they arranged a ride for me. As I walked out into the waiting room, Azalea stood up from her seat. I didn't know she'd be there, but I was glad and walked right to her.

"Oh, Maisie," she whispered, folding me into a warm hug. With our height difference, I felt almost like a child with how my head came to her chest, her hand smoothing my hair. "I'm so sorry." Her body quaked from holding back emotion.

I broke the hug, groggy with pain meds. "How did you know to come here?"

She squeezed my arm with a soulful look. "Dane sent me. He told the cops you didn't know anyone else in town. They don't want you staying at his cottage. And you need some rest."

"But I . . . He didn't do anything wrong. I want to see him."

"I know you do. I would, too. But he can't come right now."

"Why?"

She hooked her thumbs in her pockets nervously. "He's still at the station."

"Was he arrested?" I whispered.

"I don't think so." She guided me away from the sterile surroundings of the hospital, wrapping her arm around me protectively. "This place is awful. Let's get you out of here. You can come and stay with me at the inn."

I stopped us mid-stride. "Okay, but I have one condition. You have to tell me if you find out anything else about Dane. Can you promise me that?"

She nodded, her healthy brown hair shiny in the fluorescent lighting. "Yes, I promise."

"You know he's innocent, right?"

"Of course."

She had a forest-green Subaru that was probably as old as I was. It was covered in tree-hugger bumper stickers. Luckily, she wasn't super inquisitive on the way back to Pine Bluff. My body felt lethargic. The doctors had explained I would experience malaise because of the Taser, concussion, and just flat-out adrenaline crashing. Getting out of the car, I wasn't prepared for the exhaustion that swept over me.

Azalea held open the car door, offering a hand to help me. "The inn is booked, but I have a cot I can set up in my apothecary so you can sleep in my room. I promise you'll be safe and away from all the guests."

I nodded, unable to say much else.

Her room was at the very top of the Victorian house, her wrought-iron bed in a circular alcove that made up one of the turrets. She pulled down the canvas blinds on the surrounding windows, drawing the lacy curtains that still left the room saturated in the golden light of sunset. I'd usually bemoan trying to sleep without blackout curtains, but for once, I didn't want any darkness.

I all but collapsed onto her bed that was layered with soft quilts that smelled like rosemary. I didn't have the deep sleep brought on by exhaustion. I was pushed to the point where I was so tired I couldn't rest. I'd jerk awake every hour.

Later on, the shift of Azalea sitting at the foot of the bed pulled me from another chunk of fidgety sleep. The room was lighter with dawn. My stomach grumbled with the smell of warm bread. She had brought me a tray with some bland food, like oatmeal and toast, along with tea. I thanked her and scarfed it down while she explained she'd gotten my car keys from my purse and fetched it to park it at the inn. And when she saw my suitcase, she couldn't help herself and threw some clothes in the wash because she knew I'd lost some in the incident. Maybe it was my mommy issues, but Azalea's thoughtful nature choked me up. Aside from Kaylee and now Dane, I wasn't used to people caring for me. Even my ex-husband couldn't be bothered to do laundry or unload the dishwasher.

Azalea's mouth tilted in a pleasant smile while I sat down the now empty bowl of oatmeal on the tray. "You just keep sleeping. I have a shift at Silver Springs today, so I won't be here, but my great aunt, Eugenia, is around. She owns this place, and she can help you with anything. You can stay at the inn as long as you need. You hear me?" She dipped her chin with her question.

I nodded.

She took the tray away. "Oh, and I already checked in with my dentist and she can fix your tooth with something temporary. I'll take you to her office tomorrow, okay?"

"Thank you." I ran my tongue around the jagged edge. "You have to promise me you won't tell Kaylee what happened."

Azalea sat back down on the bed, shifting uncomfortably. "I don't know if I should do that. I don't want to lie to her. You don't need to be ashamed of what happened to you. It wasn't your fault."

I inched closer to Azalea at the foot of the bed. "I know, and thank you for saying that." I swept some of her pretty brown hair over her shoulder, the faintest hint of something clean and herbal floating from her tresses. "I don't want to ruin her honeymoon. It would be awful to look back on it and only think of your best friend almost getting raped. If we mention anything now, she'd be on her first flight back home. We both know it."

She picked at the seam of her Levi's in silence.

I really didn't want to pull out the big guns, but I knew I had to, and I knew it was going to be manipulative as fuck. "Remember when I fished that period cup out of you?"

We both fought a chuckle.

"Yes, is this how I'm paying you back? With my silence?"

I bobbed my head. "Blood for blood. I'm not asking you to lie to her. I'm just asking that I get to tell my own story, with my own timing."

"Okay, I'll respect that." She gestured to a slender vase of four white lilies on the nightstand I hadn't noticed. "I put white lilies from my garden near you. They're a flower for grief and mourning." She gathered a breath, floating her gaze from the flowers back to me. "But they also symbolize innocence. It's important to me that you know you didn't do anything wrong, Maisie. You didn't deserve what happened to you. No matter what you did or said, nothing justified what that monster tried to do."

"Thanks for saying that. And thank you for being so sweet with me."

She got up and picked up two photos from the dresser. "I developed these after I saw you at the parade. I was going to mail them to you, but I think seeing them now will be helpful."

She extended them to me. Tears instantly pooled in my eyes while a silent sob shook my shoulders. The first photo was Dane and me dancing at the wedding, giving cheesy smiles, and the second was candid, my head on his chest, his face turned sweetly in toward me as he held my hand against his heart.

Azalea gave me a sympathetic look. "I wanted to remind you that people care about you and there's men out there who won't hurt you."

My chest squeezed with too much emotion and love for Dane. A burning rolled up my throat, making its way to the edges of my eyes where tears flowed.

Would I ever see him again?

Where was he?

## Chapter Thirty-Four

The days following the incident pushed me to my limit. Even though I'd called the cops myself, I'd still been taken into custody. When you were a felon found covered in blood next to a cop with a knife still sticking out of his throat, they took it seriously, as they should.

But I wasn't a stalker or rapist like Boyd. I was a man who'd fixed up some sketchy, stolen cars and sold a little too much weed when I wasn't even old enough to drink. There was a huge difference. I was a man who'd defended a woman, and I'd do it again. Regardless, I knew it was going to be a process until my ass saw the light of day.

Luckily, a couple summers ago, I'd hooked up with a really pretty lawyer, Lacy, who lived in Saco. She was one of those tightly wound executive types. We'd stayed in touch because I kept her BMW running and didn't speak to her like a condescending prick like most mechanics. Having her help me came in clutch.

The county and state police had to step in since Pine Bluff PD would be biased since it was one of their guys. That hadn't stopped them from roughing me up unnecessarily while they'd taken me in. Typical.

The first investigator I talked to was named Chuck. I told him the whole story about how Maisie and I knew each other and how she'd been acting dodgy when I'd found the note on her windshield. Then I explained we'd been on the trip because she'd run up to me at the parade, asking for help to hide from Boyd. I'd known about how she'd reported Boyd to the state police. Then once we'd been back in town, how I'd seen her slumped over in the back of his car at an intersection and known something was wrong.

The only detail I left out was seeing Noah right after the stabbing. No one had brought him up, which was fine by me. I told them to contact Lennie for a statement because Boyd had harassed him while looking for us.

Then I had to tell the same story to four other people, frontwards, backwards, deconstructed, and every gritty detail even down to my "relations" with Maisie.

I asked each person if they'd noticed Boyd's pants had been undone and how the idiot hadn't even kept his gun on him because he'd been too busy trying to choke Maisie and get his limp dick out of his pants. I also asked if they'd thought to check porch cameras from the houses near the cottage to prove it was Boyd who'd left the note. Needless to say, they didn't like my questions.

At one point, an investigator woke me up by poking me in the ribs with his pen, telling me I was free to go but I couldn't leave the state and there would be an ongoing investigation.

I assumed Maisie had presented damning evidence to the investigator, like the note and ticket from Boyd. Leave it to her to cover her own ass in a cunning way. Not that that always worked. Two more minutes in that forest would've ended very differently.

I was frustrated that as a woman, she had to think like that, but God was I grateful. It saved my ass. I couldn't be prouder.

Even if she wasn't mine, I was glad I'd saved someone so smart and resourceful from ending up in a shallow grave.

Azalea promised she'd take care of Maisie and send her back to Texas once she was able to travel. Zay was such a nurturer; I knew Maisie was in good hands. It was the only relief I got from the entire process, other than knowing Boyd would never harm her again.

While incarcerated in my formative years, I'd witnessed some brutal shit. I'd watched barbaric things happen at the hands of men. I thought that was why I'd subconsciously surrounded myself with women when I'd gotten out. Along with that, the corruption of cops had become undeniable. Being around them again with the pending threat of imprisonment drummed up a lot of trauma I wasn't ready to process, along with heartbreak.

I was free but unable to escape my own personal hell.

I felt like a leper coming back to my shop. Lennie only got the most basic details—I was involved in Boyd's death but not guilty. I could tell by the way he looked at me, he had so many questions, but his tender heart knew I wasn't in a place to talk. He just hugged me and fed me his new recipe for tabouli. For once, his hippie side paid off. I needed gentleness.

With my absence from the trip and the incident, work had stacked up, so I wasn't even given the chance to rest. All I had was time to stare at projects, thinking about the woman I loved and the murder. It replayed over and over again in my head. It had been such a knee-jerk reaction. I hadn't even known what had been happening until blood had been spurting out of his neck. Thing was, I'd do it again. I didn't know if that certainty should scare me, but I couldn't change it anyway.

I still had Maisie's clothes from our trip. She'd left them in the rucksack when she'd left me. I'd never admit it to anyone, but I slept with her sundress bunched up near my face. It still smelled like her mixed with the seaside cottage—sweetness and salty air. I knew the scent would fade over time, but my love for her wouldn't.

Late in the afternoon, four days after the incident, I was dropping the oil pan under a cursed Chevy Spark when I heard Lennie yell for me in the lobby. Annoyed, I sat up, wiping my hands, assuming he'd fucked up the register again, but the second I saw a burst of pink hair, my heart squeezed tight in my chest.

"Maisie," I whispered, lifting my arms to hug her, only to realize I couldn't.

"Hey," she whispered, her voice shaky. "Chuck cleared me to travel and to see you."

"I'm gonna call it a night, boss," Lennie said.

Unable to take my eyes off her, I nodded, waiting in silence while he gathered his things and went out the back door. She had bruises on her neck, broken blood vessels in the corners of her eyes, and a split lip. The sight of her injured made my stomach clench.

"I thought you'd left already."

"Um, no. I wasn't really feeling up for the drive and I wanted to talk to you." She tugged at the sleeves of her hoodie then pulled it closer around her neck.

"You don't need to thank me."

She shifted from one foot to the other, her shoulders curving in, making her look smaller than I had ever seen. "It's not like that."

"I promise I won't tell anyone, not even Kaylee," I offered.

"It's not that either."

Emotionally and physically exhausted, I stood there, unable to fill in the gaps.

"Dane, I love you. I don't want to leave this way."

A dark laugh crept out of my lips. "Maisie, we can never be together. Especially now."

"What do you mean? There's just been so much going on and I—"

"I'll never know if you love me for me or because I killed Boyd for you. It's interesting how I'm the right kind of criminal for you now."

My ears rang with my blunt truth.

She swallowed hard and flinched, like my words were bullets. "You can't mean that. You can't seriously think like that." She sucked in a shaky breath, stepping closer to me.

"I do. Since the moment your little tornado ass landed in this town, you've told me time and time again that we can't be together. That you can't stay. That you can't love me. Don't worry, I believe you now."

Grayish tears ran down her face, streaking her mascara. I felt like a cruel asshole making her cry and drive herself back to Texas freshly assaulted and heartbroken. It just added to the tally of things I'd done wrong in this lifetime.

"Why are you being like this? Why don't you believe me when I say I love you and that I want to be with you?"

"Because the only thing that's changed is I killed a man for you."

She wiped her face with the sleeve of her hoodie.

I went on, "I don't want to build a life with someone who's only with me out of obligation. How will I ever know that you love me just for me?"

"I do!"

"I don't want someone's death to tie us together. That can't be it, Maze."

"It wouldn't be. I've loved you longer than that." Tears flooded her eyes as her delicate hand tried to touch my chest, but I reared back. "Dane, please! I'm begging you. I'll move here. I'll do anything." She bawled. "Don't do this! We're supposed to be together."

"I'm asking you to leave, now. I can't see—" My voice hitched with emotion. "I can't see you ever again. Please, can you do that for me? Can you make sure I never see you again?

You're making this harder." I gestured between us. "All of this is just too painful."

She shook her head, trying to weave herself into my arms for an embrace.

I held her shoulders, walking her backwards to the front door. She grabbed my face, pulling me down for a desperate kiss, her tears mingling with my own. I winced, unable to move my mouth against hers as I slowly pushed her off me, opening the door with a loud swoosh.

"Please," she whispered, stumbling backward. "Please don't do this!"

And similar to the moment when I'd killed Boyd, the sight of her staring at me while I shut the door seared into my mind. I knew both would replay over and over in my memory for the rest of my life.

# Chapter Thirty-Five

I drove for days in silence. Every song reminded me of him. I grimaced when I got an email indicating he'd canceled my reservation at his cottage, refunding me money I wasn't even worried about. I winced again when I saw our dorky roadside selfie as the lock screen on my phone. I full-on ugly cried when I found his book on my back seat. I clutched it to my chest, praying I'd see him again.

Luckily, I'd already scouted out good hotels for my way back, so I knew where to stop, but each night I'd go straight to my room, too scared to wander around. It was the oddest feeling. I craved people, but they also scared me.

Kaylee would send me photos occasionally. She got really sunburnt, which I'd warned her about. Aside from that, it looked like they were having a blast on their honeymoon. After about two days of vague responses, she caught on and called me around midnight.

When I answered the video chat, I prayed my hoodie hid my neck as I put on a brave face. Luckily, my eyes and lips were mostly back to normal. Kaylee looked like a goddess in a flowy white dress, her hair braided in a crown around her head like a

Swedish milkmaid. Behind her, a trellis of hot-pink flowers crept up the white stucco wall of her villa.

"What are you doing? Isn't it like 9 o'clock in the morning in Greece."

"Exactly, and it's the middle of the night there. Why are you up?"

I got up from the bed of my hotel room, finding a place to prop up my phone on the desk so I could fold myself into the chair in front of it.

Kaylee's eyes darted around the screen, watching me. "Maze, babe, what's wrong? Are you okay? I can feel something is up."

I blinked back tears. Just being in her virtual presence tore down any walls. It was always someone you truly loved who could make you fall apart by just showing up for you. "I'm okay. I really am. I don't want to dump on you while you're on your honeymoon."

"Oh, sweetie, you wouldn't be. I promise. I could use the distraction honestly. I adore Harley, but we've been in this love bubble for almost two weeks. I'm touched and talked out. So is he. I sent him on a fishing trip with one of his cousins for the day, you know, man shit."

I sniffled with a little laugh. "Kaylee, please, let's just talk about this when you get home."

She walked inside her villa, setting the phone down somewhere to point at me. "Don't make me bust out my tarot cards! They will tell on your ass!"

This was the downside to having a hella psychic best friend.

Kaylee went on, "Oh, before I forget, does this have something to do with you losing that necklace I gave you right before the wedding? I had a dream you lost it, so I found you this." She held up a shimmering chain with a sun pendant, not that different from the one she'd originally given me and a good match for the silver moon one she wore. Inspecting it, she grinned. "When I saw it at a market, I just had a feeling to buy it for you."

That was the crack that broke the dam. My face instantly scrunched up as a heaving cry overtook me.

Kaylee patiently waited for me to collect myself, making little sounds of sympathy as she took her own seat, getting comfortable by tucking her sundress around her body as she sat in a lotus pose like a yogini. "Take a big, deep breath with me and hold it at the top of the inhale for three seconds before the exhale," she instructed.

We breathed together. I already felt better.

After a sip of her coffee, she folded her hands in her lap. "Now, tell me everything. We can figure it out together," she stated in a calm tone.

So I did. I explained how Dane and I had danced at the wedding, and from there I transitioned into an all-out story time. She'd already known about the creepy drink situation and my ticket from Boyd pulling me over, but I filled her in on the note he'd left me and how I'd run into him at the parade while trying to close out my tab at Tilly's Tavern. She got all swoony when I told her about Dane pulling a *knight and shining motorcycle* situation and wanted all the naughty details about hooking up with him.

She wiggled her light eyebrows. "So it's safe to say he lives up to his reputation?"

"Absolutely. I was walking differently." Since we had been friends for so long, we'd given most of our boyfriends nicknames over the years because so many had come and gone. She had an ex called Vlad the Impaler, and I had already dubbed Harley as lumber daddy. "I've already thought of a nickname for Dane."

"Do tell!"

"Dane the Satisfier."

She threw her head back with a cackle and clapped her hands. "I fucking love it!"

"By the way, he gave me a nickname, too."

She squealed. "Tell me!"

"Tornado."

"Oh, that's fucking perfect! So where did it all go wrong? It sounds like you were getting dicked down on the beach, which is honestly great. I can contest to that." A playful glimmer lit her eyes.

"Oh!" I said, holding up a finger, gathering my thoughts. "Did Harley ever mention anything to you about Dane's past?"

"Not really. I mean, he was completely orphaned by the time he was in his mid-twenties or something. I know he moved away from Pine Bluff for a couple years. He was a tattoo model down in Boston, came back to town all inked up. I guess the grannies at the knitting circle in town started a rumor he was in the mob."

"They're not wrong."

"What do you mean?"

"Dane is a felon."

Her eyes bugged out as she jolted her in seat. "You're fucking with me!"

"No, he was arrested trafficking a fuckton of weed into Maine with a stolen car. Oh, and transporting a gun that wasn't his across three different state lines. Like a little dumbass. He was barely 18."

"Stop!"

"Yes!"

"So when he went away, he was locked up?" she asked conspiratorially.

"Yes!" I hissed.

She gasped at the scandal. "This explains his obsession with *Breaking Bad*." We both snickered at her joke. "Oh my god, Maisie, you fucked a felon!"

I smacked my lips. "Oh, bitch please! Like you haven't!"

She tilted her head in consideration, stroking her jaw. "Yeah, fair enough. Okay, so wait. You were on a road trip fleeing from a cop with a felon. I take it when you found out that little detail, you left?"

"I wish it were that easy." I scrunched my lips to my nose in consideration before I launched into the rest. "So Dane drives me back to Pine Bluff. We go to his shop for our final goodbye, and he insists he didn't lie to me about the whole felon thing, just swears it didn't come up." I roll my eyes. "Which to be fair, is a good point."

"In my opinion, you normally wouldn't care, but since you were running from a cop and your safety was in his hands, it's kinda different," Kaylee interjected.

"Exactly. So he professes his love to me. Begs me to stay, offers up the cottage and everything. And I just . . . bolted."

"Oh, Maisie," Kaylee said in a hushed tone.

"Yeah, I'm not proud of it. So I ran away from him and headed to Tilly's, then on my way to the hearse, Boyd attacked me."

She unfolded her legs, lurching closer to the phone. "What do you mean?"

"He tased me and I think he hit me over the head with his baton."

"What?!"

I sped up my story, barely taking a breath because if I did, I'd have to live in the details. I didn't want that. I *couldn't* do that. Kaylee knew me well, so she followed my speech patterns and references, barely stopping to ask details. We both knew that would require a long talk in person, not like this.

When I finished recounting the attack, she sat in silence, wiping tears from her face with my truth.

"Say something," I said, feeling sick to my stomach.

She dabbed her eyes. "I'm so glad you're okay. Honeymoon or not, I would've been there. This is huge!" She started to walk around her villa.

"Don't you dare try to come here. You have another two days on your honeymoon, and I'm already somewhere in Tennessee."

She grumbled under her breath, sitting back down.

"I'm fine. Really. Azalea took care of me."

Her bottom lip trembled. "I'm glad she was there when I couldn't be. God, I feel so awful." She glared skyward, fighting back her emotions.

"Hey, look at me," I said. She pulled her gray eyes back to mine. "You've made a nice life for yourself up there in Maine. Even Rosie gave a statement about Boyd for me. You've surrounded yourself with some really nice people. I'm happy for you."

"Well, that's just it. When are you going to grant yourself something similar. If you love Dane, you should find a way to be with him. The man literally killed for you."

"I know he did. I tried to talk to him again, after everything. He said he couldn't trust that I wanted to be with him of my own free will and not out of guilt."

Kaylee swirled her coffee around in her cup, wrinkling her nose. "You'd never be with him out of obligation. That's just not your style. When you love someone, you love them hard."

I shrugged, feeling drained from recounting the entire tale. "What happened was a big moment in his life, too. I'm just trying to be understanding and patient. You know, giving him space to work through it."

She sipped her coffee pensively.

"Everyone has left Dane. I've realized now that's my biggest mistake. We belong together."

"Well, Maisie," she said, her tone more playful as she rolled her lips to wrangle a smile. "If there's one thing I know about you, it's that you always have a plan."

My entire body hummed in the potential of finding a bright spot in such a dark time. I needed lightness around me. More ease, laughter, silliness. I'd stewed in hard truths for too long, and my best friend knew that. Thank God.

Kaylee's smirk morphed into an all-out grin as she watched me fidget with my hoodie. "So, little tornado, tell me, what's your wild plan?"

# Chapter Thirty-Six

When Harley came back from his honeymoon, I ignored his texts. I didn't want to ruin his newly wedded bliss with my bullshit. It only lasted two days. He made up some stupid excuse to bring Kaylee's Jeep in for maintenance after hours. Since it was a Jeep, that was easy. There was always something I could find that needed fixing.

It ended up with us sitting on my garage floor, drinking beer and devouring two pizzas from Yeti's Spaghetti.

When he stood up to leave, he smoothed his hands over his pants. A pained look pinched his brows. "Can I keep your gun at my cabin for a while?"

I tilted my head in shock.

"It'll make me feel better. Once you've been that close to a death, it changes you. Especially if the woman you love is involved."

I glowered at him. "I'm not going to kill myself."

"You don't have to lie to me." The muscles in his neck worked as he gulped. "Lord knows I've thought about it," he murmured.

"Really?"

All he did was nod, his eyes flat. I knew he had PTSD from being a first responder as a forest ranger, but I guessed I'd never thought it had pushed him that far.

Since I was a felon, and owning a firearm wasn't possible without jumping through some major hoops, I didn't have one legally, but Har knew I had an old hunting rifle that had belonged to my dad. I dug it out of the back of my closet and gave it to him.

The next night, he showed up and sat with me while we watched *Breaking Bad*. The following, he was on call for work, and I didn't realize how much his presence soothed me. The next night, I asked him to come over. The night after that, I showed up to the Kouris family dinner. Everyone treated me like normal, even Carson—well, his version anyways, which included acting like I didn't exist. Rosie gave me a jar of herbs and a metal strainer to make relaxing tea. She swore it had helped her sleep in the past. Kaylee was conveniently stuck at work doing after-hours inventory. I thought that was her self-aware slant on not rubbing Maisie in my face. I loved her for it, and it was nice to be welcomed back into the fold without any questions.

I started seeing my therapist, Joyce, again to talk through my guilt, but I knew I had a long road ahead of me. Noah avoided me like the plague. He didn't show up at Tilly's for the pub quiz, he didn't return any of my texts, and when I saw him at a red light, he made a right-hand turn just to get away from me.

This was some next-level shunning. I guessed all his time disappearing into the forest for work had paid off. I wondered if he'd asked Azalea about it. She knew everything. When I'd grab a coffee at Silver Springs, she'd look at me with an expression like she was about to say something but wouldn't. It was irritating. I could always depend on her kindness. Even after we'd dated in high school, we'd remained friendly. Azalea was just that kind of girl—she didn't have enemies or bad blood. I didn't normally care what people thought of me, but I wanted to know her take on it.

Had I rescued a woman? Or had I killed a man?

I guessed it was both. I would have to live with both. Living with Maisie would sure as hell make it a lot easier, but that wasn't an option. Still, I'd do it a thousand times over for any woman, but especially her.

Finally, I spotted Noah leaning against his truck, filling it up with gas. I pulled up to the pump behind him, damn near ambushing him. Noah's face went placid as he stood up, squaring his shoulders.

"Hey, man," I said, trying to sound neutral. "We need to talk."

Noah let out a noncommittal sniff, looking in my general direction. "Sorry, haven't seen you around much. Been busy with work. Summer and all."

I looked around, grateful that out of the six pumps, we were the only ones parked. I stepped closer and whispered, "You can cut the shit. I know you saw me that night. I know you know what happened to Boyd."

Noah messed with the gas pump, clicking it and pulling it out of his truck. "His wife thinks he went on a bender and that's why he was acting so erratic. A fifteen-year-old girl in New Jersey just gave birth to his baby and served him paternity orders. She visited Maine last summer for a family reunion."

"Fifteen?" I whispered in horror. "That's a child!"

Noah nodded, looking past my face. "He was a creepy bastard. I searched the forest for him with Storm. Didn't find anything."

"What do you mean you didn't find anything?" I hissed.

His chestnut-colored eyes finally set on mine, intense and unblinking. His voice, which was usually so warm and patient, was now stern. "I said I didn't find anything and I didn't."

"But we both know you saw me. Why didn't you call it in? Where you just going to let him disappear in that forest?"

His jaw muscles ticked as he gritted, "We both know no one is missing Chase Boyd. It was obvious to me as a newcomer that as a town, you let him get away with too much for too long. The world has a way of righting itself, and I'm not going to get in the way."

He folded his arms over his chest, holding my gaze, letting the loaded silence ease my worry. He was a smart man. Leave it to Noah to side-step something like this.

I cleared my throat. "Well, if you say you didn't find anything."

"I didn't." He wrapped me in a quick hug, slapping my chest afterwards. "I'll call you when things slow down at work. Take care of yourself."

And with that, he rounded his truck, hopped in, and let the engine roar.

Summer inched on with lots of loaded looks from others and a hush sweeping over a room when I entered it. Some people were bold enough to ask me what happened, others, mostly women, just nodded with an expression I could only guess was a mixture of gratitude and unease. I felt like I was walking on eggshells. I didn't think people saw me as a threat, but regardless, it was a well-known fact I'd killed the town cop.

I finally got a letter indicating the investigation was closed. A couple days later, I bumped into Carson at Pine Mart. He had a couple boxes of different pregnancy tests along with a Gatorade and some saltines in the crook of his arm, unable to conceal them quickly.

"I guess congratulations might be in order." I gestured to the loot, knowing it was about to get really awkward.

He curled them further under his arm with a nod. "Hopefully."

It was always weird being around Carson. He looked like my best friend but meaner. We'd never gotten along, even as kids. With our shared history, I decided to cut right to the chase.

"So, do you know?"

"What happened with Maisie?" His mouth went in a firm line. "Yeah."

A tingle ran from my chest all the way down my arms. "What do I do? I spread rumors about you killing people, now I actually have."

He sighed, his eyes bouncing around us. "Boyd was a fucking creep. You did the right thing. Any woman within a hundred-mile radius would agree." He poked at my chest with the box of crackers. "Listen, fuck this town. I know now why I stayed in Pine Bluff. Rosie was going to come here, and that's how I was going to find her. Maybe that's not the case for you. Maybe you need to leave, you know, for a fresh start. I remember craving that for the better part of a decade. Maybe the best way to honor your dad is to leave, even if it's just for yourself."

His phone buzzed. "Sorry, it's Rosie. I gotta get this." Without so much as a glance back at me, he turned to answer the call. "Hey, love, what's up?" He continued booking it down the aisle. "Yeah, I can look for Jolly Ranchers."

I dropped my basket to leave. Hearing it from another man who was carrying out his dad's legacy hit differently. In such a simple statement, Carson had helped me see that by staying in Pine Bluff, I wasn't preserving my dad's memory. I was hurting it. And if anything, my parents would want me out living my life, not trying to force it to work here. Before the murder, I could justify staying, now I couldn't.

I needed to talk to someone who'd known my parents before I had even been a glimmer in the cosmos. I waited until ten minutes before All Booked Up closed, just like I always did. It was the best time to catch Viviane and bum a smoke off her when I really needed it. She knew all about my arrest. Hell, she was part of the circuit.

"Dane!" Her little voice shook as I walked up to her counter. "I've been waiting for you to come see me!" She held out her arms for me. We didn't hug much, we just didn't have that kind of relationship, but she must've known I needed it because when I all but squatted to embrace her, the second her frail arms encircled me, my eyes got misty.

She patted my back, not breaking away until I did. Her cold, little, arthritic hands held my face. "You did the right thing," she said with vehemence.

I nodded. "I tried."

She all but smashed my cheeks. "No, you didn't try. You did the right thing. Do you hear me, son?"

"Then why does it feel like I've ruined everything?" I blinked back tears. I was secure with my manhood, but crying in front of a geriatric town treasure was not something I wanted to do after almost losing it in front of Carson.

"You didn't ruin anything!" She freed my face, swatting the air. "Well, hell, I'm going to have to break out the big guns for this one."

She shuffled to an old filing cabinet to the side of her front desk. It was the wooden kind they'd use at the library to keep track of the catalog cards that told you were books were located with the Dewey Decimal System. She pulled out a drawer, then opened a little tin to present a strip of paper she placed in my hand.

I held it up, recalling it was a fortune I'd gotten from a fortune cookie once. I'd used it as a bookmark but had lost it somewhere in the shuffle of exchanging books.

*Be bold and totally worth the chaos.*

Maisie, my favorite little tornado, spun around in my head. Memories of her dancing with me at the wedding, chasing me around our hotel room with a bleached mohawk, smashing glass bottles in the rage room, making love as waves thundered against the shore.

My eyes lifted to Viviane's that were electric blue, just like the letters on the fortune. Her face crinkled with a knowing smile. "I think you've read enough Western novels. Maybe it's time to go west to find your own story."

"Just run away?"

"Sometimes, to follow your path, you need a little chaos to clear it first."

"Be bold and totally worth the chaos?"

She nodded, closing my hand around the fortune.

# Chapter Thirty-Seven

August—three months after the wedding

Me: Who the fuck is this guy again? And what kind of name is Thom? Do I pronounce it like Tom?

Dom: Yes, pronounce Thom like Tom. He's very sensitive about his name. I dated his best friend and then ended up housesitting for him while he was in Europe for the summer. He has great taste.

Me: And?

Dom: He even has one of those fancy massage chairs from Sharper Image. Maybe he'll fuck you in it.

Me: You can't be serious.

Dom: Shiatsu and chill.

**Me: He's twenty minutes late. You know my impatient Aries ass hates waiting on people.**

**Dom: He's a very important businessman.**

**Me: I'm a very important businesswoman.**

**Dom: Maybe he needed to charge up his Tesla.**

**Me: Oh, god.**

I sighed, thinking about how much I missed a certain blue-collar boy who'd never kept me waiting.

Later that night, I sat across from Thom at a pretentious bistro in downtown Austin. The aggressively industrial metal barstools made my bony ass hurt, and he made a snide comment about me not ordering a cocktail. Forty minutes into him yammering on about how Texas was a great place for tax shelters, I stood up.

"Where are you going?"

"Somewhere I give a fuck. I'm sorry, I just . . ." I gestured at him with my clutch. "I feel like I'm in a boardroom. Nothing about this is sexy, dude."

His brows went into this weird squiggly line. "I'm trying to show you I'm a wolf in the workplace."

"I'd rather have a fucking, I dunno, metaphors are hard." I flung my arms around in discomfort. "A crow in a conversation."

"I don't think I follow."

"Listen, during the talking stage of dating, guys are either way too sexual or they're acting like it's LinkedIn. There's no middle ground."

"I was told you owned some businesses. I thought this would interest you."

I shifted my weight from one stiletto to the other. My high heels, although high-quality, were pinching my toes. Times like this, I missed my favorite cowgirl boots that I'd lost in Maine. "Yeah, when I'm at work. In my free time, I like to think of other things."

He shot me a snotty stare as he picked up his gin.

I scoffed. "What was your favorite picture book as a kid?"

"What?"

"What book did you make your parents read you over and over again. Mine was *Chicka Chicka Boom Boom*."

He stammered, "Um, I guess, *The Very Hungry Caterpillar*."

I flashed him my best smile. "See! It would've never worked out," I said, earning a chuckle. "But for real, lead with stuff like that, you know, authentic information."

He brought his drink to his lips, trying to flash me a sexy look, if I had to guess. "Want to try again?"

I couldn't even fight the freeing feeling of advocating for myself as I fished out a couple bills to pay for the meal. "Yeah, but not with you. Take care!"

# Chapter Thirty-Eight

### August—one year later

 The Sulphur Creek Café looked like a saloon straight from the 1800s, and they had a bomb-ass rodeo burger with honey bourbon BBQ sauce and onion rings. I treated myself to it every Friday night after work. It was a ritual at this point. I hadn't made many friends in Wyoming, but I was living a quiet, honest life.
 When I'd applied for a job at Cedar Mountain Auto Service, they hadn't brought up my record. I guessed a small town in butt-fuck nowhere couldn't be too choosey when it came to a mechanic with a past in grand theft auto.
 It was the Wild, Wild West.
 No one knew I was a felon.
 No one knew I had killed a cop.
 No one knew I was an orphan.
 No one knew who I had or hadn't slept with.
 Truth be told, I hadn't even looked twice at a woman since Maisie. Sure, some of the women who dropped off their cars wrote their numbers on the bottoms of their receipts when

they signed, but I couldn't even bring myself to think about dating.

It was either work, working out, or working on myself. I had wasted too much of my life on cheap thrills. I tried to really slow it all down and take in the new scenery and way of life. The sunsets here were incredible. I'd hike after work and sit and watch them with too many thoughts in my head that I'd pour out in a notebook. I told myself no one had to read it, and that really gave me the freedom to dump out all my secrets.

Through word of mouth, I ended up helping some farmers and ranchers with fixing their equipment. Tractors are surprisingly finnicky. One of the guys, Mr. Felton, had a bunch of horses. I'd hang around in the stables after fixing stuff for him, just observing them. He taught me the basics on how to brush and ride, and we had a standing agreement that after my work was done, I'd get to ride a horse. After spending some time with the majestic creatures, I completely understood why people claimed they healed a part of you.

I thought about adopting a dog but felt bad knowing it would be stuck at home alone all day. I thought about adopting a cat, then realized I didn't want to deal with the whole litter box situation. A fish somehow seemed sadder than just being alone, so I got a houseplant instead. I watered it every Sunday after I finished meal-prepping for the week. So far, so good.

I didn't have much in regard to possessions. I'd sold the cottage to Rosie's mom, who'd moved to Pine Bluff to be closer to her grandchildren. Lennie hadn't wanted to take over the shop, so I'd given him a chunk of money and told him to get his hippie ass back on the road again. I'd sold the building to the fire department. They'd needed a second station with bays and housing upstairs, so it'd worked out. It'd left people in Pine Bluff without a mechanic, which made me feel a little guilty. Harley got my dad's toolchests. I cried a little when I had to finally sweep away the cobwebs to move them because it was basically erasing one of the last physical reminders of my father.

The next hardest thing to sell had been the bike. I'd known I had to. It had reminded me of Maisie, our love story embedded in leather and steel. While I was glad it had helped us get away from Boyd, I'd known my dad's GTO was rarer than some Bonneville Triumph, so it had been a decision I'd had to make.

Now I lived in some sad apartment because I wasn't ready to commit to buying a house until I found exactly where I wanted to be. I didn't even have a garage to tinker in, which honestly was driving me a little crazy.

My phone buzzed in front of me on the table.

It was a video of Harley's boat motor. I'd given him a couple ideas on how to fix it over a video call a couple days ago.

**Harley: I got this POS to work for now. Thanks again.**

**Me: No problem.**

**Harley: Are you enjoying your Friday night burger?**

**Me: You know it.**

The server hadn't brought it to me yet, so I just snapped a photo of a bison bust on the wall to send him. I was tucked away at a small booth, facing the swinging saloon doors that led to a modern lobby entrance. It was my usual spot. I'd hardly been ever alone in Pine Bluff, so when I'd moved, I'd challenged myself to enjoy my own company. I'd forced myself to go out to eat alone. To movies. To rodeos. It had been awkward at first, but then I'd realized no one cared. Everyone was too busy thinking about their own experience.

I zoned out waiting for my food. Footsteps rippled the golden light peeking through the cracks around the creaky saloon doors before they swung open. Cowgirl boots strutted the hardware floor, with tanned legs disappearing under a white, fluttery, floral sundress. A golden sun pendant glimmered on her delicate neck.

I stood up as she made her way to me. Her hair was my favorite shade of pink, and her eyes searched my face in wonder before her lips tilted up as she made her declaration.

"I'm hellbent on loving you."

The air caught in my lungs as I held her face, unsure if I was hallucinating or dreaming. She smiled up at me, lovingly touching my arms.

"Hi," was all I could manage. It was barely a breath of a word. Thoughts swirled in my head too quickly, and the rest of the world faded out. All I could fathom was that Maisie Quinn was in front of me.

"Hi, handsome."

I crushed her to me in a bear hug, lifting her so her feet dangled as I wrapped her in as close as possible. I breathed her in, the same sugary sweetness I remembered so well returning.

"I missed you so damn much," she whispered, her subtle Southern drawl making me melt even more.

I broke the hug, setting her down. I needed to stare at her a little longer.

My palms got sweaty, and I could feel my heart slamming against my ribs. "How did you—Did you come here for—" I stuttered.

"Harley told me you'd be here. Can I join you?" she asked, pointing to the table.

We each took our respected seats on either side of the booth that had high, rustic wooden walls with lanterns. We sheepishly smiled at each other when we realized there was too much space between us, and it was a little awkward.

I beckoned her over to me. "Get your little ass over here," I said playfully through gritted teeth.

She settled next to me, turning toward me in the booth, her back to the rest of the world. That simple gesture showed she still trusted me. She knew I'd always have her back. That thought alone made me feel like a swoony idiot.

As the shock wore off, my doubts crept in. Maisie had left me several times over. How could this time be any different?

"I know what you're thinking," she said. "How are things different? How could you possibly trust me with your heart now? I get it. I'm not asking you to force anything. I'm asking for you to hear me out on what I've changed in my own life so I can show up and love you like you deserve."

She took a breath and rolled her shoulders back. I could tell she had rehearsed that or something. It was kinda cute, really.

"I'm all ears."

"For starters, I'm sorry for running away from you when you told me you loved me. I'm sorry I never wanted to talk about the hard stuff with you. I know it's not an excuse, but no one had ever done that with me. My mom basically ignored me and was emotionally immature. Conner was the same way. I picked the pattern because it was familiar."

She rested her hand on one of my pecs. It heated my heart.

"But you were different. You always tried to talk about the difficult stuff, and I'd shut you out. I'm so sorry. I'm committed to not shying away from those kinds of discussions anymore."

"It was hard because we got off on the wrong foot."

She pulled back her hand, using her other arm to lean against the table, turning toward me even farther, creating more of a bubble around us.

"Right, but I could've met you halfway. I've had to learn reconciliation. In my family, no one ever outright said they were sorry about things. My grandpa would take me to Build-a-Bear when he hurt my feelings. My mom would offer to crimp my hair and let me wear makeup if she needed to mend things. I learned just to brush things under the rug. You made me realize I had to learn how to apologize."

"So far, so good."

She chuckled at that.

The server came, interrupting us. I couldn't stop staring at her as she ordered the same burger as I had with a Coke.

"I thought you liked Diet Coke? It was like your crack."

"Riots not diets!" she whisper-screamed before slipping back into a reflective smile. "In all seriousness, my mom always forced me to drink Diet Coke to 'watch my figure,' but I've decided to not partake in diet culture, so I stick to the real thing now."

"Wow, you have changed!" I joked, earning a playful swat on the arm from her.

She went on, fiddling with the edges of her napkin. "On my drive back to Texas, I came to the conclusion I wasn't choosing you, and it's because I wasn't choosing myself. So I did. I'm going to therapy for emotional neglect and my mother wound. And to process the assault. That's been really hard but worth it. I also did one of those DNA tests and found my father." Her face pulled into one of the biggest grins I'd seen. "His name is Miguel Alesandro Cortez. And he's honestly one of the nicest humans I've ever met."

"That's fantastic! I'm so glad." I wanted to touch her but fought it. "Was he searching for you, too?"

"He had no clue I existed. My friend Dom and I visited him in Mexico. I look so much like him and my aunts, it's not even funny. I'm learning all about my Mexican heritage now. It's opened up this whole new side of my story I was too scared to look at."

"Did he ever marry or have other kids?"

"Yes. After the initial shock wore off, his wife was really understanding about it. He has two sons who are a couple years younger than me."

"So you have brothers. I mean, you already kinda had a sister with Kaylee, but brothers are new."

"Yeah, they're nice, but I can't tell if they've really warmed up to me." She shrugged. "I get it. It'll take time."

She said a quick thanks to the server who brought over her Coke. She speared the ice with the straw and swirled it around in the cup. "What's funny is right after the one-night stand with my mom, he met his wife. He's absolutely crazy about her. It's like she hung the moon. My mom would have had zero chance pulling him from her."

"So she spent her whole life pining over some mystery man who would've never been interested in a second chance?"

"Yep! I don't plan on ever speaking to her again, but if I have to, I'm going to throw it in her face." She snorted and sipped her soda.

"As you should. So what else is new? Did you sell Pretty Kitty?"

"Yeah. They've already opened two more. I took the money and rolled it into some new investments, like a carwash and a booth at the huge state fair in Dallas that specializes in deep fried food."

"Deep fried food?" I asked incredulously.

"Yeah, ridiculous things like Snickers and birthday cake."

"Are you for real?"

"I'm pretty sure you could deep fry a shoe and someone would eat it. Did you close down your auto shop?"

"Yeah. Sold the cottage, too."

"Did you just need a fresh start after everything that happened?"

All I could do was nod.

"That makes sense," she said. "Are you glad you did it?"

"For the most part."

"Would you ever want to work somewhere else?"

"Like?"

"Well, I'm currently working on a passion project." She rolled her eyes, playing with her straw. "It's this wacky idea. I got it from some goof once."

"Oh yeah?" I asked, already amused. I knew where this was going.

She pursed her lips to sober, committing to the bit. "Have you ever needed to get an oil change, but you'd really love a big, juicy burger while you wait?"

As if orchestrated by the universe, our server slid our burgers across the table.

I grinned down at my plate. "I feel like that's a niche need that should be tapped into."

"Me too. So I'm opening this place called—"

"Fill'er up," I interrupted, holding up my burger.

"Yep!" She beamed. "It's still in the beginning stages. I wanted your input on the build and whatnot. But I really don't want to hire another mechanic. I want it to be you. This is your brainchild. Plus, you'd have space to rebuild classic cars when you want. Regardless of if you want to be a part of it or not, I'll give you a cut."

"You want me to move to Texas and work for you as a mechanic?"

"If you want. And you'd be co-owner, of course."

"So you're gonna be my sugar mama?"

"Well, you *did* kill a man for me," she joked under her breath.

I all but choked on my food. God, I'd missed her.

Wiping my mouth with my napkin, I mumbled, "I'm going to hell for laughing at that."

Her eyes searched my face for an answer to the original question.

"You already know my answer, tornado."

"Really?" Her pink eyebrows raised, then she drew them together on second thought. "Wait, what is it?"

"Yes. My answer is yes."

She picked up a fry, offering it to me since I'd ordered onion rings. "You sure?"

"Yes. I spent the better part of the last year and a half wondering how I could come back to you."

"You said you'd never know if I loved you for you, not because of what you did to protect me. I want you to know that you protected me because you loved me. I know that. I always knew that. It's not like I'm indebted to you. I'm simply in love with you, Dane."

"I think I was just horrified that I did that without thinking. It scares me how much I love you." I lowered my tone, putting a hand on her thigh. "I killed for you, Maisie. But what scares me is I'd do it again in a heartbeat. I'd do anything to protect you."

Her eyes went all doe-like.

I kept going. "I also remember you wanting to take the fall for me so willingly. You were ready to claim you had the knife and everything."

She bobbed her head enthusiastically.

"That alone should've told me everything I needed to know. I'm sorry for pushing you away. I was disgusted with myself."

"It was traumatic for you, too. I get that," she said in a tiny voice.

We stared at each other, memories and emotions swirling around us.

I skimmed my knuckles across her cheek. "I want to be with you."

"I want to be with you too. I want to experience life, not avoid it." Her gaze fell to my lips as she licked her own. "You were set free by walking away from your past. I was set free when I learned more about mine. Now I'm thinking about the future."

"I don't want this to be some fling or business venture. I need more than that."

"We're more than that," she affirmed.

"If we're going to do this, I want all of you. Not some weird long-distance thing. Or casual dating. I want you in my bed when I wake up in the morning. I want to hear all about your crazy theories while we dye your hair. I want to spend holidays with you and go on more adventures."

"Yes, I want that too," she said, inching even closer to me.

"And I'm going to put a ring on that little finger of yours because I want to call you mine for the rest of my life."

She breathed in my words, her eyes soft and full of love. "That's all I needed to hear." She picked up her Coke. "To the future."

I clinked her glass with mine. "To the future."

We spent hours catching up and talking nonstop. We were laughing so loud that at one point, people were side-eyeing us. It had been about a year and a half, but it was like barely any time had passed. Eventually, we got up to leave together. I loved how easy it felt to slip my hand in hers. How good it was to hold the door open for her.

The warm summer night hit me. The heat was different here in Wyoming. Drier. Like being baked in an oven, not sweltering in humidity. The world around us was golden with the pending sunset and the soft hum of nature mixed with Maisie's voice.

"What are you driving nowadays?" Her eyes scanned the brown, dusty parking lot.

I gestured to my GTO parked away from everyone else to avoid dings. "I'm sorry, baby girl. I sold the bike. I couldn't even look at it without thinking of you. I regret it now."

"Oh, who did you sell it to?"

I fished for my keys. "Kaylee's dad, so I promise it's in good hands. He's still in Maryland so we met halfway before I moved."

"Interesting."

Rounding the corner, I stopped dead in my tracks, staring at the all-black Triumph. My bike, *our* bike was parked in the sandy gravel.

"No way!" I bellowed.

She threw her head back in a musical giggle, clapping. "You did sell it to Kaylee's dad, but he turned around and sold it to me." A sparkle lit Maisie's eyes.

"Are you fucking kidding me?"

It had gutted me to make that decision. I had sentimental attachments to the bike and my car, but I knew my GTO was rarer. I'd had to give up my dad's shop, and the idea of giving up his car had just been too much to contend with in the swarm of change.

"Check the plate."

I got closer to read the small plate that had **HLL BNT** punched into the metal in black letters.

"Hellbent?" I asked with a grin.

She walked toward me with a nod. "Hellbent. Reckless and stubbornly determined."

"Yeah, that sounds like us." I hooked an arm around her waist, pulling her closer to me.

# Chapter Thirty-Nine

I let Dane drive the bike. My whole body was vibrating in disbelief as I pressed myself against him on the back, wrapping my arms around his ripped body. He was still sexy as fuck and all tan from summer. It made his green eyes and bright smile pop. And his scruff was still covering that little dent on his chin I had to fight to keep from kissing.

I couldn't believe my plan had worked. I'd been half worried he'd say no or ask for my number to ghost me and make it awkward, but deep down inside, I knew Dane wasn't really that kind of guy. It was worth the risk. I squeezed him tighter, promising myself I'd never let him go.

The sunset in my eyes made me squint and curl into him further, pressing my cheek against his back. After a few seconds, I could feel his heartbeat thump. His large hand went to where mine clasped his chest. He gave an affectionate squeeze and accelerated. We ended up at his place. He showed me his depressing apartment. He couldn't decorate if his life depended on it. He had a single houseplant on his bar as décor.

"What kind is this?" I asked, turning the plant around to inspect it.

"I had no clue, but then this white lily sprouted up last week. It was so cool. When I Googled it, it turns out it's a peace lily."

A gentle knowing washed over me, recalling the white lilies Azalea had put next to my bedside when I'd recovered from the assault. She'd promised me I was still innocent and that people like Dane would still protect and care for me. This was the synchronicity I needed.

Testing my theory, I picked up the cheap plastic pot. The tag on the bottom had it marked at $4.44. My angel numbers.

"Is there something I'm missing?" Dane asked.

I shook my head. "No, sorry, just caught up in my thoughts."

I wandered into his room that still consisted of his simple wooden bed and nightstand. Next to a stack of Westerns was the black 8-ball I'd stolen from the pool hall from our trip. I picked it up and inspected it in disbelief.

His voice came out thick. "I considered it a souvenir. From loving you. I looked at it every night and wondered how I could get you back, but I worried seeing me might make you think of what happened."

I kissed it and put it down. "I'm glad you thought of me, but I want you to know I don't associate you with Boyd."

He gave me a half-hearted nod and went to the closet. "I made this for you. In hopes maybe I'd be able to give it to you." Swinging a jean jacket out on a hanger, he held it against his body as he looked down at it. "I found this at a flea market in Pennsylvania. The lady swore it was a vintage Wrangler. I know yours got ruined when, you know, that night."

"Yeah, yeah it did." My voice got thick as I ran my fingers over the denim. "And you put patches on it?"

"From all the places I stopped along the way."

"Oh, Dane." I said, swallowing hard, unable to stop touching each patch. "You moved to Cody because it was my favorite patch, didn't you?"

"It just stuck with me." He flashed me a bashful smile, helping me into the jacket.

He smoothed out the shoulders then pressed his firm chest against my back. "I know it doesn't replace your dad's and all the memories, but I was hoping it would help prove that another guy in your life loves you."

"This is so thoughtful. Thank you." Something shiny on the breast pocket over my heart snagged my attention. Instead of a patch, it was a pin with a long silver encasement. I twisted the fabric of the jacket to inspect it.

"'Be bold and totally worth the chaos.' Oh my god! it's the fortune from the book of yours I bought, isn't it?"

"Yes! I covered it with glass then electroformed the edges in metal to protect it."

I looked over my shoulder at him. "The little old lady at the bookstore totally stole it from me, didn't she? I was so bummed when I didn't find it as a bookmark."

"Viviane is very sneaky. She gave it back to me. I guess I needed the words more than you." His kissable lips screwed to the side as he considered the papered fortune.

"Well, you're certainly bold."

He wrapped his arm around me, his hand possessively holding low on my tummy. "And you're certainly worth the chaos."

His eyes simmered on my lips. I tilted my chin up, giving him permission. His mouth covered mine as his hand boldly slid up and down my torso. I held the back of his head, keeping him in the kiss. His tongue traced the line of my lips. I opened to him with a relieved sigh as he kissed me deeper. Everything was alright in the world. I was back in his arms, covered in his adoration.

We pulled apart, fighting for air. His pupils were blown out, wide with love and hunger.

"We still got it, don't we?" he said roguishly, hinting at our natural chemistry.

"I feel it. God, do I feel it." I turned to face him, wrapping my arms around his neck, pushing my aching breasts against him.

He picked me up and walked us to bed. Before he could lay us flat, he cleared his throat and sat me down. "Wait, we should wait."

I tried my best to ignore the warmth pooling between my legs. I was so ready for him already. We'd talked for hours this evening and covered all my questions, but I had to respect his decision. I was a flight risk. I got it.

"Right," I lied in agreement. Feeling too hot, I took off my jean jacket. I knew I couldn't be alone with him. We'd be too tempted. Scrambling for a plan, I went with my first idea. "Can I maybe get a ride in your car?"

His face broke into a boyish grin as he took my hand.

We rode the motorcycle back to the café, leaving it there to pick up the car. The late summer heat was no joke, so we drove around with the windows down. The night was dark, with sprinklings of stars and a paper-white crescent moon on the western horizon. I snapped a photo of it and sent it to my moon maiden.

**Kaylee: OMG, did it work? Are you with him? Harley and I are dying over here.**

**Me: Yes. I'm riding shotgun in his car. He said yes. We worked it out.**

**Kaylee: That's the best news ever!**

Along with the text, she sent a photo of her and Harley mock screaming together on their couch.

**Me:** Hey, remember when you found some asshole cheating on you with your favorite barista, in the beloved coffee shop of all places?

**Kaylee:** Yes! And remember how I took off like a banshee and crashed my car in Maine and this super hunky forest ranger rescued me? It could've been so bad. What if I'd driven south and gotten stuck in New Jersey?

I giggled, staring at my phone, loving how Dane's calloused hand floated over to hold my knee.

**Me:** Yeah, and isn't it great how that ranger just so happened to have a gorgeous mechanic friend who looked at your wrecked car?

**Kaylee:** Luck was on our side!

**Me:** Thanks for inadvertently introducing me to my other soulmate.

Kaylee sent me a moon emoji, code for *I love you so much I can't stand it*. I sent her a sun one right back.

"Take it that's Kaylee?" Dane asked, his hand traveling under my sundress to clutch my inner thigh.

I was glad I wasn't the only one fighting the attraction. In the dark with him, it was even harder.

"Yeah, just telling her and Harley."

"I need to call and thank him."

"It was way too easy to find your ass."

"I'm a simple man."

"That's not true."

His wide shoulders bounced. "If you say so."

He pulled up to a grove of trees that had a river glimmering just beyond the leaves. Putting the car in park and killing the engine, he looked me up and down.

"You look so good sitting there in the passenger seat." I put my phone in my purse, letting it fall to the floor of the car. "Thank you."

"I want to thank you for finding me. For understanding how I wasn't in the right place to show up for you either."

I reached out, skimming his scruff and strong jaw. "We just weren't ready."

"But we are now." He kissed my palm.

"Mm-hmm."

He pulled me closer to him. His fingers trailed the sensitive skin over my shoulder, up my neck, and over to the edge of my ear. Goose bumps erupted along my skin, my nipples stiffening under my sundress. "Are you ready for other things?"

"Mm-hmm."

In a rush, we made our way to the back seat.

"You've always wanted to do this, haven't you?" I asked, straddling him.

"You have no clue," he said, squeezing my ass. A clouded look traveled over his eyes as he brought his hands up to cradle my face. "Wait, did you?"

"What?" I said, breathlessly undoing his pants.

"Did you—not that it matters." His face twitched. "Have you been with anyone else since me?"

"No. Have you?"

"God no," he spat. The information registered in his mind, softening his features. "Good." He pulled me back in for a kiss as we started to grind. "By the way, Maisie," he mumbled against my lips.

"Yeah?"

"The cowgirl boots stay on. It's fucking hot."

"Deal!" I wound my hips, all my thoughts and worries disappearing as I felt him stiffen against my core. "Dane," I whispered. "I missed your big cock."

I yelped as he plopped me on my back on the upholstered seat, shimming my panties down my legs. "Good because I missed the way this pussy tastes. I dream about it."

"I know classic cars are supposed to be roomy, but you really fill this thing up." I squeezed his shoulder, loving the solid muscle.

He murmured something about filling something else up as he knelt on the floor, kissing up my legs. Making his way to the straps of my sundress, he playfully tugged on one with his teeth. A giggle rippled through me. God, I missed how playful he was during sex. I loved that about him.

When he yanked off the other strap in a similar fashion, my breasts were exposed to the warm summer breeze coursing through the windows. He pulled the dress down even farther, causing me to slip my arms out of the straps.

"Wait!" he said. "Is that what I think it is?"

Realizing what he'd seen, I lifted my arms over my head. "Bright pink armpit hair? You bet it is!"

"Still fucking hot." He nuzzled my neck.

"You make me feel alive," I whispered.

"You're worth living for," he said, covering me with a kiss before he traveled lower. I held his head to my pussy, jerking my legs with how sensitive I was before I melted into a yummy, mindless fog of pleasure.

I loved the view of him between my legs, but he was wearing too much clothing.

"Take off your shirt," I demanded, interrupting him.

He fisted the fabric behind his neck and tore it over himself, causing all his muscles to shift in the process. Butterflies erupted low in my belly at the sight as he returned his mouth to my center.

"Baby, I just need you in me."

I couldn't wait any longer. I wanted no frills, just hot, needy sex in the back of his car.

I straddled him once more, the flicker of the coursing river reflecting in his green eyes as he brushed the tip of his cock against me. Sliding down on his length, I fought a shudder. It felt so damn good being this close again.

"I love you," he murmured.

"I love you, too."

We nodded in unison and started to move together.

"Dane, I'll love you until the day I die, do you hear me?"

"Yes. I'll love you forever, Maisie baby."

# Epilogue

"I never thought I'd be paying a shaman for anything," I told Kaylee. "That's more your gig."

She fixed the elaborate body chain I was wearing almost like a cape over my bare shoulders. It was dainty and gold, with double-sided diamonds dappling my clavicle and scalloping over the caps of my shoulders.

"You're a gorgeous bride." Kaylee sniffled with misty eyes.

"You said you weren't going to cry!"

She huffed, now clucking at my hair. "I lied, okay!"

A scratch at the canvas of our glamping tent caused her to fan her face. "Come in!"

Harley tentatively ducked in the flap. A proud smile pulled at his face as he saw me in my gown. It was the faintest shade of pink, my favorite color. It had an exposed bodice with a sweetheart bust that morphed to chiffon floating to the bottom.

"You look gorgeous, Maisie."

"Thanks, dude."

Kaylee sniffled as he gave me a hug. "I can't handle this!" She gestured to us in the embrace.

"Are you sure you want to marry this guy?" Harley teased, breaking the hug.

"Yeah, but I heard he lied to my friend about her car being wrecked while she was snowed in with some Grizzly Adams type."

Harley playfully rolled his eyes, looping his arm around Kaylee. "We're never going to live that one down, are we?"

"Hell no!" Kaylee and I said in unison.

"Are you able to hike in that dress?" he asked.

Since we were eloping outside, we had to hike to our destination.

"Yes! I'm prepared." I stuck a leg out of one of the slits, revealing a white cowgirl boot that secretly had 444 carved on the heel.

"A true Texan." Kaylee beamed with pride as she looked up at her husband. "We just need, like, five more minutes."

He held out his hand. "I was told to get your ring."

I slid the dainty gold band off my finger, the one-carat solitaire glinting in the low light. Dane had proposed using his mother's wedding ring a couple weeks after we'd nested in Texas. It was an honor to have it, and its timeless elegance was just more proof the woman had taste. Forty years later, it was still a flashy stunner.

His dad's ring was a bit outdated and beat up, so we reconstructed it to be a simple brushed gold band that had *hellbent* engraved on the inside. Since he was a mechanic, he'd be wearing one of those silicone rings at work most of the time anyways.

Ringless and clad in a wedding gown, I felt my nerves morph into excitement. I was so grateful to have Kaylee and my dad at my wedding. The energy and circumstances were drastically different from my first one, where I'd schlepped off to Vegas. I was grateful I did the whole girly thing this time around—the dress, jewelry, shoes, nails. It was fun, and I shouldn't be ashamed to celebrate and take up space.

We had chosen to elope in Sedona, Arizona. On one of our road trips with the bike, we'd fallen in love with the place. Although we weren't as woo-woo as Kaylee, even we could feel the sacred energy here. To honor the history, we had hired a local Native American shaman to conduct the ceremony on top of some of the iconic red rocks at sunset.

We'd invited my dad, Dominique, Harley's and Kaylee's parents, and a couple of my closest friends from college and Texas. Not wanting to leave out those who couldn't be with us, we arranged to have three bouquets of white roses around us to represent Dane's parents and sister.

Harley and Kaylee helped me hike up, all three of us holding my dress and bouquet of blush peonies and white lilies. I gave them each a final kiss on the cheek before they left me. I wanted to walk myself down the aisle, or rather up the pathway, and luckily no one seemed to take offense to that.

The shaman played a flute as I made my way to Dane, who was already waiting at the top of the cliff with the rest of the small crowd. As I approached, he wiped his eyes, trying not to lose it. He looked dashing in black slacks with a black dress shirt that I'd told him to leave unbuttoned a little so I could see his sexy chest.

The desert sunset lit up Dane's green eyes as we exchanged simple vows. We hiked back down with all our friends in good spirits. At the base of the trail, our bike was parked in the lot with a sign that said *just married* in cutesy scrawl tied to the back.

Dane extended a hand for me. "Are you ready to hit the road, tornado?"

"Yeah, sometimes you just gotta get the hell out of Dodge."

Reviews are immensely helpful to me as an indie author. Please consider leaving a review on Amazon and Goodreads to help this book find other readers, such as yourself.

Catch Azalea and Noah's story in the fourth book in the Pine Bluff series, coming 2025.

Sign up for the latest book news and upcoming releases at MaggieMaren.com

Listen to the Hellbent playlist.

# Acknowledgements

I want to first thank my husband and family for their unwavering encouragement. I appreciate how you always remind me who I am on the days when self-doubt and frustration creep in. And an extra, special thanks goes to my husband who helped me get through a tough, scary winter. When things get gnarly, you're always prepared and patient with me. Thank you for showing me gentle love.

I also want to thank my beta readers Cas, Kim, and Lakshmi. Each of you held down a different side of the fort for me this time around. Cas, thank you for always reminding me to fuck 'em if they can't take a joke and for letting me bitch and moan about Leos for months on end. Kim, thank you for listening to my podcast-length voice notes and for always being a calm, steady, perceptive presence who is unquestionably in my corner. I know Carson is your favorite but thank you for entertaining me with Dane. I'm so lucky you always pick up what I'm putting down. Your annotation hearts live rent free in my mind. May the tapestry continue to unravel. Oh, and Theodore sends his best wishes. And Lakshmi, thank you for letting me go dark. It is comforting knowing I can bring the most scandalous ideas to you, and you never think it's too much. I appreciate your openness and ability to keep my secrets. You are an angel (with the mind of a devil).

A big thanks to my fellow indie author, Victoria Moxley, who provided great insight into the Latina and Texan aspects of Maisie's character. I owe you a crawfish boil and a Big Red.

An extra special thanks goes to my editor, Norma, for pushing me to make this book better. Your insight was priceless and spot on. Purple people unite!

And lastly, thank you to all the readers who send me sweet messages about how my books inspire you to live a more sensual, spiritual, fearless life. You deserve all the good things you desire.

# Also by Maggie Maren

Pine Bluff Series:

Stormbound
Feverburn
Hellbent

Yule with the Wild God

## About the Author

Maggie Maren is a lifelong weirdo and misunderstood mystic. Combining her deep love for nature and romance, she enjoys playing mountain man matchmaker. Her stories transport readers to cozy cabins and the great outdoors, where kooky characters find love.

While earning her English literature degree, she worked as a bookseller, because clearly temperance isn't her strong suit. Her curious ways have led her to some interesting forays as a librarian, professional tarot reader, crystal merchant, and some dark ages in corporate America.

She spends her time tucked away in the wild woods of Maine, with her own mountain man. If she isn't writing or reading, she is either dancing, sipping iced coffee, yipping at the moon, adventuring, or ugly crying over a majestic sunset. She loves to hear from her readers, preferably in the form of a haiku, but hey, no pressure.

To stay connected, visit her at [MaggieMaren.com](MaggieMaren.com)

Made in the USA
Columbia, SC
18 March 2025